GLOBAL WAR

GLOBAL WAR

A TEAM REAPER THRILLER

BRENT TOWNS

WOLFPACK
PUBLISHING
— EST 2015 —

Global War
Paperback Edition
Copyright © 2024 Brent Towns

Wolfpack Publishing
701 S. Howard Ave. 106-324
Tampa, Florida 33609

wolfpackpublishing.com

Paperback ISBN 978-1-63977-370-1
eBook ISBN 978-1-63977-916-1
LCCN 2024931684

AUTHOR'S NOTE

Although this is part of the Team Reaper series, I've jumped forward to the year 2030 to give a different perspective of what I think the world and the team might look like at that time. Yes, some of the personnel are different, as is the equipment. But the action you have become accustomed to is still there. They wage war differently. They've had to adapt because the bad guys have grown their business.

Readers will also note I have taken liberties with a little Saudi project called The Line.

So, join Kane, Knocker, and Cara as they dive once more into the seedy underworld of bad guys and take the fight to their doorstep with a few surprises along the way.

TEAM REAPER

Command:
Mary Thurston
Cara Billings

Team Reaper:
Reaper One: John "Reaper" Kane
Reaper Two: Raymond "Knocker" Jensen
Reaper Three: Grace Henderson
Reaper Four: Red Ryan
Reaper Five: Ken Welsh

Bravo:
Bravo One: Patricia Houlihan
Bravo Two: Mike Tanner
Bravo Three: Crystal Garcia
Bravo Four: Molly Wilson

Capt. Eugene Potter: Pilot Boeing C-252 (Skyhammer)
Lieutenant Commander Leslie Groves: Co-Pilot Boeing C-252 (Skyhammer)

WEAPONS

- *Global Viper (Viper)*—Manually operated robotic system.
- *Global Viper (Ivan)*—Heavy Assault manually operated robotic system. (Twin Miniguns, Anti-tank, Flame Thrower)
- *Global Viper (Ares)*—Heavy Assault manually operated robotic system. (Twin Miniguns, Anti-tank, Flame Thrower)
- *Lockheed Martin F-56*—Fighter Bomber.
- *Lockheed Martin F-60 (Black Cat)*—Unmanned Fighter Bomber.
- *GAU-2/A minigun*—Belt-fed rotary weapon.
- *Boeing C-252 (Stratomaster)*—Mobile forward operations base. (Skyhammer)
- *Heckler & Koch G550*—Next Generation Assault Weapon.
- *Heckler and Koch P756*—Team handgun.
- *AT-120*—Anti-Tank weapon which fires depleted uranium rounds.
- *AG-666 Missile (Lucifer)*—Hypersonic air-to-ground missile.
- *AA-696 Missile (Raptor)*—Hypersonic air-to-air missile.
- *LCV Scorpion Landing Craft*—High-Speed stealth landing transport for the Viper Robotic Systems.
- *30 mm ATK GAU-23/A*—Autocannon. (Striker)

- *105 mm M102*—Howitzer. (Thor)
- *Phalanx CIWS (M85 Vulcan Rotary Cannon)*—Anti-Missile Defense System. (Ripper)
- *Type 763 Remote Controlled Submarines*—Armed remote-controlled miniature submarines.
- *Type 1000 Hunter/Killer Submarine*—Larger smuggling platform heavily armed.
- *T495 Panther*—Armored Car with a 30mm autocannon.
- *Star Hawk*—Unmanned Combat Aerial Vehicle (UCAV) with stealth capabilities.
- *General Electric Hanson Rapier*—Unarmed Aerial Vehicle (UAV) with stealth capabilities.
- *Walter*—Small, compact drone named after explorer Sir Walter Raleigh.
- *Tamworth-Class Destroyer*—Australian Guided Missile Destroyer.
- *HP433 Battle Droids*—Remote-Controlled Armored Battle Droids.
- *Houdini*—Experimental cloaking ability for Skyhammer.

*Almost all of the weapons and military items do not exist.

GLOBAL WAR

PROLOGUE

The Mexican sun was sizzling, but the man called John "Reaper" Kane seemed oblivious to its scorching rays. Not inside the Global Viper Robotic System. Its automatic coolant conditioner saw to that. The external armor was constructed of a new alloy that had been developed and tested by Global and was now operational.

Inside the helmet was a full Heads Up Display, HUD, on which the wearer could see at a glance threat warnings, ammunition count, battery life, and whether the armor was compromised. And no matter the build of the wearer, the adjustable armor gave them an operational height of almost eleven feet and a sustained ground cover speed of thirty miles per hour.

This was the future. A necessity for operators to take on the heavily armed threats now expanding operations across the globe. Someone at Global had taken a Dale Brown novel and brought it to life. Team Reaper—

the *new* Team Reaper that is—was the beneficiary of it all.

And Kane and Raymond "Knocker" Jensen had been brought back to lead the fight. Even though both men were in their forties.

The HUD was sensor-operated from a small pad at the operator's temple. It sensed thoughts and reacted accordingly. Right now, Kane's HUD was scanning the terrain for life forms and armed threats.

From his earbuds, a hopping tune filled his head. "What the hell are you humming now?" Kane asked Knocker.

The Brit stopped. "Sorry, Reaper. I've been listening to Creedence, and 'Fortunate Son' is stuck in my fucking head."

"Hey, I like that song," a voice replied. "Old music like that is cool."

The words were spoken from the third Viper operated by Grace Henderson. She was a former Air Force pilot who'd flown Lockheed Martin's F56s before the F60 Black Cats came out and were totally automated. Flown by stick jockeys half a world away from whatever combat zone they were in.

She had been hand-picked by Global for the Viper Program the year before. The twenty-five-year-old Idaho native had jumped at the chance. After all, Global Corporation was the best on offer, and they only selected the best.

Or rather, Mary Thurston did.

"Shit," Knocker muttered. "Young people these days."

"Can I help it if I am, old man?" Grace asked.

"Keep it up, Reaper Three, and I'll spank you."

"Promises, promises."

"All right, knock it off," Cara Billings said, interrupting their banter. "Heads in the game. Morenos and his soldiers are heavily armed. It's not like the old days."

No, it was nothing like the old days. Cartels were now using tanks and helicopters and shoulder-launched missiles. A heavily armored wall had gone up along the US-Mexico border, but the drugs still managed to get in. Everything south of that wall to the tip of South America was cartel country. They ran it all.

Two weeks before this operation, the DEA had sent a covert team in to assassinate the cartel leader, Juan Morenos. Fifteen experienced, heavily armed men who never came home. Each had been killed and their bodies displayed as an example. Hence, the request for Global to intercede using their high-tech assistance.

There were two more Vipers, both on standby, circling at 40,000 feet above the earth. They were operated by former Australian Special Forces Red Ryan and former British Commando Ken Welsh.

Each Viper was armed with a GAU-2/A minigun housed behind the robot's right shoulder and then deployed. It was belt-fed from a 3,000 round pack fitted on their backs like a school backpack.

Additionally, under the left arm was a weapon able to fire 30mm depleted uranium rounds. All were aimed and fired using the HUD.

"Bravo One, I need a sitrep."

"Copy, Reaper One. I have three guard towers all loaded with fifties. Lots of movement around the perimeter. Looks like they know you're coming."

"Don't they always?" growled Knocker. "Ready to go to work, Gracie?"

"Turn me loose, Governor."

"Your British accent is horrendous."

She grinned. "So is yours."

"Commencing attack, Bravo," Kane said and came erect. "Move out."

Then they were running. The Vipers swiftly traversed the desert toward the large compound.

On Kane's right, Knocker crashed through a large bush and smashed an even larger saguaro. On the inside of Kane's helmet, his HUD detected movement from one of the towers as a shooter started bringing his fifty-caliber heavy machine gun around.

Within a heartbeat, the minigun on Kane's shoulder fired a short burst of fifty rounds. The tower was immediately shredded, and the guard simply vanished. Meanwhile, the second shooter opened fire from his tower, sending geysers of sand and stones erupting around Knocker's Viper as it rapidly closed the distance.

"Not so fast, mate," he snapped, and his minigun came to life. In a serious moment of déjà vu, the tower was destroyed, and the shooter torn apart.

"RPG on the wall!" Houlihan called out over the comms.

Kane picked it up on his HUD, but the warning came too late as the rocket-propelled grenade streaked across the desert floor toward the charging Vipers. It flew straight and true, hitting Grace's exoskeleton like a runaway truck.

The Viper stopped as though colliding with a brick wall and went down. The comms broadcast a cry of pain, causing Kane some concern. "Reaper Three, are you okay?"

"I'm all right," Grace grunted, sounding a little shaky.

"What about your Viper?"

"Armor integrity down to sixty percent but still operational."

Knocker opened fire again, and the RPG user died in a cloud of red. "Got the bastard."

"There is movement inside the compound, Reaper One."

"Copy."

Kane's HUD zoomed in on the compound in time to see the main gates open. Emerging through the opening, like being projectile vomited, raced four heavily armed vehicles. The real problem, however, came in the form of three Russian-made T-90 tanks with reactive armor. Just another string to the drug cartel's bow.

"Ah fuck a duck," Knocker growled. "Someone has brought out the Tonka toys."

Kane muttered a curse and then said, "Launch Reaper Four and Five. I say again, launch Four and Five. We're about to have a bad day. Out."

———

ABOARD BOEING C-252 STRATOMASTER OVER MEXICO

They were chalk and cheese. Red Ryan was a big man, strong and confident. Ken Welsh was thinner and not as tall, but as they said in his unit, the man was a goer. And right now, they were at 40,000 feet in the belly of a Boeing C-252 Stratomaster called Skyhammer. Basically, a Globemaster on steroids.

Cara watched the pair insert themselves into their Vipers. Her hair was pulled back into a ponytail, and she wore a headset with a boom mic. "You boys have comms up?"

"Yes, ma'am," they replied.

"Red, take the AT-120."

"Yes, ma'am," Ryan replied, and the Viper locked him in.

The AT-120 was a belt-fed anti-tank weapon which fired depleted uranium rounds capable of disabling, if not destroying, the heavier tanks of the day. However, to sustain a direct hit by a shell from a main battle tank, you were as good as dead.

With the press of a button on the two handheld joysticks, the Viper closed up and Cara was looking at a giant robot. "Gentlemen, ready to deploy?"

"Copy."

"Stand up."

The Vipers came to their feet. Although they were eleven feet tall, the top of the operations and control room deck was still well above their heads.

Moments later they were armed and ready for battle.

"Good luck, Vipers, deploy."

The two machines turned to face the rear of the plane. While they did this, Cara hooked herself to the safety strap attached to the hull and put on one of the oxygen masks utilized by the crew.

When everything was ready, she hit the ramp's down button and watched as the rear of the plane opened.

Moments later, both Vipers were gone.

Cara closed the back of the Stratomaster and went upstairs to the second deck. Along each wall were banks of computers and screens operated by her new Bravo Team. She said into her comms, "Reapers Four and Five are on their way down into the zone. Keep them alive. Bravo Three, I need a sitrep on vitals."

Bravo Three was Crystal Garcia, a former UAV pilot for the RAF (Royal Air Force) in another life. Now Global had retrained and reassigned her. She hit some keys and said, "All systems look to be normal except for Reaper Three. She took an RPG. Her armor integrity is down to sixty percent but holding. Her heart rate seems a little elevated."

"Keep an eye on her. Pull her out if you need to."

"Yes, ma'am."

"Reaper One, copy?" Cara said as she looked at the screens in front of her. Each was linked to a Viper and saw what they saw.

"Read you Lima Charlie, Bravo," came the reply.

"Four and Five are airborne. Expect them to arrive directly."

"Roger that."

Suddenly Kane's camera went down, and his vitals went crazy. Cara could hear intermittent radio transmissions but that was all. Then the link went dead, and every reading for Reaper One's vitals flatlined.

"Reaper One, copy?"

Nothing.

"Ma'am, I've lost everything from Reaper One," Crystal said, her voice holding more than a hint of concern.

"Get it back," Cara said helplessly. "Reaper One, copy? Do you read me?"

Nothing.

Then came the call she dreaded, hoping never to hear it. It was Knocker. "Reaper One is down, I say again, Reaper One is down. He took a fucking tank shell."

The blood in Cara's veins turned to ice, and she felt her heart sink. "Oh, no."

———

MEXICO, ON THE GROUND

Kane's head swam. He was lying on his back. The blast had knocked him senseless, and it looked as though his Viper was offline. "Christ," he groaned as he tried to reset. Moments later, his HUD came back up, along with his comms.

"Reaper, you there, buddy?" Knocker asked.

"Yeah, I'm still here," Kane replied.

"That fucker rang your bell. Time to get back to work. What's your status?"

"Give me a few."

Moments later, another display came up on the HUD. "Armor integrity down to ten percent. I've got warnings everywhere, and the link to Skyhammer is down. Thank God it wasn't a direct hit."

"What about your weapons?"

The display changed again. "They look to be all right."

"Good. Now let's get back into the fucking fight. Four and five are one mike out and these bloody tanks aren't messing around."

Kane looked over at Grace. Her minigun fired a short burst, and then she raised her arm. BOOM—BOOM! Two 30mm depleted uranium rounds reached out like long lances and impacted one of the T-90 tanks, penetrating the armor and catching fire, incinerating the crew. Outside everything looked fine. Inside was a different story.

The tank lurched to a stop, black smoke rising from the gaping hole into the clear desert sky, a dark stain forming against the bright blue.

"Incoming!"

Kane looked up and saw the two parachutes, the two Vipers beneath guiding them in. They hit the ground with an audible thud, and the pair immediately disengaged their parachutes.

Ryan took a knee and opened fire with the AT-120, its booming sound rolling across the dry landscape. The two T-90s stopped dead as they were knocked out. Ryan then shifted his aim to find another target. As he did, he heard Knocker say, "Bollocks, a fourth fucking tank."

It fired.

A huge explosion threw dirt and debris skyward, twenty meters short of where the team was. Ryan's HUD indicated he was locked on, and the AT-120 mailed two more tank killers. One hit the tracks while the other ricocheted off the armor, leaving the T-90 in the fight.

"Smoke out," Knocker said, and a small smoke grenade was shot out of the grenade launcher on the Viper's right arm.

It obscured their position from both the tank and the armored vehicles coming their way. Kane said, "Red, flank that bastard. Ken, Knocker, push right and take out the technicals. Grace, with me. We form a base of fire from here."

Red pushed left along a deep dry wash, not that the eleven-foot Viper was easy to conceal. Knocker and Ken went in the other direction, moving as fast as the units would go. Meanwhile, Kane and Grace's miniguns rattled to life and began finding targets.

There was a big boom, and Kane heard Knocker curse. Over his comms he heard Bravo Three say,

"Reaper Two, your armor integrity is down to seventy percent, are you all right?"

"Close call, Bravo Three."

"Roger that."

"Talk to me, Knocker," Kane said as he switched targets to a new threat.

"I'd be fine if Red would take out that fucking tank," Knocker snapped.

"Red?"

"Working on it." Red's voice held a tone of frustration at being interrupted.

"Work faster."

The situation became dire as several of the operators noticed a First Strike helicopter sweeping low over a ridge to the east.

Knocker said, "You have got to be bloody kidding me. This bastard has a fucking arsenal. And I don't mean the football team either."

Kane turned to assess the incoming threat for himself, taking in the rocket pods beneath each wing. This was indeed a major threat to the Vipers. "Reaper Two, I need the hand of God on this one."

———

ABOARD A BOEING C-252 STRATOMASTER OVER MEXICO

Cara turned to the operator seated on the second console. "Tanner, I need an F6o right now."

Mike Tanner, also known as Bravo Two, was a stick jockey out of the Royal Air Force. He was arrogant and confident because he was good at his job. He wore his wavy black hair like a movie star, and a square jaw set off his good looks. And as Knocker liked to joke, it made a perfect target for a punch in the mouth.

"I have one ten klicks out and inbound, ma'am," he said without looking up from his screen.

"Get that damn First Strike out of there."

"Ma'am, we've got another three tanks inbound," Houlihan called out.

"Ammo status, Crystal," Cara demanded.

"They're running down, ma'am," came the reply.

"Damn it," Cara hissed. "Tanks first, Mr. Tanner."

"Yes, ma'am."

"Reaper Two, copy?"

"Read you Lima Charlie, Bravo."

"Hang on to your shorts, things are about to get bumpy."

———

MEXICO, ON THE GROUND

Another explosion put Knocker's Viper off-balance. "Come back to Global, she said. It'll be fun, she said, get the shit blown out of you, she said."

"You do know I can hear you, right?" Cara said.

"You do know these wankers are trying to kill us and we're low on ammo, right? We're strike fighters, not fucking war machines."

"I'm well aware of that fact, Raymond," Cara replied tersely.

"There she goes, calling me Raymond—"

BOOM!

"What was that, Reaper Two?"

"Have a nice day, Boss."

Out on the flat, the new tanks had fanned out and

were preparing to fire. Meanwhile, the helicopter was coming back around for another run. Add to that the three remaining technicals.

And they needed to get through all of those to reach their target. "Reaper, I have an idea."

"Send," came Kane's reply.

"I'm going to break the line."

"What?"

Then came the three words that Kane dreaded to hear. "Hold my beer."

"Oh hell," Kane growled, and when he next looked, he could see Knocker's Viper running across the plain toward the compound two klicks distant where Juan Morenos assumed his sanctuary and security would keep him safe.

"You stupid son of a bitch, there's a damn Black Cat inbound."

"Tell Tanner not to miss."

Kane shook his head in disbelief, and of course the Viper did as he did. He tried resetting his uplink again, and it came to life. Kane said into his comms, "Bravo Two, we have a Viper running across the target area. Check fire."

"Check fire bollocks," Knocker growled. "Tanner, you frag their asses."

"Copy. First Lucifer away."

The AG-666 Lucifer was a hypersonic air-to-ground missile which was radar-guided and would penetrate its target before detonating.

Ahead of Knocker, as he ran toward the tanks, one exploded into a fireball. Flames and black smoke rose into the air, staining the sky once more. The other three were firing freely at the running Viper. Suddenly the earth erupted around the Brit as the rotary cannon on the helicopter joined in. Kane snarled into his comms, "All Vipers target that damn helicopter. Open fire."

Soon the air was filled with tracers from the Vipers' shoulder-mounted miniguns. The Strike Helicopter flew into a wall of fire, and for a moment seemed to hang in the air before its nose dipped and it fell to earth, exploding on impact.

Kane's HUD display flashed red with a low ammunition warning. His pack would be empty after ten more rounds. What was even worse, for some reason the Viper's integrity had dipped even further and was down to five percent.

"This is Reaper One. Footloose, I say again, Footloose."

"Copy, Reaper One," Cara said in reply. "Footloose."

Then the Viper opened, and he climbed out into the steaming, hot desert.

———

MORENOS CARTEL COMPOUND

Juan Morenos watched the battle unfold in real time from inside his operations room. Things weren't going well, and he was far from happy about it. First, they had decimated his opening tank assault, then his strike helicopter had been destroyed. Now they were going after his other tanks. "What are those things?" he asked out loud.

"Vipers," one of his men answered.

"What are these devil machines?"

"They are like battle robots controlled by a human inside. They are fast and very combat-effective."

As he watched a screen, another technical erupted in flames and then he saw one of the Vipers running through a curtain of explosions. "You tell my men to destroy them now or I will kill their families. Understood?"

"Yes, Patrón."

———

ABOARD A BOEING C-252 STRATOMASTER OVER MEXICO

"Mike, get that damn Black Cat back in the fight," Cara growled as her eyes flicked from one screen to the next. "The Vipers are taking hits that are bringing down their integrity."

"Yes, ma'am, Black Cat is inbound."

"I'm sick of fucking around." Cara changed channels on her comms. "Eugene, take us down. It's time for Skyhammer to flex her muscles."

"Yes, ma'am," replied the pilot, Eugene Potter.

Skyhammer's muscles were a 30 mm ATK GAU-23/A autocannon and a 105 mm M102 howitzer. The same as the now obsolete Specter Gunships. They were fully automated and operated by Molly Wilson, a tough female aviator from Sussex.

The plane started to lose altitude immediately.

Cara said, "Bravo Four, you're up. Punch a hole wide enough for our crazy friend to get through."

"Roger," Molly replied with a smile, glad to be doing something useful.

Fingers danced over her console, and an aim point on the screen moved across it before a beep indicated that it was in position. Then she fired with devastating accuracy.

The technicals disintegrated under the intense and lethal fire from the autocannon. The desert floor exploded upward all around them, and one by one the vehicles joined it.

"Targets destroyed, ma'am," Molly said to Cara.

"Bravo Two, what about the Black Cat?"

"I have a Lucifer in the air, ma'am."

Moments later, the screen lit up and a tank disappeared. "Two T-90s left, ma'am."

"Copy. Bravo Three, I need a sitrep on our people on the ground."

"Ma'am, Reaper One is Footloose. Reaper Two's Viper is down to fifty percent integrity. Reaper Three under twenty percent. Reaper Four and Five are comfortable at eighty-five percent."

"Ammunition?"

"Minimal."

Cara looked at the screen and watched as Knocker's Viper continued to streak across the battlefield. "What are you up to?"

———

MEXICO, ON THE GROUND

Another RPG tracked in his direction and Knocker managed to roll the Viper to avoid it. But only just. Prior to that, the minigun had locked itself down. He never worried about the shooter, just concentrated on pushing hard forward. He looked ahead. The compound wasn't far away.

Numerous 50 caliber rounds swarmed around his

Viper, one impacting the armored casing. He looked at the tower and saw it still stood proud. The minigun unlocked itself and tracked left. *Target Lock* came up on the HUD, and the weapon opened fire.

Man and weapon disappeared.

Now Knocker turned his attention to the main gate. His face took on a grim expression and the Viper increased its speed, closing the distance between itself and his focus.

"Reaper Two, sitrep?"

"Hang on, cock, I'll be with you in a moment." And the Viper crashed through the gates.

———

"One, did you see that?"

"Fuck me," Kane growled from his hiding position. He brought up his automatic Heckler and Koch G550, looking through the scope. "Reaper Five, move to the compound in support."

"Copy, One."

"Four, what's your status?"

A loud explosion erupted across the desert. Kane saw the black smoke rising skyward, and a voice said, "The last tank is out of action, boss."

"Good. Move on the compound. Reaper Three and I will meet you there."

"Copy. Moving on the compound."

Kane started running across the desert. Without the comfort of the Viper, he inhaled the heated air, almost searing his lungs as he drew each breath. "Bravo, I need to know what you see."

It was Cara's voice that came back to him. "Knocker is taking heavy fire, Reaper. His armor integrity is down to thirty percent and dropping. Your people need to get in there now."

"Four and Five, move faster."

"Already balls to the wall, skipper," Ryan replied.

"Knocker, speak to me."

The Brit's transmission came across garbled, and Kane cursed. He tried to run faster, but he had no hope of keeping up with the Vipers. "Reaper Two, get the hell out of there."

"Lucifer away!"

Kane skidded to a stop. "What the fuck? Bravo Two, what did you just do?"

A blinding flash, and the compound erupted in a ball of fire.

Kane stared in horror at the compound. "Bravo Two, copy?"

"Copy, One."

"What did you do?"

"What does it look like?" Tanner replied.

"Son of a bitch. Who gave you the order to fucking fire?"

"I did," replied Cara. "It was me."

———

Knocker groaned. "Fuck me."

The Viper was on its back, and the HUD was flashing a warning that the armor's integrity was down to five percent. Rolling the Viper over, he came up onto a knee. He looked around and saw the devastation surrounding him. Buildings were shattered, piles of rubble and debris were burning, and bodies, or bits of bodies, lay everywhere.

"Anyone out there hear me?" he said over his comms.

All he got back was static.

Finally standing erect in the Viper, it was as though the machine groaned with him. He looked at the battery status and saw that it was draining fast, which meant something else was compromised. He opened the Viper and climbed out, taking the H&K 550 with him.

Smoke hung heavily in the air like a thick fog. Knocker took a couple of steps and then turned to face the gates he'd crashed through in his Viper. A giant figure emerged from the dense smoke. It was Ryan, followed closely by Ken Welsh.

Their Vipers opened and they climbed out. "Are you all right?" Ryan asked.

"My bell has been rung, my Viper is about rooted, and some prick fired a fucking Lucifer on top of me. Apart from that, I'm fine." He waved his hand dismissively.

Knocker sat on the ground, his head on his knees, just as Grace entered the compound. Moments later, Kane appeared, approaching Knocker. Hauling the Brit to his feet, Kane punched him in the mouth.

Knocker sat back down hard, looked up at his friend and said, "I guess I deserved that."

"You dumb son of a bitch," Kane snarled at him. "What the fuck am I meant to do if you go and get yourself killed?"

Knocker gave him a wry grin. "We won."

Kane looked around at the compound. "I guess we—"

Suddenly an armed, bloodied, dust-covered figure came screaming out of the smoke. Kane whirled and fired his 550, the rounds hammering into the shattered form of Juan Morenos. The cartel boss collapsed to the ground, unmoving.

Kane nodded. "Now we've won. Prepare for extract."

CHAPTER 1

They called it Happy Days. It had nothing to do with the 1970s and 1980s television show. This was much more sinister. Happy Days was a synthetic drug that had taken the globe by storm. It was the latest party drug sold in pill form, providing the user an unbelievable high. And the purported best part about it was the slow release. Taken two hours prior to heading out, there was no chance of it being found on the user as they entered the nightclub.

The substance also had another name, one that was only spoken quietly. Roulette. For the simple reason that it killed one in ten users. Most users, however, were willing to take the risk as the high was so good.

Users like Jerry Randall. Lawyer, partner, highflyer, and all-round ladies' man. He adjusted his hair as his reflection stared back at him from the mirror in his bathroom. Happy with the result, he winked at himself and said, "Look out, ladies, Jerry is on the loose tonight."

His cell rang. A high-pitched jingle that drove him nuts. But the ladies liked it and that was all that mattered. He looked at the screen and hit answer. A face appeared. "Leo, my man. What the fuck are you doing?"

"Just making sure you're getting ready for the Dark Room."

The Dark Room was the nightclub they were heading to tonight. Sure, they could go to any one of the many clubs in the area, but all the young crowds, drunk and stoned, made it almost unbearable. The Dark Room had a policy of no one under thirty-five. And with a door charge of two hundred dollars, that kept the rest of the riffraff out. "Almost there, my friend. All set to sweep the ladies off their feet and out of their knickers."

"Don't forget your Viagra," Leo joked.

"Viagra, my ass," Jerry grunted. "One little red pill and I'll be hard enough for whatever comes my way. You got yours?"

"Shit, yeah. Fucking price has gone up to five hundred a tab."

Jerry chuckled. "Next time you want one, give me a call. My dealer is selling for three-fifty."

"I'll do that. Hey, did you see that Global took out Morenos in Mexico?"

"Yeah, I saw it on the BBC."

"That might make prices go up. Seems to happen every time they take out a major supplier. Remember when they took out El Lobo? Fucking prices doubled."

Jerry grunted. "We'll see."

A doorbell rang in the background. "I'll see you at the club. Have to go."

"Is that Mary?"

Leo nodded eagerly. "She's early. With a little luck I can bone her before we go."

"You're a fucking animal."

"One who loves eating pussy. Happy Days."

Jerry grinned. "Happy Days."

The call disconnected, and Jerry shook his head. He walked out of the bathroom and into his living room. Reaching under a cushion, he found what he was looking for. A small box that looked like a battery charging pack. He opened it and tipped the content into his hand.

One small red pill. Jerry grinned and put it into his mouth. No need to worry about it, he'd had them before.

"Happy Days."

———

HER NAME WAS LUNA. It should have been Lunar for she was as high as a satellite circling the earth. But right at that moment, her tongue was circling the head of Jerry's cock as she kneeled under the table out of sight.

Jerry was high too. He just sat there enjoying the heightened sensation and staring at the mirrored ceiling of the club. He reached down and stroked her blonde hair, forcing her lower so that she gagged.

"Hey, you want another fucking drink?" Leo called across at him from the opposite side of the table.

Jerry looked at him as he swam into focus. Jerry nodded. "Sure. Fuck it."

"Are you all right, mate?" his friend asked.

"Yeah, just bloody hot."

Leo nodded. "I'll be back in a minute."

He turned and looked at the line up at the bar. Then added, "I might be a while."

Jerry gave him an absent wave and then stared down at Luna as her head kept bobbing up and down.

"Hey, sweetie, you don't look so good." Mary had slid around the table to sit next to him. She was wearing a red dress with a plunging neckline, which needed invisible tape to make sure it stayed in place so her breasts remained covered.

"That's a lovely dress, Mary," Jerry said, staring at her tits.

"Would you like to see what's in it?" she asked cheekily.

He smiled. "Happy Days."

"Happy Days."

Jerry reached out and pulled the dress away from the tape, revealing Mary's breasts. She leaned forward and kissed him, her tongue snaking out between her parted lips into his mouth. She pulled back and said, "Do you want to bite them?"

"Fuck yeah."

Mary locked her fingers into his hair and pulled him down to her chest, waiting to feel his teeth on her nipples. But nothing happened. She repositioned his head trying to encourage him, but again, nothing happened.

At first.

Then she felt a tremor ripple through Jerry's body, which suddenly became quite violent. Mary grew scared. "Jerry?"

She looked down at him and saw that his eyes were open, but they were rolled back inside his head. Then he started foaming from the mouth.

"Jerry!" Mary exclaimed.

Under the table, Luna stopped sucking and looked up. "What's going on?"

"I don't know."

The tremor grew rapidly into a full-blown seizure and Jerry whacked his head on the table, opening a gash just above the right eye. From there, he slid onto the floor and continued thrashing around.

Then, with Mary shrieking his name, Jerry died thirty seconds later.

Happy Days.

———

JACK HOLLAND, MP, sat in his office, behind a dark-stained solid oak desk, half undressed, watching porn on his computer. As he masturbated, he imagined that his secretary, Alice, was sliding up and down his cock, calling out his name.

Happy Days always did this to him once it kicked in. It turned his nearly seventy-year-old body into that of a raging teenager.

His desk intercom buzzed. Holland reached out and said, "Yes?"

"Are you being a bad boy, Jackie?"

Oh god, it was Alice. "Y-yes."

"Would you like me to come in and watch?"

He felt himself get harder. "Y—" He swallowed. "Y-yes."

The door crashed back, and Alice stood in the door-way, legs wide, black latex shining. She walked toward him, and his hand moved faster. She looked down at it and gave him a look of disdain. "What the fuck are you doing?"

Alice Roberts was in her late twenties and had

curves in all the right places. Nobody could expect that the normally quiet secretary would ever be capable of something like this. But Happy Days had a way of removing inhibitions and transforming the meek into a whole different beast.

She brought the short whip down across his white stomach, hard enough to make him lurch. She did it again, twice more, each time eliciting a gasp of pleasure from the old man.

"Do you want me to suck it for you, Jackie?"

"Y-yes."

"Yes what?" Alice snapped.

"Yes, please."

"Fuck off."

It was part of the game. She would deny him any physical contact until he could stand it no more. Then, when she did initiate touch, he would be so turned on that ejaculation was instantaneous.

Happy Days.

Then they would have sex.

Alice walked around his desk until she got back to where he sat. "Open the drawer."

Holland did as he was told, revealing the bundle of cable ties he kept there. She reached in and removed two. Then, being careful not to touch him, tied his hands behind his chair.

Alice turned it on its swivel so that Holland was facing her. The MP licked at his top lip which was showing a thin bead of sweat. She reached up and pulled the top of her strapless latex suit down, revealing two firm, rose-colored tipped breasts.

Sweat formed on Holland's brow, and Alice thought fleetingly that she might have gone too far. She looked down at his throbbing cock expecting it to spurt to life, but to her surprise as she watched, it was getting soft. "What the fuck are you doing, Jackie?"

"I-I—" He stammered.

"Don't you dare go soft on me now, or I will beat you for being a bad boy."

"I-I—"

Alice frowned, the Happy Days ecstasy suddenly draining away. Holland started to tremble, and his head went back, eyes rolling.

"Jackie?"

The seizure took over. Moments later, Jack Holland, MP, was dead.

Happy Days.

———

"YEEAAHHH!"

The Maserati 790 boomed through the night streets of London at an unbelievable speed, leaving a trail of destruction in its wake after many near misses and avoidances. Somewhere behind the blue streak was a handful of police vehicles that had no hope of intercepting it. And with the disabler itself disabled, they were pushing shit uphill.

Behind the wheel of the beast sat a man in his early twenties. Joel Keller. Beside him sat his girlfriend, Helen Morse. It wasn't his vehicle. What Oxford student could afford to buy such a machine? His father, however, could afford it, and that was how Joel had procured it.

"HAPPY DAYS, BABY!"

Helen shrieked from the passenger seat with glee as Keller swerved violently to miss another vehicle which seemed to be standing still, such was the pace of the Maserati.

"Go faster, baby!" Helen cried out.

Keller's foot went down further, and the seemingly impossible happened. The Maserati went faster.

"Happy fucking Days," Keller muttered to himself as his face took on a grim expression.

Ahead of them, flashing lights appeared. The Maserati slowed, and Keller went back through the gears and swung hard right. The vehicle slid on the wet road suddenly and started to spin. Helen cried out with glee as her world turned. Keller laughed and waited for the spin to stop before flooring the gas pedal again.

Overhead, a helicopter appeared, its bright light flooding the street the Maserati traversed. Keller's foot went down further, and the speedometer hit one-thirty miles per hour. It was suicidal but his drug-addled brain was getting the biggest high of its short life.

"Woohoo!" Helen cried out as she ripped her top off and threw it out the window, the wind whipping it away. "Go faster, baby. Go faster and I'll take my bra off."

Happy Days.

———

THE POLICE HELICOPTER pilot looked down at the Maserati and shook his head. "Who the fuck does this guy think he is?"

"Richard Holly, obviously," the copilot replied.

Holly was a racing car driver who'd won the British Grand Prix three years previously. The pilot, Mark Lister, shook his head once more. "The stupid prick will be jam on the pavement if he keeps this up. What was that? What just came out of the passenger window, Pete?"

"Looked like an item of clothing."

"Shit. How fast is he going now?"

"One-fifty."

"Christ. All cars be advised, target vehicle is now doing one-fifty."

"He has to be high," Pete replied.

"Try that bloody disabler again."

"It's no good, Mark. The thing is rooted."

"Macca, do you think you can put a round in the block when he slows down for the next turn?"

"I can try," Macca replied.

Macca was the onboard sniper. Former SAS, he was well-schooled in the dark arts. The pilot nodded. "Give it a go."

Macca slid the door open and picked up his SciOps .308 sniper rifle. He brought it up and started to track the Maserati.

"Speed is one-eighty."

"Shit," Macca muttered. "The passenger just threw her bra out the window."

"Get ready, there's a corner coming up."

"One-ninety."

"Shit, he's not slowing down," Lister said.

"One-ninety-five."

"There go her panties," Macca said.

"He's running out of room."

However, the Maserati wasn't slowing, if anything it gained speed, and the concrete wall at the end of the street would not be forgiving.

As the three men in the helicopter watched on, the Maserati finally ran out of road and blew into the concrete wall at just over two hundred.

———

KELLER GLANCED over at Helen just as the bra came off and went out the window. She bounced in the seat, making her breasts jiggle. She smiled at Keller and said, "Panties are next, baby."

His foot went down even more, and the Maserati's speed picked up again. Streetlamps flashed by in a blur along with the storefronts. Keller thought his heart was about to explode from his chest, it was beating that hard. Beside him in the passenger seat, Helen was wriggling and tugging at her final undergarment.

"There!" she exclaimed and held a pair of pink lace panties in the air between her thumb and forefinger. Then she tossed them out the window. "What is next, honey?"

He looked over at her and gave her a troubled smile. He started to stiffen, and his foot jammed the gas pedal all the way to the floor. The tremors came next, followed by the seizure.

By the time Helen realized she was about to die and opened her mouth to scream, the concrete wall was already impacting the front of the Maserati.

Happy Days!

———

THE BRITISH PRIME Minister put the report down on her desk and stared at the pair standing opposite. Polly Yates was the MI5 chief. Oliver Preston, MI6. Both had been called to the meeting to discuss the next step in the war on S-24, or Happy Days.

Millicent Stride was, at thirty-five, the youngest prime minister in British history. It was a sign of the times. She sighed and said, "Well? What do we do? These were just three out of twenty-four deaths last night alone. Is it my imagination, or is this stuff becoming even more toxic?"

Yates nodded. "It would seem so, ma'am. We intercepted a shipment two nights ago which had a street value of almost a billion pounds."

"And what are we doing about it?"

"We're doing our best, but it's complicated."

There was disgust on the prime minister's face. "That always seems to be the excuse."

"Ma'am, if I may?" Preston asked.

"What?"

"Polly is right, it is complicated. We know that the pills come from somewhere in South America. We also know that there is a link to Saudi Arabia. To send people into the Hot Zone, we would almost need to put an airborne battalion on the ground. Also, if the government is linked to an operation in Saudi Arabia, then it could damage relations irreparably for years."

"Then send someone not linked," Millicent said.

"That would seem to be the best option." He looked at Polly Yates, who got up from her seat and went to the door.

Moments later, a third person entered the office. She was athletically built, hair down to her shoulders streaked with gray and her face with shallow lines, with her age being a shade over fifty. The prime minister took one look and said, "Oh, fuck no."

The head of Global Private Security sat down and waited to be spoken to. Former general Mary Thurston had been called into the meeting because Global was the only company outside of the government capable of getting the job done.

Preston said, "Mary's people are the only ones who can kill the situation."

"Kill is bloody right," Millicent said bitterly. "Wherever her people go, chaos ensues, followed closely by international incidents. If I had my way, Global would be kicked out of the country."

Thurston said, "Ma'am, if you want British citizens to stop dying hand over fist, then you need to let my people take care of it. If that means starting a war inside the Hot Zone to get done what needs to be achieved, then so be it. This isn't the old days. We're fighting tanks, fighter jets, guided missiles, armed drones, and anything else they can get their hands upon. It's a new fight that calls for new methods to counteract it."

"Out of the question. Find another way. I won't have it."

Thurston got to her feet. "Then your people will keep dying. And I am wasting my time."

Millicent nodded abruptly. "Indeed, you are. Everyone out."

Once outside the room, the three stopped in the hallway. Polly Yates shrugged and gave Thurston an apologetic look. "I'm sorry, Mary, I really am."

"Not your fault, Polly."

"If she only knew," Preston said.

"She'd have a calf," the Global boss said.

"Probably two."

"Then we're agreed?" Polly Yates asked. "We carry on?"

Thurston nodded. "I have no issue with continuing. Just be aware, this thing will get worse before it gets better. I need to know you have my back."

Preston nodded. "If you go down, Mary, we'll go

down with you. Rest assured; we won't abandon ship before you do."

"Thank you."

Polly looked at her and asked, "Did I hear that Global was testing some kind of landing craft off the coast the past few days?"

Thurston nodded. "The Scorpion. It is a high-speed stealth landing craft which allows us to get the Vipers onshore if the need arises. Once we perfect it, I'll pass the plans on to British intelligence, and you can see they get into the right hands."

Preston nodded grimly. "It'll be like the rest. Filed never to be seen."

"I won't be accused of not trying."

Polly nodded. "Good luck, Mary, keep us updated."

Thurston left the building and climbed into the waiting SUV. Cara looked across at her. "Well?"

"As usual, we go it alone."

"I'll put the team to it."

Thurston's expression grew serious. "Be careful, Cara, this won't be easy."

"They never are, Mary. They never are."

CHAPTER 2

The Frog and Toad was busy for a Tuesday. People seemed to filter through the front door with regularity, and as the night progressed, the volume increased. Kane and his team sat at a corner table out of the way. The center of the scarred tabletop was filled with empty beer bottles.

Knocker winced as he adjusted his position in his seat. He scratched at his beard and sighed. "I'm getting too old to be shot, Reaper."

Kane nodded. He was a touch taller than Knocker but just as solid, and like his friend, unshaven. Both men bore tattoos, Kane had one of the Grim Reaper on his back which gave him his nickname. "Aren't we all?"

Grace gave them a pitiful look. "Aw, is Grandpa One and Two feeling their age?"

Knocker's stare hardened. "Careful, lass, I'll pull your pants down and spank that rump of yours."

"You'd pull my pants down, old man, but the plan would probably alter from there."

Welsh said, "From what I've heard, Knocker has a lass in every port."

The former SAS man looked offended. "Not true."

"Really?"

"Yes, it was every second port."

They all chuckled.

Kane took a pull of his beer and looked at the Australian, Ryan. "What's up?"

"I've got a feeling," he replied.

"What kind of feeling?"

"One that very rarely ends well."

Kane nodded. "Drink your beer, worry about it tomorrow."

"You got any family, Kane?" Ryan asked.

Knocker lowered his beer and looked at his friend. Kane shook his head. "No."

"I heard you had a sister."

"She died. Two years ago."

It was a lie. Knocker knew it was. Family for an operator like him and Kane was a weapon to be used by their enemies. Ryan nodded, seemingly satisfied with the answer. Kane on the other hand, looked at Knocker who said nothing.

"God bless Ireland!" The words came from a large, solidly built man at the bar.

There was a man behind him who turned to look and then said, "Fuck off, spud."

The Irishman rotated to face the man and calmly shot him in the chest.

Knocker reacted instinctively, but Kane was expecting it and grabbed his friend by the arm. He gave him a slight shake of the head and nodded toward a man standing near the log fire. He was holding a weapon.

There was a third blocking the door and a woman standing near another door, which led out to the rear of the building. This was more than a random incident.

"Now, everyone just remain calm and it will be fine," the Irishman ordered. "We are just here looking for one person, and then we'll be on our way."

A nervous murmur rippled through the bar.

"Are you here, Professor?"

"That can't be good," Knocker whispered.

"Professor Julius Altman."

"Foreign professor. Things just got worse." Knocker gripped his half-full beer bottle.

The big Irishman started walking through the crowd. He stopped in front of a couple seated at a table. The man had gray hair. "Are you Professor Altman?"

The man shook his head. "No."

The Irishman shot him. "Too bad."

He looked around at the rest of the people in the dark pub. "I'm still looking."

"What do you want with him?" Knocker asked.

Kane muffled a curse.

The Irishman walked over to their table. "Who are you, big man?"

"I'm Ray."

The Irishman looked at the others. "Are these your friends, Ray?"

"You could say that. You lot IRA?"

"A new brand of IRA."

"New, new, or just new? I mean, it's hard to tell because there is always a new one appearing every couple of months."

The Irishman raised his gun and pointed it at Knocker. Kane said, "I wouldn't do that."

The killer turned to Kane. "Really?"

"Yeah, if you do, I'll have to kill you."

The Irishman grinned coldly before he moved the weapon. As he did, Knocker threw the bottle of beer at him, and Kane smashed his. As the man staggered backward, Kane followed his movements and drove the jagged part of the bottle into the Irishman's throat, twisting it as he went. Blood spurted, and the shocked Irishman grabbed at the gushing wound.

Kane moved again, grabbing the handgun and twisting it so that it came free. No sooner had he gained possession when he turned it and shoved the barrel into the Irishman's face. Kane pulled the trigger.

Twice.

Blowing the man's brains out the back of his head.

However, there was no time to relax, there were still three others. Kane swiveled and picked a second target. He fired once. It was safer that way. The bullet punched into the chest of a second killer who dropped where he stood.

Meanwhile, Knocker was moving, taking the third killer by surprise. Before the man could recover, Knocker hit him flush in the face with an elbow, stunning him. Then with fluid movements, Knocker turned him and gripped his head. With a violent twist, the man's neck snapped, and Knocker released him, sending the body slumping to the floor.

This left Grace rapidly closing on the woman. Grace hit her with a shoulder, just as the woman's weapon discharged, knocking the gun up and sending the bullet plowing into the ceiling.

"Fucking bitch," Grace hissed and hit her in the face.

The woman staggered back, and the Team Reaper operator followed her with a snarl on her face. She brought a knee up into the woman's stomach, making her double over. The knee came up again and impacted the woman's jaw. The shooter's head snapped back, and she dropped, out cold.

Grace adjusted her ponytail of dark hair and sneered at the woman at her feet. "Fuck you."

"We all good?" Knocker asked from where he stood.

Ryan and Welsh casually took a sip of their beers. Welsh put his bottle on the table and said, "Knocker, it's your shout."

CARA WAS SHOWN into Thurston's office at Global by a young woman wearing a dark pantsuit. Closing the door, the woman left them to their meeting. Cara sat in a comfortable leather chair and let herself relax.

"How is the team?" Thurston asked.

Cara nodded. "You know."

"Reaper and Knocker settled back in?"

"You read the report of the last op. What do you think?" Cara replied.

Thurston gave her a wry grin. "I'd say just like old times."

"Except it isn't."

Thurston's head bobbed. "Yes, except it isn't."

"How is the testing coming along for the landing craft?" Cara asked.

"Good. Is there anything you need?"

"Better logistics?"

"Working on it."

They spent a few more minutes skirting the main reason for Cara's visit. Then she asked, "What's up, Mary?"

"Off the books mission."

"How far off the books?" Cara asked, her interest piqued.

"The dark side of the moon off."

"You'd better fill me in."

"Happy Days. We're going to work alongside MI5 and MI6 to rid it from the face of the earth."

"Unsanctioned, of course."

Thurston nodded. "Of course. We'll do all the heavy lifting. You and your Vipers."

"Where do we start?"

The Global boss sighed. "That is the question. Get your people onto it and see where it leads you. There is a link to Saudi Arabia and another to the Hot Zone."

"Just so you know, Molly has picked up chatter that the cartels in the Hot Zone have acquired some new weapons."

Frowning, Thurston said, "New weapons? I've not heard anything as such."

"They're trialing unmanned combat robots. Nothing as sophisticated as ours, but they could pose a threat."

"Where the hell are they getting them?"

"Underground out of China. Ever since the Chinese economy had their downturn, they're shipping weapons to the Hot Zone for billions, which in turn is propping them up."

"How are they operating them?" Thurston asked.

"The biggest commodity the world has to offer. Underground gamers."

"You are shitting me."

"That's not all. They also have the capability to deliver them to any combat zone they are required. We've been lucky not to have come across them yet."

"I'll get our intel officers onto it. After I kick their asses. In the meantime, you've got forty-eight hours to get everything together and get your command airborne. Time to go to work, Cara."

————

CARA FOUND Crystal Garcia in the Global operations room, going through files. She looked up, her brown eyes looked tired. "Hey, Boss."

"How long have you been at whatever it is you're doing?"

"I'm looking into the intel on these combat robots the cartels have supposedly got."

"And?"

"Nothing definitive."

"So it is a rumor?" Cara asked.

"Where there's smoke..."

"I get it. However, I have something else for you. Forty-eight-hour turnaround."

"Let me have it."

"We need a lead on Happy Days. Where they're producing it, transports, apparently there is a Saudi link as well. Anything you can come up with."

"Yes, ma'am."

"Great. Have you seen Houlihan?"

"In the gym, I think."

Cara nodded and left her to it.

Cara found Houlihan where Crystal said she would be. Dressed in sweats, she was working over a bag. She stopped and turned to Cara. "I'm guessing you are here for me."

"I need you to get everything prepared to fly."

Crystal nodded. "By everything you mean..."

"Eight Vipers, enough ammunition for them, any spare parts we'll need, small arms, the usual. We'll also need Black Cats on standby wherever we go."

"I can do that."

Cara stared at her. "Everything squared away at home?"

Houlihan nodded. "Yes, ma'am."

"You sure? I need Bravo One's full attention this time out."

"My mother has maybe two weeks left to live. We've said our goodbyes. She doesn't want me around for the end."

"And you're good with that?" Cara asked, raising an eyebrow.

"Rather remember the way she was, ma'am."

Cara nodded. "It's the only way to remember them."

"How long do I have, ma'am?"

"Forty-eight hours."

"Then I'll get right to it."

———

CARA's next stop was Kane. She found him drinking beer with Knocker and watching a John Wayne western. "What is it?"

He looked up from where he was seated. "Comancheros."

"I don't think I've seen it."

"There is a beer in the refrigerator," Knocker told her. "Take a seat."

She grabbed one and sat in a lounge chair. The Comancheros were just attacking a small farm, crossing a river to do so. Kane looked across at her. "What's up?"

"We're being deployed."

Knocker pressed pause, and the movie froze. "When?"

"Forty-eight hours."

"Where?" Kane asked.

Cara sighed. "That is the million-dollar question. I'll know more when Crystal is finished."

"What's the target?" Kane asked.

"We're going to war with Happy Days." Knocker grinned and opened his mouth to speak. Cara held up her hand and said, "You crack a Fonzie joke and I'll smash you in your bollocks with a baseball bat."

"I wouldn't dream of it."

"Liar."

"Are we going unsanctioned again?" Kane asked her.

"Yes." She took a drink of her beer and nodded.

"We'll be ready."

"I hope you are."

———

JAKARTA, INDONESIA

His code name was Chelsea. He was an Indonesian national working deep cover for MI6, currently monitoring the uptick of piracy in the waters around the archipelago. Short, slim, and dark-haired, he was the right hand of a local smuggler.

They were currently at a small airstrip outside Jakarta, waiting for a private jet to land. Chelsea was in the driver's seat. Beside him was Lombok Charlie, the smuggler in question.

"What are we doing here?" Chelsea asked his boss.

"Meeting a plane."

"What is so important about a plane?"

"It's not the plane, it's who is on it."

"Who is on it?" Chelsea asked.

"Majed Abdullah," Lombok Charlie said as though Chelsea should know who he was. When he saw there was nothing forthcoming, Charlie said, "He is from Saudi Arabia. He is setting up a new route for important shipments to Europe. He has heard about my business and has come to talk."

What kind of shipments?

"It will be worth a lot of money for me. Millions, in fact."

A private jet touched down on the end of the runway in front of them. The pair watched as it started to taxi before coming to a stop on the apron, and the screaming engines shut down. As the steps were lowered, a bearded man appeared, followed by three others.

Charlie climbed out of the SUV he and Chelsea were sitting in and walked swiftly toward the group. Chelsea checked his mirrors and saw that from the three SUVs accompanying them, every member of the armed escort had climbed out.

Charlie and Majed shook hands, and they walked toward their waiting vehicle. The two men climbed into the back, and one of the Saudis climbed into the front beside Chelsea. He gave the agent a hard stare before focusing forward.

"It is good to have you with us, Majed. I look forward to our meeting."

"And I you," the Saudi replied. "My colleagues are most anxious to get started."

"A boat is waiting," Charlie explained to the Saudi. "We can discuss along the way."

"You will be an important link in the chain," Majed told him. "From here, the shipments will go to Somalia and distributed."

"It will be a pleasure to work for you," Charlie replied.

Majed shook his head. "You do not work for me. You work for the same people I do. I am a link, the same as you."

"My remote submarine fleet will not let you down, Majed. I promise you that."

Chelsea listened as the conversation continued for the next forty minutes before they arrived at a secluded area. They climbed onto a cabin cruiser and left the dock. Two hours later, they arrived at a place known as The Hub. It was an underground complex complete with concrete sub pens in which there were no less than six Type 763 remote-controlled submarines. All were armed. This gave the miniature submarines bite. But they weren't the reason the Saudi was there. In a separate dock was a much larger sub. A Type 1000 Hunter/Killer.

Majed nodded. "I am impressed."

"It has been modified to carry ten thousand pounds of product for you without compromising any of her armaments."

The Saudi was more than happy. The Type 1000 carried six guided torpedoes as well as a further six guided surface-to-surface anti-ship missiles. Much like the Harpoon missiles of old, but smaller and with more impact.

The Type 763s were only armed with torpedoes.

Majed turned to Charlie. "When can you start operating?"

"Whenever you want."

"There will be a shipment here in five days. I want it transferred to Somalia. If it is successful, you will be given more work."

"Wait," said Charlie. "I thought this was a permanent thing."

"Nothing is permanent in this business," Majed said. "Even life. If you keep my bosses happy, then I am happy. If that changes, my employers will be unhappy with me, and I will terminate our agreement."

"I understand," Charlie replied. "Trust me, I have more than enough people to make sure that doesn't happen."

"I will be counting on it. Now let's go over details."

Chelsea looked into the mirror and saw Charlie smile. "Happy Days."

Majed nodded. "Happy Days."

———

THURSTON CALLED the teams together in the briefing room the following day. She waited for everyone to be seated before starting. "Crystal, tell me what you have."

Crystal leaned back in her seat and said, "Not much. I've been digging as deep as I can and have come up with nothing, not even a name. These assholes are good. I've been trying to find a thread to pull on, but, well..."

Thurston nodded. "I might have something for you.

Oliver Preston from MI6 reached out to me last evening. They have an asset embedded with a smuggler in Indonesia by the name of Lombok Charlie. He has a hi-tech setup. It seems Charlie had a meeting with a Saudi named Majed Abdullah."

The Global commander paused, waiting for Crystal to catch up as her fingers worked. Moments later, two pictures appeared on a large screen. "Charlie is on the left."

Everyone stared at the screen while Crystal did some more digging. Then, after only a few moments, she said, "Ah, fuck it."

"Who is he?" Thurston asked, knowing what the answer would be.

"Majed is Saudi Royal family."

"Could create problems," Kane said thoughtfully.

Knocker shook his head. "Fuck it, the prick is a drug runner. Treat him like we would if he was one of us."

Cara shook her head. "Reaper is right. If we go after him, we do everything in our power to take him alive."

"What else do you have, General?" Kane asked Thurston.

"There is a shipment of Roulette expected in Indonesia in the next few days. Charlie is to transport it from there to Somalia using his remote-controlled subs."

"If they get the drugs aboard, we will pay hell finding them," Knocker pointed out.

Thurston nodded. "Especially when he's using a Type 1000."

"Sounds new," Molly Wilson said.

"It is. Not only does it carry torpedoes, it also has anti-ship surface-to-surface missiles."

Knocker snorted. "You have to love these guys.

Why couldn't it be like the old days? We parachute in, shoot them, blow up their shit, and leave."

"Not that simple, otherwise we'd be using Tomahawks."

"What's the plan?" Kane asked.

"Intel gathering. If you can, take Charlie and blow the shit out of his operation."

"Why not Majed?" Knocker asked.

"Because he's vanished again. Hopefully Charlie will know something."

Cara said, "Come up with a plan to go in without the Vipers. Gather intel, and then we strike when the shipment arrives."

Kane said, "I'm not going in with all my teeth pulled. I want one Viper on standby. I'll take a four-person team."

"Work out a plan, and I'll look at it. In the meantime, we're wheels up in twelve hours."

CHAPTER 3

"All links are up and operational," Crystal Garcia said from her console in the dark sky, forty thousand feet up, on board the Stratomaster. "Reaper One, copy?"

"Copy, Bravo Three. Read you Lima Charlie."

"Excellent. Will keep you updated."

The Stratomaster was circling in lazy figure eights, its stealth capabilities keeping it cloaked. Reaper had dropped in twenty-four hours before and made contact with a local asset named Theo, who had set them up with wheels and a place to put their heads down.

Crystal went back to work doing what she did best— six things at once. An alarm pinged on her console, and she brought up a hidden window. Staring back at her was the mean-looking face of a man wearing an Indonesian uniform. "This just gets better. Ma'am I need a word."

Moments later, Cara was beside her. "What's up?"

"This is Stefano Solossa. He is our friend Lombok

Charlie's brother. I'm guessing he is the reason Charlie doesn't give a shit about much."

"Indonesian military."

"Which means if shit blows up, he can have assets on us within a very short time."

Cara nodded. "Reaper One, copy?"

"Copy, Bravo."

"Be advised that our friend Charlie has a brother named Stefano. He is a general in the Indonesian military."

"Roger that."

"Any movement?"

"No, ma'am."

"Keep me updated. Out."

There was a ping on Cara's encrypted cell. She checked the message. "It's from Chelsea. They're moving."

"Did he say where to?"

"No."

"Reaper, heads up, target on the move."

———

JAKARTA, INDONESIA

"There," said Knocker, pointing out through the windscreen of the Toyota van.

Inside were Kane, Knocker, Grace, and Welsh. Red Ryan was on the command platform as a one-unit quick reaction force.

They were all dressed in civilian clothing but also wore vests and carried suppressed G550s. Beneath their clothing were bulletproof suits made of a synthetic material. Grace engaged the van into gear, and they fell in behind the target convoy.

"Don't get too close," Knocker said. "Remember, we have eyes in the sky."

Grace rolled her eyes. "No shit, Sherlock."

"You two should be married," Welsh said. "You both carry on like a married couple. The only thing you aren't doing is bumping uglies."

Grace dropped back and let the convoy pull further ahead. She said into her comms, "Bravo Three, I'll leave them in your capable hands."

"Copy, Reaper Three. Just hang back, I'm picking up a weird electronic signal."

"Roger that."

They continued tracking the convoy by using the guidance from above. When they reached their destination, it was a dock with a cabin cruiser waiting for Charlie and his crew.

"Bravo Three, they're getting on a boat."

"Copy, I can see that on ISR."

"What do you want us to do?"

There was a pause and Crystal said, "Hold position and—"

"Say again," Kane replied.

Static.

"Shit," Kane growled. "Prepare for contact. Knocker, get us out of here. They were tracking us."

"That's what you get for sharing military secrets with the pricks."

The van slammed into gear and shot backward just as the windscreen shattered. Knocker cursed as the Toyota hammered into a tree behind them.

"Everyone out," snarled Kane.

Doors flew open, and the team tumbled out as

bullets cut through the air. Welsh grunted and fell as a bullet hammered into him. "Shit, I'm hit."

Knocker stopped firing and grabbed him by the collar. "Come on, you bastard, get up."

"It hurts."

"Tell me about it."

The bulletproof undersuit had stopped the round, but with pliability came disadvantages. The pain factor was one of those.

Kane fired at a muzzle flash and growled into his comms. "Bravo, this is Reaper One, we're taking heavy fire. I say again, we're taking heavy fire."

"Roger, Reaper One. We're on it."

Kane urged his people back, and they took cover behind some rocks. Kane reloaded, and as he did, he called across to Welsh. "Are you all right?"

"I'll live."

"He's a big pussy," Knocker called back.

They kept up their rate of fire, holding their own against what seemed to be a superior force. Moments later, Kane's comms came alive again. "Reaper One, from Bravo One."

"Send traffic, One."

"There are vehicles inbound from the west. Looks to be five of them."

"Roger that." Kane called out to Knocker, "Hey, we've got five vehicles inbound from the west."

"Great. I'm between the proverbial rock and a hard place, and I'm low on ammo."

"And we're outnumbered," Grace called out as she reloaded.

Kane nodded. "Roger that. Bravo, request you launch Viper Four."

"Copy, Reaper One. Understood, out."

———

40,000 FEET ABOVE JAKARTA, INDONESIA

Cara looked at Red Ryan. "Gear up."

Ryan nodded and disappeared from the mobile TOC. Cara turned back to the screen and said, "Get me a look at those vehicles."

Houlihan zoomed in, and the ISR feed sharpened. It was immediately evident to Cara what they were, and she cursed. "Shit, they're Panthers."

The T495 Panther was an armored car with a 30mm autocannon, mainly for troop support on the battlefield. They were old but still effective. "Reaper, your visitors are Panthers."

"Just what we need, Bravo."

"Red will be on his way directly."

"Copy."

Cara turned to Molly Wilson, their weapons tech. "Tune up our weapons package and give our people some help until Ryan can get on the ground."

"Yes, ma'am."

"Eugene, take us down."

"Yes, ma'am."

Cara felt Skyhammer begin an immediate descent.

Molly's fingers danced across her console, and her screen changed. The Panthers appeared on the ISR feed. A few more buttons were pushed, and the 105 was online. "Thor ready. Reaper One, this is Bravo Four, copy?"

"Copy, Four."

"Thor is online, keep your heads down."

"Let loose the God of Thunder, Bravo Four."

Thor cleared his throat.

On the screen, Molly saw the first Panther disappear in a cloud of fire and smoke as 105 rounds rained down upon it. The weapons tech had already programmed the rest of the targets so when the first Panther registered as destroyed, the weapon automatically shifted to the next. By that time however, the Panthers had scattered.

The howitzer crashed incessantly; the automated system was fed by a belt. The second Panther vanished in flames, and the system searched for the third target. Moments later, it locked on.

Molly said, "First two targets destroyed, third acquired."

Cara nodded in satisfaction. "Crystal, do you still have eyes on Charlie and his boat?"

"It's pulled away from the dock, ma'am, and headed on course—"

Suddenly, an alarm sounded, and the interior of Skyhammer turned red. Lieutenant Commander Leslie Groves' voice sounded over the internal comms system. "All crew, brace. Missile inbound, taking evasive measures."

Even before she had finished speaking, the Stratomaster was making its turn and launching a curtain of countermeasures.

Cara grabbed hold of a panic handle and said, "Molly, where did that bitch come from?"

"Tracing now," she replied as she canceled the current commands for Thor and searched for the missile launch site. "I have it, they're trying to kill us with our own bloody SAM system."

"Take it out," Cara snapped.

Molly said, "Eugene, bring us around to zero-three-three."

"Copy. Turning—"

"Two more missiles in the air," Groves said in a calm voice.

Molly picked the trajectory and range on her system. Her fingers attacked her keys furiously. "Eugene, turn left now."

There was no questioning the order even though he was the captain of the plane. Their world was built on trust, and no sooner had Molly spoken than he started the left turn. By the time he was halfway through it, the updated Phalanx CIWS M85 Vulcan Rotary Cannon anti-missile system came to life with a tearing sound.

Flames erupted from the muzzles, and tracers shredded the sky. The first of the SAMs disappeared in a fiery explosion. The guidance system tracked the second missile, and once more, the system known as Ripper did its work.

"Threat neutralized," Molly said calmly.

"Right, get that launcher," Cara snapped.

The 105 came to life, and within moments, Thor did the same. Molly nodded. "Target destroyed."

"Reaper Four, ready to launch."

Cara adjusted her boom mic. "Reaper Four, launch."

———

ON THE GROUND

"Reaper One, you still have three Panthers inbound."

"Copy, Bravo One," Kane replied as bullets hammered the shipping container where he was sheltered. "I'll throw rocks at them if they get too close."

"Won't have to, my friend. Captain America is inbound to save the day."

"Say again, Reaper Four."

"I was just saying—"

"Just shut up and get your ass down here," Knocker growled, interrupting the transmission. He reloaded his G550. "Last mag."

To his left, Grace reloaded as well. "Same here. I knew I should have brought double ammo."

Suddenly a Panther appeared, bursting through some brush out onto the approach road to the dock. Its main gun opened fire in haste, and the shell impacted to the right of where they were.

"Pull back," Kane snarled.

"What I'd give for a Viper right now," Grace said.

There was a thump close by, and a voice said, "You called."

The Viper looked bigger in the darkness, and it whirred as its GAU-2/A minigun appeared. It came to life, ripping apart everything it touched. Metal, flesh, bone. One of the Panthers stopped, and its turret started to turn. Ryan lifted his arm to expose the 30mm. It fired twice, and the Panther exploded.

Inside the Viper, Ryan turned his head, looking for more targets. The minigun followed his movements, and three shooters appeared. They looked to be military. The minigun opened fire, and all three vanished.

The Viper was a mechanical beast. Even one, if used properly, gave the team on the ground an advantage, provided the operator could detect its targets. Which was why Ryan was surprised when the Viper was thrown back as it was hit by a 30mm round from a Panther. The only bonus was that the Indonesian Army wasn't using depleted uranium rounds. However, the integrity of the armor was compromised a great deal.

On the HUD display, a warning flashed, indicating that the armor integrity was down to thirty percent. That meant another direct hit, and Ryan was in trouble.

"Reaper Four, are you all right? I'm reading armor integrity at thirty percent. Confirm."

"Roger that. I took a direct hit from a Panther. At the moment, I'm immobile."

"Copy. I'll see what I can do. Just sit tight."

Moments later, Thor threw hammers at the nearby Panther, and it exploded under the onslaught. That left just the one, and above at her console, Molly rectified the situation. "Reaper Four, you're clear."

"Copy."

Ryan had worked on getting his Viper back online and now had it up again. It came to its feet and was mobile once more. On its armor, he could hear the impact of the small arms fire. The minigun came around and once more blazed its own fire.

Bullets ripped through the attacking soldiers, driving them back. Ryan turned, looking for more targets, but his HUD was clear. Suddenly, he realized that the shooting had stopped.

"Reaper One, this is Reaper Four. It looks like your friends have bugged out."

"Roger that."

"Brother, confirm our friends are gone," Ryan said.

"Affirmative, Reaper Four. It looks like things are clear."

Cara came on the line. "Reaper One, we need to get you out of there. Prepare for extract. Will have some kind of bird there soon."

"Roger. Will be awaiting extract."

CHAPTER 4

40,000 FEET ABOVE JAKARTA, INDONESIA

Cara looked at the ISR screen and asked, "Where's our target?"

Houlihan looked up at her commander as the Stratomaster rocked on some turbulence. "They look to be headed out to an island northwest of Jakarta."

"Zoom in. Let's have a look at it."

Houlihan tapped some keys, and the picture changed. Cara nodded and said, "Crystal, are you seeing this?"

"Wait one, ma'am." A few moments later, she said, "I have it."

"Find out what you can about it."

"Yes, ma'am."

Cara frowned. "Zoom in on that there." She indicated the spot with a finger.

"Ma'am?"

"Sorry, Pat." She leaned in and touched the screen with her outstretched hand. "There."

The frame zoomed, and the picture became clearer. "What is that?"

"Give me a moment, ma'am," Houlihan said.

"Crystal, can you magic this for me?"

"On it."

The picture moved around as Crystal worked deftly to enhance the image. By the time she was finished, they were at sea level, looking along a dock into a concrete-encased opening.

"Are they submarine pens?" Cara asked.

"Could be."

"X-ray it."

"Yes, ma'am."

In the years since Reaper's inception, technology has come a long way. Part of that was a new hypersensitive ground penetrating radar which mapped everything below ground to a depth of almost a thousand feet.

Slowly, a picture began to form, and a few minutes later they could see what was below. Crystal said, "Looks like the old Nazi U-boat pens from back in the day. Complete with subs."

"Can we identify them?"

"I'm thinking three, seven-six-threes, and a one thousand."

"I wish we could get some real-time feed from there."

"What about Walter?" Houlihan asked.

Walter was the next generation in compact UAVs. Named after Sir Walter Raleigh, it was no bigger than a hummingbird and could be controlled from anywhere.

Cara said into her comms, "Reaper One, copy?"

"Copy, Bravo."

"Put Walter up for me. I have a mission for him."

"Roger that."

A short time later, Kane said, "Walter should be coming online."

Cara turned to Houlihan, their drone operator. "Pat, Walter is coming online."

The screen changed once more, and the feed came on from the drone. Houlihan took her joystick and performed a few maneuvers and said, "Bravo One has control."

"Copy, Bravo One," Kane replied. "You have control."

Walter traveled from land out across the water and arrived at the target area at the same time as the boat with Charlie and his people on it. It followed the boat in, and Houlihan found a ledge where Walter could land while using the camera to observe the operations occurring within.

Charlie and his entourage climbed from the boat onto the dock. He talked to another of his men—remonstrated would have been a better word, for he was far from happy.

"Can we get some audio?" Cara asked.

"Should be able to," Houlihan said, with a few strokes of her keyboard.

"...what the fuck that was that? Who are they? We have a shipment coming in tomorrow from our new customer and if it doesn't get out of here, then I won't be the only one to suffer the consequences."

"I will find out," the second man replied.

"Ask my brother. It was obvious he knew something I didn't."

Cara looked at Houlihan. "I need to know how they knew we were there. Find out if we're compromised or whether they were just lucky."

"Ma'am."

"*...the one thousand is ready to go tomorrow once it is loaded. Are the weapons loaded?*"

"*Yes, everything is ready.*"

"Get me a deeper look inside."

Walter became airborne once more and flew deeper into the sub pens. As he went, Houlihan took recon photos which were immediately stored at her console. Twenty minutes later, she said, "Ma'am, we need to bring Walter home."

"Has Reaper and his team been extracted?"

"Yes, ma'am."

"Deep six, Walter."

"Copy."

"Now, let's see what we have."

———

FENTON AIRFIELD, AUSTRALIA

The weather was hot and humid and would stay that way until the rain came in the afternoon, only to return once the rain was gone. The Global team was set up at Fenton Airfield in the Northern Territory. Once utilized as an air base back in World War Two, it had been reopened two years previously. Converted to take larger planes and military transports, it was now used by the Southwest Pacific Patrol, which was a conglomerate of forces from different countries monitoring China's expansion.

Kane stood beside Cara as they examined the photos of the sub pens. He said, "Come in from the sea, plant the charges, and get out."

Cara shook her head. "We leave that to the

Australians. We want Charlie, which means going back to Jakarta and pulling him out."

"We can do that."

"He has to be taken alive, Reaper." She looked him in the eye to ensure he understood. "I need to know what he has inside his head."

"Besides shit?"

"Yes."

Houlihan appeared, sweat staining her T-shirt. "The Australians just reached out. They put a team in place, and the first thing they reported was that the one thousand had gone."

"The shipment must have arrived early," Cara said. "We know roughly where it's going, but—"

"What about intercepting it?" Kane asked.

"The Australians have two of their new Tamworth-Class Destroyers in the area the submarine is likely to traverse. They've tasked them to keep an eye out for the submarine."

"I don't like their chances," Kane said.

Houlihan shrugged. "They might get lucky."

"Or unlucky."

Cara nodded. "Get your people ready. You go tonight."

"You're kidding. We've been back twelve hours."

"Do I look like I'm kidding?"

"Shit."

———

JAKARTA, INDONESIA

Charlie let himself into his dark penthouse apartment and switched the light on, throwing his keys on the wooden console table. He jumped almost immediately when he saw Majed and one of his men standing next to a chair with a bloodied figure tied to it.

There was a gag in Chelsea's mouth which had muffled his screams when they had tortured him. Charlie stared in horror at his man and demanded, "What the fuck is happening?"

"Your man is a traitor," Majed replied. "He is the reason everything is at risk."

"Nothing is at risk. The shipment is gone."

"Everything is at risk. I already told you, he betrayed everything."

"I don't believe it."

"Believe it. He is an MI6 spy."

Charlie stared at Chelsea and knew immediately what Majed said was true. He took his Glock from his pants and shot Chelsea in the head. "Damn him."

"What will you do?" Majed asked.

"I have contingencies. What will you do?"

"I will go home where they can't touch me."

"They know about you?"

The Saudi's eyes narrowed. "I'm going to take a wild guess and say yes."

Charlie's eyes grew wide as though realization was just dawning. "They will know about Somalia."

Majed nodded. "Yes, but they won't know where. Didn't you tell me when we first met that you were the only one—apart from the operators—who knew the destinations of each submarine?"

"Yes."

"Then there shouldn't be a problem. Our dead friend wouldn't have known."

"You're right."

"But remember, if something happens to the shipment, you will be held accountable for it."

"I understand."

———

HMAS GERALDTON, INDIAN OCEAN

Captain Bob Murphy sat in his chair and stared past the rise and fall of the Tamworth-Class guided Missile Destroyer's bow at the ocean as though he was expecting something to materialize. To the south of the *Geraldton* was *HMAS Corowa*, sailing the same patrol patterns as those of her sister ship.

They had been on station for six hours west of Sumatra. Their orders: intercept a suspected submarine used for smuggling drugs.

Both ships had originally been sailing out of Darwin, bound for Freemantle. However, a last-minute change of orders off the Western Australia coast had them where they were right then.

Murphy was lost in his trance when he was interrupted by his XO, Bryce Campbell. "Coming up to course change, sir."

"Thank you, Number One."

"This is like looking for a needle in a haystack, Skipper."

Murphy nodded as he felt the ship shift beneath him as it hit another swell. "A needle we're meant to find. Bring us down to twenty-knots, Bryce."

"Aye, sir."

For the next twenty minutes, the *Geraldton* kept to her search pattern and was about to make another turn when, "Sonar is picking up screw noises bearing zero-four zero. Range—missile launch, we've got two missiles in the air."

"How the hell did that happen?" Murphy demanded.

"High-speed screws in the water!"

"Shit," the captain growled. "Sound the alarm. All hands brace for impact. Weps, knock those things down."

Orders were snapped and responded to while the Phalanx came online. The missiles approached at phenomenal speed and were almost on top of the destroyer when the rotary cannon opened fire.

Within seconds, the Phalanx had turned the tables on the missiles, and both exploded in a ball of flames.

"Cox'n hard over helm, countermeasures ready to fire," Murphy snapped. "Give me a range on that torpedo."

"Range one thousand meters."

"Keep her bow coming round, Cox'n."

"Captain, the torpedo is homing, following our turn to intercept."

"Thank you, Number One."

"Range, six hundred meters."

"Thank you. Where is that bloody sub?"

"Port side bearing one-two-five."

Murphy nodded. "Prepare anti-submarine torpedoes. Launch countermeasures."

"Missiles in the air!"

"Calm down. The ship will take care of herself. Just—"

BOOM!

Everything shuts down.

"Talk to me, what just happened?"

"Working on it, sir, but we just lost all power."

Horror struck Murphy as he realized they were dead in the water. He fought down the urge to let his emotions override his calmness before saying, "All hands brace for impact. Good luck, ladies and gentlemen."

CHAPTER 5

"Listen up," Cara said, gathering all her personnel around her. "The Australians just lost a Tamworth-Class destroyer in the Indian Ocean. Everyone is assuming that it was the submarine that did it."

"Losses?" Kane asked.

"Twenty dead, times two wounded. They were picked up by her sister ship. By the time that happened, the sub was gone. We need to get our friend Charlie and put a stop to this. How are we progressing?"

"All the equipment we'll need is already aboard," Kane said.

"Do we have a location on Charlie?" Cara asked.

Crystal put her hand up to speak. "He's at a place outside of Jakarta. It looks to be an old school. It's shut down now, but I think he's using it as a base. He was in the city but moved after meeting with this man."

A picture appeared on a screen. Cara said, "Majed Abdullah."

"What kind of force is there at the school?" Knocker asked.

"Fifty, sixty shooters."

"He doesn't do things by halves," the big Brit growled.

"It would be advisable to take the Vipers," Crystal said to Kane. "I counted a couple of machine gun nests as well."

Kane nodded. "Strike hard and fast and get the hell out."

"We can do that. Any sign of heavy equipment?"

"No, not this time."

Kane said, "Knocker and Grace will go in the Vipers. Ken, you and Red can sweep the school with me. We'll go in first while the others hang back as a QRF. What about the sub pens?"

"They will be hit the moment you launch."

"Roger that. This should be interesting."

———

OUTSIDE JAKARTA, INDONESIA

"Two targets to your left, Reaper One," Houlihan said into his ear. "Both walking your way."

Kane remained silent and brought his suppressed 550 up to his shoulder. Beside him, Ryan did the same. Then, a few heartbeats later, the two roving guards appeared. Kane and Ryan stroked the triggers of their weapons, and the men dropped.

"Let's get them undercover."

Back in the darkness of the wood, the two hulking Vipers waited, Knocker and Grace within them.

"Reaper Five, we've got two snipers on the rooftop."

"Copy."

Welsh paused and searched the rooftop with his Designated Marksman Rifle, DMR. He found the first and then moments later found the second. "I've got them, Bravo. Engaging."

He hit number two first, followed by number one in quick succession. "Bravo, both X-rays are down."

"Roger that. Reaper One, Charlie Mike."

Kane and Ryan had dragged the two dead guards into the shadows, and now the three of them were rushing toward the old school. When they reached it, they halted.

Kane said, "I need to know where he is, Bravo."

"Our intel has him top floor, rear, last room along the hallway."

Kane took off his pack and reached inside. He removed an air-launched grappling hook and pointed it up. Moments later, the launcher hissed, and the compressed air exploded out of the barrel, forcing the four-pronged hook up to the rooftop.

Once the hook was set, he hooked the rope into the belt winch and set it in motion.

The compact machine lifted him toward the rooftop in a smooth motion. Once at the top, he kneeled and waited for the others to join him.

Ryan was the last man over, and from there they hurried across the rooftop to the door which accessed the stairwell to the third floor.

Kane opened the door, and Welsh entered. His white phosphor NVGs turn everything to daylight.

Welsh traversed the stairwell and stopped on the third-floor landing. He paused and, in a whisper, said, "Bravo, I'm at Teacher. I need to know what's on the other side."

"Reaper Five, you have a rover in the hallway and sleepers in the rooms."

"Copy. What's the location of the rover?"

"He's walking away from you, about two-thirds along the hallway."

"Roger that. Moving."

Welsh turned the knob and pushed the door open. It was stiff, the top hinge almost seized. Kane stopped it from slamming back as Welsh moved into the hallway.

The Brit had his 550 up as he moved silently toward his target. As the guard started to turn, Welsh shot him but said nothing.

The guard dropped to the floor of the wide hallway, his weapon spilling from his grasp and clattering on the floor. Welsh froze at the sound and waited. Kane held his breath, but nothing happened. Houlihan said over her comms, "Up ahead on the right."

The Brit kept moving until he reached the door. He tried the knob and it turned easily, so he pushed the door open and stepped into the large, what used to be a classroom.

Welsh let the 550 hang by its strap and took out his suppressed handgun. He walked across the tiled floor to where Lombok Charlie slept quietly in his bed. The Brit pressed the weapon against the man's head and said into his ear, "Wakey-wakey, moth-erfucker."

Charlie's eyes flashed open, suddenly awake. He tensed and Welsh said, "No, not advisable. Just roll over and we'll truss you up like a nice package."

"Who are you? MI6?"

"MI6 are pussies compared to us, mate," the Brit replied. "We're meaner and more fucked up."

Kane covered Charlie while Welsh secured him.

The operator was getting him off the bed when Charlie called out.

"HELP! HELP!"

"Shit," Welsh muttered and hit the smuggler hard.

Overall, it wasn't much, but enough to raise the alarm, and the school soon rang with the sound of gunfire.

———

RYAN OPENED fire as more shooters poured into the hallway. They dropped into a heap on the floor, and he pulled back as more bullets ripped through the walls. Ryan reloaded and said, "We can't bloody stay here."

Kane nodded. "Out the window. Just hold them back for a minute."

"Reaper One, you have more shooters headed toward the main building," Houlihan said over the comms. "Looks like a technical is with them."

"Knocker, time to earn your pay."

"And here I was thinking a man with your reputation could handle it."

Kane opened the window and immediately dove for the floor as a machine gun opened fire and ripped holes in the wall around it. "Nope."

A bouncing sound could be heard from the hallway as an object careened across the old tile floor. It was followed by a loud cry, *"Grenade!"*

They hit the floor as the explosion tore a hole in the wall further along the hallway. Thankfully the slippery tiles had created little friction, and it was propelled further than expected.

Dust rained down upon them, and Kane rolled over onto his knees. "Call out."

"I'm still here," Welsh said.

"Me too," Ryan said.

"Knocker, clear that fucking machine gun so we can get out of here," Kane growled.

"On it."

———

THE TWO VIPERS came lumbering out of the trees and into the light. Their miniguns were up and ready, and their pilots were looking for targets. Knocker said, "Give me a position on the machine gun, Bravo One."

"South side of the building. It looks like it's mobile."

Bullets started ricocheting off the Viper's armor as four shooters came into view. Knocker said, "Grace, take the machine gun. I'll take care of these guys."

Grace's Viper lumbered away, oblivious to the rounds peppering it. Meanwhile, on Knocker's HUD, he had a target lock, and the minigun let all hell loose.

The first shooter blew apart from the hailstorm assailing his body. Knocker looked at the second, and the minigun followed his gaze. "Night, night, motherfucker."

A short burst and number two was gone to hell, hot on the heels of his counterpart.

The remaining two shooters did the only thing they could do.

They ran. And took shelter behind an old wooden shed and thought they were safe.

The minigun came to life again, pulverizing the shed in front of them. The shooters taking refuge, no longer having cover, were taken down as well.

Meanwhile, Grace was moving quickly around to the south side of the old school. She rounded a corner and the Viper lumbered into a wall of machine gun fire from one of the nests.

The heavy machine gun was a fifty-caliber monster. Each impacting round shook the eleven-foot metal beast. She turned her head, and her HUD lit up with a threat warning. The impacts were depleting the armor's integrity. It was down to eighty percent.

The minigun roared to life, and tracers sliced through the night. The 7.62mm rounds ripped through flesh and bone. The position came apart with sudden violence as Grace raised her arm and fired the 30mm cannon with depleted uranium rounds.

The position failed to exist.

Grace lumbered on and reached the south side where the mobile machine gun was sited. It was an LMG and was firing up at the window where Kane and the others were sheltering. Once she had target lock, the minigun cycled to life.

"Reaper One, south side is clear."

"Copy, Three, we're on our way."

———

40,000 FEET ABOVE JAKARTA, INDONESIA

"Ma'am, I have Mary Thurston on the line for you."

Cara's head snapped around. They were in the middle of an operation, and her boss was calling. The question was why? "Put her through."

"Yes, ma'am," Crystal replied.

"This is Cara."

"You need to abort the operation now."

"What?" Cara was stunned. "We're in the middle

of it. I've got troops in contact, and we've rolled the package up."

"Let him go and get out," Thurston ordered.

"Ma'am—"

"Now, Cara."

Fuck! "May I ask why, ma'am?"

"Because someone knows you're there, and that someone called the British Home Office, and they called the Prime Minister, who called me and threatened to kick Global out of the country unless we got out of Indonesia. So, as you can see, I'm in the middle of damage control. Now cut the package loose and get out."

"Yes, ma'am."

The call disconnected and Cara stared at the screen, thinking about her next move. "Reaper from Bravo."

"I'm still here."

"Cut the package loose and get out."

"Say again, Bravo."

"Cut the package loose and get out. It comes from those higher than me."

"Roger that."

Cara turned to Houlihan. "Send the extract team."

"Yes, ma'am."

———

OUTSIDE JAKARTA, INDONESIA

"Let's go," Kane snapped. "Bring him with us."

Ryan looked at his commander. "Weren't we just ordered to cut him loose?"

"That's right."

"Well?"

"She didn't say where."

"You're the boss."

Welsh looked out the window and saw Grace's Viper below. "This is going to be fun."

He grabbed Charlie and said, "Out."

"How are we going to get down?" the smuggler blurted out.

"You see them bushes down there, mate? Jump."

"What?"

"Fuck it." The Brit grabbed Charlie by the collar and threw him out the window. "Grace, coming down."

"Copy."

Welsh followed him out, plunging down into the bushes below. Even though the branches cushioned the fall, he still hit hard. "Jesus wept."

"Coming down," Ryan called out and was the next to freefall into the already smashed bushes below.

That left Kane. He looked down and shook his head. "Idiots."

Then he became one of the crowd.

He picked himself up with a groan. "Is everyone all right?"

"We'll live," Welsh said.

"Fall back to the trees. Grace, where is Knocker?"

"Not far away," the Brit said as he lumbered up to them.

"Cover our fallback."

"Copy that."

They took Charlie into the trees and halted. Kane put him on his knees and said, "You have one chance before I lose patience. Where is the sub going?"

"What sub?"

"That's it, no more. Where?"

"No idea."

Kane shot him in the leg. Charlie cried out in pain and lurched violently. "Try again."

"All right, all right. Port Francis in Somalia."

"When?"

"Should be there in four days."

"Is Majed behind it?"

Charlie shook his head. "No, he's a middleman. Organizes the transport. He works for whoever is behind it."

"Name?"

"I-I don't know."

Kane raised his handgun. "Name?"

"Honest, I don't know. Majed didn't say."

"Who is your man in Somalia?" Kane asked.

"Cumar," Charlie replied. "But he is not my man. He is Majed's man."

"He is in Port Francis?"

"Yes, under the protection of Tadalesh," Charlie added.

"The warlord?"

"That is him."

"Anything else?"

"No."

Kane shot him.

"What was that?" Ryan asked.

"Fucker would have screamed the moment we left. Everyone would know it was us that did this," Welsh said. "Better him than us."

"All right, enough of the chat. Everyone to the extraction site. Move."

———

LONDON, ENGLAND

Millicent Stride was leaning back in her leather office chair, starting to feel the effects of Happy Days when the cell rang. She looked away from the gyrating, semi-naked form of Kylee, her secretary, and opened the drawer where it was sequestered. "Fucking shit."

She took it out and hit the answer button. "You have impeccable fucking timing."

"They killed my man in Indonesia," the voice on the other end said.

Millicent indicated for Kylee to come closer and turned her chair away from her desk. "I got them out of there like you wanted."

"What I wanted was for them not to be there in the first place."

"I did what I could. But your man sank an Australian destroyer. If you think that won't have repercussions—"

"You will see that it doesn't."

Millicent felt the drug surge through her veins. She indicated for Kylee to kneel between her splayed legs. "I will do what I can."

"Need I remind you what I can do, Millicent?"

Millicent pushed Kylee's head down and stifled a moan. "No, you don't."

"Good. Make sure they stay away from my drugs. I don't care how you do it, just make sure you do it."

The call disconnected, and Millicent stiffened as she ran her hands through Kylee's hair. "Don't stop. Don't ever fucking stop."

———

THE HOT ZONE, CENTRAL AMERICA

To some it would always be Colombia, but to the outside world, it was known as part of the Hot Zone, a constant state of war between the drug lords, the dealers, and the rest of the world that sent their people across the fence. The countries known before as Central America are now under the control of Fernando Torres. To those inside the boundaries, he was God. And anyone who defied God, went to hell.

He was an average-sized man with a bushy mustache and dark hair to match. He sat on a sun lounge beside a pool full of green water and lily pads. Every now and then, the water rippled from movement under the surface, the only telltale sign of what lurked beneath.

A cheerful shout from beyond the pool drew his attention to a young girl, perhaps six or seven years old, kicking a football with two men. He watched her for a while as she ran around in circles, trying to gain back control of the ball.

"That is enough, Ana. Come in and wash up."

"But, mama—"

"Now," Maria Torres said firmly to her daughter. She glanced at Fernando and waited for him to rebuke her as he normally did. But her brother-in-law remained silent.

Since the death of Maria's husband back before Ana was born, she had come to live with Torres. Although the biological father of the little girl wasn't his brother, Torres wasn't aware of the fact, and heaven forbid he should ever find out. If he did, he would kill both mother and child.

Ana ran up to her mother and said, "Can't I just have two more minutes, please?"

"No. Go and do what I asked."

The little girl disappeared inside. It was only then that Torres spoke. "A couple of minutes wouldn't have hurt."

"She doesn't need spoiling, Fernando," she replied hesitantly.

"I will do as I wish. After all, she is my brother's child."

Maria was about to speak when Torres's cell rang. He picked it up, answered, and pressed the speaker. "Yes?"

"We have a problem with our courier in Jakarta."

"What kind of problem?"

"He was killed by British mercenaries. Working for MI6."

"Are you telling me my drugs have—"

"No, no. The shipment made the submarine. But the mercenaries—"

"What mercenaries, Majed?"

"They work for Global."

Maria hesitated as she turned to walk away.

"Is one of them called Kane?"

"Yes."

"Then if you get the chance, kill him. I would consider it a personal favor."

"I have talked to our asset, and she will take care of the problem. But I'm calling you as a courtesy to inform you what has happened."

"Make sure our asset carries through with her part of the arrangement. And find someone to replace our man."

"I will see to it."

"Remember, without the pipeline, we have nothing. And if I have nothing, you will have nothing. Including your life."

The call disconnected, and Maria walked away, leaving Torres to his thoughts.

CHAPTER 6

Thurston stared at Kane and Cara from behind her office desk and held up the folder she had in her hand. "I read the report and what I want to know is how you got the information."

"He volunteered it," Kane replied.

"Just like that?"

"Just like that."

"It also said he was killed by a stray bullet from his own men. Do you stand by that?"

Kane nodded. "He was killed by a bullet."

"Monitor on," she snapped curtly. The monitor on the wall came on. "Play file."

And it played. What they were watching was an ISR feed of Kane and the others in the woods questioning Charlie. It finished when Kane shot him.

Cara stared at the wall. Thurston stared at Kane. "What the fuck was that?"

Kane remained silent.

"I'm waiting."

"The mission was compromised. That was me stopping it from getting any worse."

"By shooting the man you were told to let go."

"If we had let him go, who knows where it would have stopped. We would have lost the drugs and the transit station in Somalia."

Thurston's eyes blazed. "Your job is to follow fucking orders."

"Yes, ma'am."

The door to Thurston's office opened, and her secretary appeared. "Ma'am, we have a problem."

"What is it, Leena?"

"It is me," Millicent Stride said as she pushed past, followed by Oliver Preston from MI6.

Thurston felt the turmoil beneath the surface, but externally she showed nothing. Instead, she said, "John, Cara, excuse us, please."

"No, stay," Millicent said. "I want to hear from them as well."

"What is this about?" Thurston asked.

"It is *about* whether or not Global gets the luxury of staying in the country or I shut you down and kick you out."

Thurston glanced at Preston, whose face remained stoic. "I can assure you my people were nowhere near wherever they were meant to be."

"Bullshit. They were there and especially after I told you not to be anywhere near this. I don't want your help."

"Do you have proof?" Kane asked.

Thurton's head snapped around. Millicent glared at the big operator. "I don't need proof."

"Yes, ma'am."

"Now—"

"I'll take that as a no," Kane finished.

"Stand down," Thurston snapped.

"What did you find out?" Millicent asked.

Thurston was confused. "Ma'am?"

"You questioned and killed a man. What did you learn?"

"Who told you that, ma'am?" Cara asked.

Exactly what everyone else was wondering.

"It doesn't matter how I know, just that I do know, and I expect my questions to be answered." Her face was becoming redder, and she scratched at her arm.

"Whoever told you that, ma'am, was wrong. We were in Lithuania for the past few days helping authorities smash an arms' smuggling ring."

Preston frowned but remained silent. Thurston wondered what the hell he was even doing there. Millicent's eyes narrowed. It was obvious she'd come without proof, but even so, she was on the money. But she was conflicted whether to push it further. She made her decision.

"One more slip up, and you and your mercenaries are gone, Thurston. I was hoping we could work together at the start, but you and your people are just loose cannons causing chaos and destruction wherever you go."

"Your predecessor didn't think so."

"That was then. I see it differently. This is it. No more. Goodbye."

She turned and started to leave. Stopping, she stared at Preston. "Are you coming, Oliver?"

"I just need to tidy up a few loose ends before I return to London. I'll find my own way back."

"Suit yourself," Millicent grunted and left the room.

"Where the hell did she get her information?" Thurston asked Preston.

He shrugged. "I have no idea. How accurate is it?"

"Pretty fucking accurate," Cara said.

"What I want to know is how long she's been using Roulette." Kane said aloud.

All eyes in the room turned to him.

"Are you using it?" Thurston asked him.

"Her face was getting redder, she was scratching her arm, and she had a red tinge to her eyes. And she fidgets. I bet if you dug deeper, you would find out what I'm saying is true."

Thurston stared hard at Preston. "Can you find out?"

"No."

"Oliver—"

"She's the British Prime Minister. She wouldn't dare. She meets with foreign dignitaries almost weekly. Like next week she's traveling to Saudi Arabia."

"To meet with who?"

"The King."

"Does she have any other meetings?"

"Yes, she's going out to look at the Line."

"Why her?"

"What?"

"Don't you have people for that?" Thurston asked.

"She wants to handle it personally. She wants to secure a deal to do with the British Line."

The British Line was a copy of the Saudi model, just not as big. "Who is she meeting?"

"I don't know. They haven't let us know."

"Why not?"

"Because she's using her own security."

"Something isn't right," Kane said.

Preston nodded. "I agree, but until we know what it is, we can't do anything about it."

"You can find out if she's using, though."

"I can try."

"In the meantime," Kane said, "we're going to Somalia."

"Wait a minute," Thurston said. "We were told to stay away from this."

Kane smiled. "We are. MI6 is sending a team to look into a threat arising from a well-known warlord in the region. Right?"

Preston shook his head. "What the hell. But we do this right. We run the op from my center."

Cara nodded. "I can live with that."

"Send me what you have, and I'll look it over." He looked at Kane. "Did you kill that bastard Lombok Charlie? Off the record."

Kane nodded. "Seemed like the thing to do at the time."

"Thanks. He killed our man in Jakarta."

"In that case, my pleasure."

———

OVER PORT FRANCIS, SOMALIA

It was a deep-water port south of Mogadishu in a disputed territory, with the concrete skeletons of war-ravaged buildings overlooking it. The port itself was surrounded by anti-aircraft batteries and machine gun posts. This was going to be one of those missions where the Vipers would come into their own.

Too dangerous for the team to go in without the robots, this would be a blunt instrument raid. Bash their way through into the port, destroy what they can, and get out. Tanner would have a Black Cat in the air with a fifty-minute window to stay on station. Other than that, they had the Stratomaster and its toys.

Meanwhile, back in England, Thurston and Preston were linked into the live feed and comms.

Cara faced her people. She was about to send them into harm's way, and she wanted to face them before she did. "Are you all set? No last-minute problems?"

Knocker grinned. She looked at him and said, "Shut up."

"I never said a word, darlin'."

"Call me that again, and I'll cut your balls off and feed them to you."

"I guess a parting kiss is out of the question."

She glared at him.

"Fine, but just remember, when the chips are down and poor old Knocker is about to breathe his last, you had the chance to be the last one to kiss him goodbye."

"Are you done?"

"Yes, ma'am."

"I swear you're getting worse as you get fucking older."

"I do have a question though."

"Ask it," Cara said with a sigh.

"Are there any fucking tanks?"

"No. No armor whatsoever. However, there are anti-aircraft weapons. Mostly SAMs. And you can bet they'll have some kind of anti-armor weapons. Just don't get shot."

"Bollocks," Knocker grunted.

Grace chuckled. "You're screwed. I think you get hit nearly every time we've been out."

"Don't remind me."

Kane turned to Crystal. "Can you bring up the photo?"

"Wait one."

The Stratomaster lurched from turbulence as it circled out over the darkened desert. A couple of moments later, a photo appeared on the screen. Kane pointed at what looked to be a street in it. "We bust through here. If Tanner can hit it with a Lucifer, we'll be able to walk through. After that, we'll hit the machine gun block houses. Red can take the AT-120 with high-explosive rounds. That should be enough. Then we hit the docks, blow the sub and the drugs. That'll be Red's job too."

Cara nodded. "If it goes off like that, I'll take it. Once Tanner takes out the SAMs, I'll bring Skyhammer in. Until then, you're on your own."

"We'll manage," Kane replied. "We'll glide in over the town and take it from there."

"What is your backup plan to get out?" Preston asked.

"Run like your bollocks are on fire," Knocker said.

"Are you sure your machines are up to it?"

"Boy, are you in for a treat," Grace said. "Just sit back and break out the popcorn."

"I'm glad you sound confident."

"Wait until you see us in action."

"All right," said Cara. "Get ready. We jump just as soon as the sub is confirmed as being in harbor."

———

"Suit up," Cara said into their comms, and each member of the team went to their Viper and climbed in.

Once they were locked away, they stood erect and

prepared to jump. Kane said, "Bravo Three, Viper check."

Crystal looked at her screen and said, "All Vipers look to be sound, Reaper One. Team vitals look good too. Except..."

"Except what?" Kane asked.

"Give your friend a kick. His heart rate is down so far, I'd say he was asleep."

"I'm too old to be getting all worked up about jumping out of a plane from forty thousand feet," he said tiredly. "If my ex-wife was on this flight, then that would be something else. I'd just jump. Forget the parachute."

"Which one?" Kane asked.

"Wife?" Knocker asked as he checked his HUD display.

"Yeah."

"Number two."

"How many do you have?" Grace asked.

"Three," Cara supplied. "Every one of them suffered terribly."

"Shit," the Brit muttered. "You really know how to hurt a man's feelings."

"Just don't get yourself killed."

"Just for that, I think I might."

Cara rolled her eyes. "Move to the ramp. Prepare to launch. Good luck, people. Crystal?"

"Good to go, ma'am."

They all moved forward toward the opening ramp. Once it was down, they disappeared out into the night.

———

PORT FRANCIS, SOMALIA

The streets were dark except for the fires, which burned to light the night. On the outskirts of the port town, the Vipers gathered, ready to assault the port.

"I've got a roadblock on the main road into town," Knocker said over the Vipers' intercom. "Four X-rays and fifty cal."

Kane said, "I'm looking at another roadblock to the east. We go on my command. Bravo Two, how far out is that Black Cat?"

"Reaper One, Black Cat is two miles out."

"Copy. Bravo One sitrep on the sub?"

"Sub is docked and about to be unloaded. There is a heavily armed presence, Reaper One. At least five technicals with heavy machine guns on them."

"Copy. All Reaper elements standing by."

———

ABOARD SKYHAMMER

"There's a lot of activity around that port," Cara said as she stared at the ISR feed. "Once those SAMs are out of action, we need to get in there."

"If we get in there too close and we miss one, they'll have us for dinner," Houlihan said.

"Then don't miss."

"Black Cat one mike out, altitude fifty meters," Tanner said.

"All right, let's go to work. Molly, all weapons on standby."

"Yes, ma'am, already there."

"Crystal, monitor their vitals and look out for any threats we don't see."

"Ma'am."

"Eugene, get ready to take us in on my command."

"Yes, ma'am."

"Mike, let's do this."

Tanner pulled back on the joystick to bring the plane up. "Black Cat starting first run."

———

PORT FRANCIS, SOMALIA

The boom echoed over the port as the Lockheed Martin F-60 Black Cat went supersonic. The vibrations from it rattled everything it touched. Startled people on the ground looked up automatically, searching for the origin. Even as they did so, the first of two Lucifers were impacting their targets: a SAM launcher and the roadblock to the port.

Kane said over the Viper's intercom, "Ground units move in. Primary target is the sub and the drugs."

All the Vipers called in as they started forward. Each machine had the power of a mechanized infantry platoon. Moments later, the first of the enemy combatants opened fire, and battle was joined.

———

ABOARD SKYHAMMER

Warning lights flashed, and an alarm beeped incessantly at Tanner as he brought the Black Cat back around. "SAM inbound, firing countermeasures."

Fifty miles to the east, the Black Cat released its chaff and pulled into a steep climb before rolling into a dive to evade the missile. Behind it came the explosion, and the alarm on the console ceased. Tanner said, "Missile down."

He rotated the joystick and brought the F-60 back around for another run at the remaining SAM launcher. He flicked a switch and said, "Remote jamming engaged."

"Don't know why you didn't have it on in the first place," Cara said bluntly.

"Won't do much good if they're using radar or heat-seeking, ma'am."

"Pat, sitrep on the ground?"

"Team is pushing forward, ma'am. Looks like light resistance so far."

"Not for long," Crystal said. "Pat, transferring to your screen."

A picture evolved inside the picture already there, and Houlihan saw what was happening. "It looks like they're taking to the rooftops."

"If you look closer, I can see RPGs and other missile launchers."

Cara's face grew grim. "Damn. Tanner, knock that SAM out now. I need you to do a strafing run. There's more than one of them left."

"Ma'am."

"Crystal, inform Reaper of the shitstorm he's walking into."

———

PORT FRANCIS, SOMALIA

Heavy caliber rounds ricocheted off Kane's Viper, forcing him to readjust his target package. The minigun came around toward the rooftop as he aimed with his 30mm at the technical further up the street.

Both targets disappeared at the same time, and he gave a grunt of satisfaction. Over his comms, a reassuring voice came with some not-so-reassuring news. "Reaper One, copy?"

"Copy, Bravo Three."

"The fighters are taking to the rooftops with heavies and missile launchers. Advise you hold position until we can get a strafing run done to thin them out. Over."

"Copy," Kane said grudgingly. "All Vipers hold and consolidate."

"Consolidate fucking what?" Knocker asked. "As they say in the classics, we've only just begun."

A mound of roadway exploded upward next to Kane as an RPG round bore in and detonated. "Just do it, Two."

"Copy. Holding and consolidating."

Each Viper crouched down onto a knee and waited as though they were metal reincarnates of Rodin's statue, The Thinker. Moments later, the sky above lit up as the Black Cat unleashed its version of hell.

"All Reaper callsigns proceed," came the blanket call, and the crouching metal monsters unfolded themselves and returned to the fray.

———

KNOCKER WALKED THROUGH A WALL. Just literally walked up to it and went on through. It was either that or get hit with a shoulder-launched rocket. However, on the other side, there was nothing. What had once been a warehouse of significant size was a pile of rubble. So, he turned and walked through the only other remaining wall, which stood alone.

"You're a child," Grace said to him.

Knocker's face remained passive inside his Viper. "You followed me."

His eyes worked tirelessly as he sought targets, eliminating them one at a time. Grace followed his movements.

Suddenly, Knocker's Viper seemed to be punched back by a giant explosive fist.

"Knocker!" Grace exclaimed.

"I'm still alive," he groaned and tried to get his machine to crawl behind the cover of a debris mound. Grace reached out and went to help, but another explosive round detonated close by and threw her machine to the ground.

"Leave me, girl," the Brit said. "Take cover and get us some support. Someone missed a fucking blockhouse."

"Reaper Four, copy?"

"Copy, Three."

"We've got a situation over here on the right. We need your assistance."

"On my way."

"Be aware, it's a concrete block house throwing explosive trains."

"Sounds like fun, Three."

"Reaper Two, copy?" It was Crystal.

"I'm here," Knocker said with a cough.

"I'm reading your integrity took a dramatic drop down to sixty percent. Are you combat-effective?"

"My bell is rung, but I'm otherwise fine."

"Roger that."

Rounds came in all around the Brit and his machine. He knew that if he moved, the heavy gun in the blockhouse would hit him again. All he could do now was wait for backup.

––––––

ABOARD SKYHAMMER

"Ma'am, the team is virtually static," Houlihan said to Cara as they studied the screen before them.

"I am aware," Cara replied.

Knocker was pinned down, and so was Grace. Ryan was moving to help out, and Kane and Ken Welsh were crashing up against a strongpoint, which had suddenly become apparent.

"What seems to be the issue?" Preston asked over the uplink coming in from the UK.

"Our warlord and his friends seem to be a little more determined than first anticipated," Cara replied.

"Then do something about it."

"I will if you shut the fuck up," Cara snapped.

The MI6 man was taken aback by the harshness of her words. Beside him, Thurston grabbed him by the arm, stopping any reply. The Global boss said, "Let her work."

Cara's eyes danced across the screen. The situation with Knocker and Grace would resolve itself eventually. But then they would run into another strongpoint behind the first. She turned to Tanner. "Mike, unload everything you have left on the secondary strongpoint."

"Yes, ma'am."

"Pat, you're in command."

"Ma'am, where are you going?"

"If you want something done, you have to do it yourself. Someone has to save their asses. Get Six ready. Full package."

CHAPTER 7

PORT FRANCIS, SOMALIA

"Reaper Six is airborne."

"Here we go," Kane muttered to himself as he looked up from where he was crouched. The HUD recalibrated, and he picked out the Viper as it descended beyond the normal vision of the human eye.

"Reaper Two, sitrep?"

"I'm still here, playing with my johnson, hoping some Somali prick doesn't get lucky. But don't you worry, I'm sure Red will be here any *fucking* time now."

"Red, what's the holdup?"

"Another blockhouse that no one told us about."

"Christ. Intel was all fucked up on this one."

"It will be looked into, Reaper One," Houlihan assured him.

"I'm not blaming anyone. As much my snafu as anyone's. Ken, I'm sick of dicking around. Time to go ballistic."

"Roger that."

Both Vipers came erect and unleashed with their 30mm cannons while their miniguns tracked other targets. The Viper started to move fluidly, taking rounds but avoiding any major impacts. Soon the strongpoint ahead of them was silenced, and the ground around it was strewn with dead and dying Somalis.

Kane said into his comms, "Five, push forward. I'll cover the flank."

"Roger that."

Moments later, another voice filled the airwaves. "Ivan is down."

———

IVAN WAS UGLY. Unlike the more streamlined Vipers that the rest of the team used. Ivan was ugly because of the equipment and firepower it packed which meant it had to be bigger and wider.

And heavier.

It crashed down onto the top of the concrete block-house that had Knocker and Grace pinned down. It came erect like a giant sentinel, a full foot and a half taller than the others. But that didn't mean that it was slow or cumbersome.

Immediately, two miniguns appeared and started picking targets from the automatic search system. Cara extended her arms out from her sides and let loose the twin 30mm cannons with their depleted uranium rounds. She opened fire and blew holes through the concrete ceiling of the blockhouse, mincing anything inside.

Ivan was a brute of a machine.

Cara said, "Reaper Two, blockhouse is clear."

Without waiting for his reply, she turned and

headed for the next line of defenses the warlord had in store for them.

———

"Sɪʀ, they are into the second line of defenses," called out a nervous-looking Black man in his combat fatigues.

Tadalesh shook his head in frustration, removing his bright red beret, and said, "What are these monsters?"

"They are some kind of robot."

Standing beside Tadalesh on the dock was Cumar. "Majed told you about these people. He said they would possibly come after the drugs and the submarine. They must be stopped."

"Stopped? They are wiping out everything I have fucking built." Tadalesh shook his head once more and picked up his radio. "Omar, bring up the tanks."

Three miles away from the port, large blast doors in the earth rumbled open as though the sky was filled with distant thunder. There were three of them, and moments later, a pair of outdated Leopard tanks emerged from each.

"Tanks are deployed, sir."

Tadalesh nodded with satisfaction. "Now, let's fight metal with metal."

———

ABOARD SKYHAMMER

"Oh, you have got to be fucking kidding me," Crystal blurted out.

"What?" Houlihan asked, not taking her eyes off the screen.

"Now we've got tanks."

Houlihan moved to the screen where the tanks were showing. "Where the fuck did they come from?"

"Out of the ground," Crystal replied.

"What?"

"Literally, out of the ground. Some kind of underground bunker."

"Mike, what have you got left on Black Cat?"

"We're dry, One."

"Shit. Did we get all the SAMs?"

"All SAM activity would indicate that."

"All right then. Eugene, copy?"

"Copy."

"Take us in over the target. Shit just got worse."

"Skyhammer inbound."

"Molly, get your toys ready. Crystal, let them know they've got tanks inbound."

"Bravo Three to all callsigns, you have tanks inbound your position. I say again, tanks inbound your position."

———

PORT FRANCIS, SOMALIA

"So much for no fucking tanks," Knocker growled. "Where are they?"

"They're going to come at you from the rear," Crystal replied.

"There's only one thing to do then," Kane supplied.

"I agree," said Knocker.

"Mind telling the rest of us?" Grace said.

Cara gave them the answer they searched for. "We punch through to the docks and make our stand there."

"Got it in one," Knocker replied. "Damn good to have you on the ground, Reaper Two."

"Don't you mean Bravo?" Grace asked.

"Nope, she'll always be Reaper Two. The only woman I know with her head screwed on in the right direction."

"Gee, thanks," Grace replied.

"You'll get there, kid."

"Are you two done?" Kane asked.

"Let's do it," Knocker said.

"Cara, open a door for us."

"Follow me."

Ivan lumbered forward, eliminating strongpoints as it crashed against them. The twin miniguns, along with the cannons, ripped everything apart. Ahead of her, two technicals appeared, and the CHUG-CHUG of .50 caliber machine guns thumped in the night.

Cara felt the impacts of the rounds as they crashed into the Viper's armor. She raised her arm to fire the 30mm when one of the rounds hit the left cannon.

A warning came up on the HUD. All indications were telling her that the cannon was disabled. Her armor integrity was down to eighty percent. "Fuck you," Cara hissed.

Suddenly, from the same arm where the cannon was housed, a foot-long tube appeared. Moments later, Ivan's flamethrower came to life, engulfing the two technicals.

Explosions followed swiftly as human torches staggered in circles.

She kept Ivan moving until she came upon a wall of shipping containers blocking her advance. However, with a hard shove like a human putting their back and shoulder into moving something heavy, the shipping containers moved back and created an opening large enough for them to pass through.

On the other side was the dock. Kane said, "Set up a perimeter."

From above, looking down, the Vipers spread out with their backs to the bay. In front of them, the skyline burned orange. Tracers cut across it, and not for the first time, the team felt like they were at war.

Flashes winked at them from the tops of buildings, and pale lines could be seen from the trails of shoulder-launched rockets. Explosions started to erupt around them as a wave of mortars came in.

A warning flashed up on Kane's HUD. He was running low on ammo, and he wasn't the only one to spot it. "Reaper One—"

Kane muttered a curse. "I see it, Bravo Three. All callsigns, I need immediate ammo status."

As predicted, everyone, apart from Cara in Ivan, was running low. Ivan not only packed extra grunt, he packed extra everything.

Cara said, "Reaper, get everyone into defensive positions. I have a feeling we're going to be swamped with targets soon."

"You heard the boss. Conserve ammo." Kane watched as his people, still under fire, took up positions. Then he said, "Bravo One, what's the sitrep on the drugs and submarine?"

"They're still unloading."

"Any possibility of pulling actionable intel at this stage?"

"I don't know."

"You're in command, Pat," Cara said. "Make the call."

"I would say it's highly unlikely."

"Are you sure?" Thurston asked.

"Ma'am, we lost the element of surprise. Any hope of taking a HVT is all but gone on the scrap heap. Best case, we hit the sub and the drugs."

"Roger that. Make the call."

"Bravo Four, destroy it all."

———

It was like hell raining down on those below. The dock became a burning furnace that only Satan or his spawn would inhabit.

Figures staggered among the violence and carnage birthed by Thor and Striker. Flames and smoke leaped skyward at least one hundred feet in a massive conflagration. The submarine was sinking, and the drugs, along with the trucks, were all on fire. Tadalesh was lying behind a container with his hands over his head beside the quaking form of Cumar. Two of the tanks were inoperable, but the other four were still in the fight, looking for targets.

For the past hour, they have been heavily engaged. Early in the fight, it had been sporadic, but the tanks had made a concerted effort. Nearly every Viper was close to being bingo on ammunition. Ivan was still in the fight but had taken a glancing blow from a Leopard tank and was seriously compromised.

Skyhammer was still circling but would have to leave the station soon. The sun was rising in the east, and the sky was smudged with clouds of smoke.

"I'm fucked," Knocker said. "I'm bingo on ammo."

"Reaper Five is the same," Welsh said. "All I've got are personal sidearms."

Kane cursed. How could things be so fucked up?

Simple. It was a sign of the times. Well, it wouldn't happen again. "Two and Five, remain inside your Viper. More protection that way."

"Copy."

"Bravo One, anything on that extract?"

"Shouldn't be far out, Reaper," Houlihan replied. "Hang in there."

"It's about all we're doing."

Kane's minigun whirred to life and cleared two shooters from a building—what was left of it—two hundred meters out.

But it was about then that the remaining tanks broke cover and settled on a coordinated attack.

———

ABOARD SKYHAMMER

"It looks like our armored friends have popped back up," Molly said from her station. "Shit, they're putting something together."

Houlihan brought up the feed. She saw the tanks and said, "Can you stop them?"

"I'm low on ammo, and Skyhammer is—"

"Bravo One, this is Eagle Two. We're about out of playtime unless you want us to start flying on fumes."

"I have a refueling flight inbound, Eagle Two. Can't we hang on?"

"No, ma'am. We need to meet it. If we stay here, we'll be dead in the desert."

"Crystal, how far out is the extract?"

"Ten mikes, ma'am."

She thought for a moment, then nodded. "Molly,

drop everything you have on that place. Eagle Two, let's go have that drink."

"Copy."

"Reaper One, Skyhammer is bingo fuel, sorry. Your extract is ten mikes out. Good luck."

"Copy, Bravo. See you on the other side."

"Roger th—"

Man down! Man down! Reaper Five is down!

Things just got a whole lot worse.

————

PORT FRANCIS, SOMALIA

Ignoring orders, Knocker came out of his Viper and rushed to Welsh's machine. It had been blown open, and the inside was a mess. It was another reminder that the Vipers were not indestructible, but it was the first time one had been devastated in such a fashion.

He took one look at Welsh and saw that he was beyond help. Knocker said, "Reaper Five is Cat One. I say again, Reaper Five is KIA."

There was a brief silence as they all took in the devastating news. But the sorrow would have to wait because the threat was still real and present.

Kane pushed the news aside and said, "Red, what have you got left?"

"Down to three rounds."

"Get me a fucking tank. Cara, how's Ivan doing?"

"Integrity down to forty-five percent and AT ammo sitting at five rounds. Miniguns down to five hundred, and I'm out of flame."

"Can you get us another tank?"

"Damn right."

"All we have to do is stay alive for ten mikes," Kane said.

"Technically, seven," Grace said.

Kane said, "Bravo One, do you still have ISR?"

"I wouldn't leave you totally blind, Reaper."

"What do you see?"

She told him.

"Knocker, you still got that crazy steak we all love?"

"As silly as a two-bob watch."

"What?"

"Had an old Aussie mate who used to say it."

"Okay. Listen, when I tell you to go, I want you to break cover. That tank on the left, distract it."

"How?"

"You'll think of something," Kane replied. "Get ready. Red, you're up."

"I'm good."

"Knocker, go."

Everyone expected the Brit to break cover and draw fire while his Viper ran across the battleground. However, that would have been too easy.

"Jesus Christ," Kane groaned.

"Am I really seeing that?" Grace asked.

"I'm afraid so."

Knocker had trained relentlessly in the Viper when he and Kane had been drawn back into the Global web. He spent hours every day trying to get used to the mechanics of it all, and after a while, he had the machine mastered so that it moved fluidly. He even bragged that he could make the Viper dance if he wished.

Well, he was right.

"He's fucking—" Grace started.

"Dancing," finished Kane. "Red, get that tank."

The main gun of the Leopard had been trying to track the movements of the Viper while the others had been stunned by the Brit's lack of grace.

Red opened fire with his AT-120 and hit the metal beast with his remaining depleted uranium rounds.

The tank exploded in a ball of flame as it rocked under the impacts. Then with the job done, Fred Astaire took cover once more.

"You are a dick, Reaper Two," Grace said.

"It distracted him."

Cara said, "I've got a second target in need of distracting."

"I've got it," Grace replied, and she broke cover, taking the Viper up to full speed.

As the tank tried to track her movements, Cara and Ivan blew the shit out of it with their AT.

"Oh, bloody hell!" Grace exclaimed.

Through his HUD, Kane saw her deviate dramatically and then saw why. A third tank had appeared almost in front of her. It opened fire just as she cut to her left, throwing the Viper out of the way.

When the tank fired, the shell crashed into a freighter anchored in the bay. The plume of smoke which rose from it added to the curtain of murky air now hanging over the bay.

Kane blew through the last of his minigun rounds without any effect. Except for attracting the attention of the tank turret swinging in his direction.

The tank fired, but he had the Viper moving—right into the path of the remaining tank.

Which fired.

He felt the impact of the round.

And the Viper crashed down, disabled.

"Reaper's down! Reaper's down!"

Kane knew the Viper was done for, so he hit the release switch and climbed out just as the tank was lining him up again.

This time, he was helpless.

As good as dead.

Until what sounded like a freight train seemed to rip the air above him open and the tank, which was to be the death of him, exploded.

Kane flinched, then heard through his comms someone say, "Did someone call for a cab?"

Their extract had arrived. "You could say that."

"Keep your heads down, and we'll take care of things first and come get you."

Out on the bay, a stealth Landing Craft Vehicle, LCV, codenamed Scorpion let loose with all of its defense weaponry, from mortars to rotary cannon, and surface-to-surface and surface-to-air missiles.

The Scorpion laid down a tremendous rate of fire as it came in. Then within five minutes, the shore fire was suppressed, and all of the team was aboard the landing craft, including Welsh's remains.

Kane looked down at the black body bag that contained his teammate. It wasn't the first time he'd lost someone. But the Vipers were meant to prevent this from happening.

Knocker looked up from where he was seated. "Mission fucked."

Kane nodded. "Just makes me more determined."

"I hate this part," Cara said.

"The only upside was we smashed the drugs and the submarine," Grace said solemnly. "But was it worth it?"

"Not yet," replied Kane. "But it will be."

THE HOT ZONE, CENTRAL AMERICA

Wild screams emanated from the man strapped in the doctor's stirrup chair. Castration was the consequence of his actions. Not that he could close his eyes against the pain because his eyelids were gone. Carnicero, or the Butcher, had seen to that.

Fernando Torres had to admit that his man had talent when it came to inflicting pain. However, former surgeons always knew just where to cut when it was required.

Carnicero cut some more, and the man once more cried out, begging for his life. Imploring the torturer to stop.

But there was no stopping. The man had been Torres's accountant and had been funneling money into an account for his brother and his wife. They were already dead, hanging from an overpass in Mexico.

Torres's encrypted SAT phone rang. He answered it and found Majed on the other end. The only time Majed called was when something was wrong. "What is it?"

"We had a problem in Somalia."

"No." Torres started slowly. "You. You had a problem in Somalia."

"It affects both of us."

"This sounds like it will be interesting."

"The submarine and the drugs were destroyed."

Torres felt his anger surge. "What do you propose to do about it?"

There was silence. Majed knew when silence was the best answer.

"Who was it?"

"The ones I told you about before."

"I thought you were taking care of it?" Torres's voice was a hiss.

"I thought so too."

"Then take care of it like you were supposed to. Just because you are who you are does not mean I cannot get to you if I wish to."

Torres ended the call abruptly. He looked at the tortured figure before him and said to Carnicero, "Finish it."

The former surgeon grunted and used his scalpel to cut the man's throat. The cartel boss said, "Put him in the pool."

———

TORRES SAT at the head of the long dining table. At the other end, Maria did the same, Ana sitting beside her. Cutlery tinkled on the china as they ate their meals. Theirs was an awkward silence.

"Ask him, Mama," Ana whispered.

"No, Ana," she whispered back, glancing nervously at the cartel boss.

"Come on, please."

"Hush."

Torres put his cutlery down and dabbed at his mouth with the blue linen napkin. "What is the problem?"

"Uncle Fernando—"

Maria stayed her daughter's words as she placed a hand on the girl's thin arm. "I wish to take Ana to the Caribbean for a break. A reward, if you will, for her great behavior over the past few months."

Torres nodded slowly. "How long would you be gone?"

"A week, maybe ten days," Maria said.

"I think that will be fine."

"Yippee—" Ana burst out.

"But you must take a personal bodyguard with you."

And there it was: the boom that was always hanging over them suddenly lowered. Maria nodded. "I guess we don't have a choice."

"Not if you want to go to the Caribbean."

Maria looked at her daughter. There was only one choice.

————

LONDON, ENGLAND

The phone rang just after midnight. Millicent Stride untangled herself from her maid who lay across the large bed, the wash of silvery moonlight glowing on her ebony skin. She stirred with the movement. Her name was Honey. "What the fuck?"

Millicent placed a hand on her shoulder. "Go back to sleep, honey."

The maid rolled over, and the moonlight reflected off her lithe back.

"What is it?" Millicent asked as she answered the phone.

"What happened to you taking care of our fucking problem, Millicent?"

It was Majed. "What? Have some damn respect."

"Respect? We're beyond that, Millicent," Majed

hissed. "I lost a whole shipment in Somalia thanks to the very people you were asked to stop."

"But I did put a stop to it. I went and did it personally. The only thing that came across my desk today was —oh fuck."

"What was that?"

"An MI6 operation against a warlord who had hostages."

"Someone has fucked you over, Millicent. And I don't mean the bitch you have in your bed tonight."

"I will fix it."

"No. But you will help. I want you to replace your bodyguard for your visit to Saudi Arabia."

"What?"

"You will bring them with you to The Line, and my people will take care of the rest."

"I-I don't know if I can do that, Majed."

"You will have to find a way, Millicent. Find a fucking way."

Majed hung up, and Millicent lay there on her back, staring at the light from outside dappling the ceiling. How had she ended up here? How?

CHAPTER 8

HEREFORD, ENGLAND

Why did it always rain when they buried one of their own? As was the case during the starkly quiet funeral. Just those of the team and a handful of others. No family as Welsh didn't have any. Waiting until the priest finished, Kane walked away from the grave site toward a waiting SUV he and Knocker had come in. He climbed in, wet and solemn. The door on the other side opened, and the Brit climbed in. He leaned back against the seat and said, "Fuck, I hate these things."

Kane nodded. "We've been to a few. Too many."

"Axe was the worst," Knocker said. "I miss that big lummox."

Kane did too. He started the Land Rover and was about to drive off when the rear passenger door opened, and Cara climbed in. "I hate these fucking things. It makes me think of Axe."

"We were just talking about the big lummox," Knocker said.

"Pub?" Kane asked.

"Yes," Cara said. "But what about the others?"

Kane shook his head. "Nope. This one is for us. They can hang out with the rest of Bravo."

The trio left the cemetery and drove out into the countryside along a narrow road until they reached a small village with a stone-built pub named The Yeomanry. They bought beers and found a table by the fire.

The place was quiet, just the way they wanted it. A young waitress with long, red hair and freckles served them. Once they had their drinks, they toasted Welsh, then sat in silence for what seemed like an eternity.

"How's your sister, Reaper?" Cara asked.

He nodded. "She's good. The second baby has slowed her up a bit. Being married to an SAS operator has made things interesting for her. I tried to warn her, but she never listened."

"Is she happy?"

"Without a doubt."

Knocker chuckled. "Uncle Reaper."

"Shut up."

"Anyone hear from Brick?" Cara asked.

"Not as of late," Knocker replied.

Kane shook his head. "I haven't really talked to him since the 'incident.'"

Cara nodded understandingly. "I might have a need for him."

"Doing what?" Kane asked.

"You'll see."

Kane left it at that, not wanting to press it any further. The waitress brought them another couple of drinks, and Cara looked as though there was something else troubling her. Kane said, "Out with it."

"What?"

"We've known you long enough to tell when there's something bothering you."

"Millicent Stride wants us for her security detail in Saudi Arabia."

"Be fucked," Knocker said in disbelief. "First, she wants us shitcanned, and now she wants us on her team? This smells like a big shit sandwich."

"What he said," Kane replied.

"Mary thought so too. That's why she agreed."

"Ah, fuck," the Brit growled.

"But she only approved the two of you to go."

Kane stared at Cara. Knocker said, "I have a feeling, Reaper, you and I have won the jackpot in the shit sandwich lottery."

Kane stared at Cara and waited for the hammer to fall. She nodded. "You two are the only ones I trust to go."

"I'm thinking you won't be far away," Kane said.

"Just below the horizon in Skyhammer. We won't leave you hanging in the wind."

The door to the pub opened, and Preston entered. Knocker stared at him. "What's he doing here?"

"I asked him to meet us here," Cara replied.

"How—" The Brit just shook his head.

The MI6 man took a seat and ordered a beer. His first order of business was to confirm Kane's suspicions. "Millicent Stride is using."

"What are you going to do about it?"

"Keep an eye on her."

"That's it?"

"Yes. She's bound to come undone of her own accord. She sleeps with her secretary, her maid, and her bodyguard."

"All of them?" Knocker asked, impressed.

"Only the ones who will accept the invitation."

"The silly cow is unhinged," Knocker growled and took a sip of his beer.

"Which is why I urge you to be careful with this detail. She had her security team pulled and asked—no, demanded—that you were to be their replacements."

"But why?" Kane asked.

"The official line is that she wants you there because she wants the best," Preston replied. "Unofficially, I wouldn't expect to come back alive."

For the first time, Knocker grinned.

The MI6 boss frowned. "What are you smiling about?"

Kane shook his head. "He's taken it as some kind of personal challenge. She's just let the genie out of the bottle without any hope of getting it back in."

"Christ."

"What's the plan?" Kane asked.

"Just a few diplomatic things, and she is visiting The Line for inspiration for the British one."

"Sounds interesting," Knocker said. "I always wondered what that thing was like."

"They've completed seventy kilometers of it so far."

"Seventy kilometers is a lot," Cara said.

"It was meant to be nearly three times that by now, but they had issues," Preston said. "It's only a few hundred meters wide all the way along. It's totally run by renewable energy, and both sides are mirrored. Inside, it's a different world. No vehicles, just an underground electric train."

"This is going to be an interesting trip," Kane said.

Preston nodded. "I concur."

———

PARIS, FRANCE

Richard 'Brick' Peters opened the door and saw Mary Thurston standing in the entryway. His face grew dark, and he said, "What do you want?"

"A chat," she replied.

"Five years since I heard anything from you or anyone else. Why now?"

"That was my bad," Thurston said. "I can't speak for the others."

Brick grunted.

"Why are you here, General?" he asked again.

"I want to offer you a job."

"This ought to be good," Brick said skeptically and turned his wheelchair away from the door.

Thurston followed him inside and closed the door. She stared at him from behind, her memory flashing back to the day of the incident. Team Reaper had been on a mission in Brazil. They were being inserted by fast rope when Brick lost his grip and fell, and the wheelchair was the result.

Global had taken care of everything. He wanted for nothing, except his friends. Brick turned his chair. "There's beer in the refrigerator if you want one."

She grabbed two beers from the kitchen, approaching him in the living room and handing him one before taking a seat on the sofa opposite him. He cracked the bottle and took a pull.

"Well? Let's hear what you're handing out."

"This will not be a handout," Thurston said. "If you take this on, you'll earn every bit of it."

"Uh, huh."

"What do you know about the Viper program?"

"Not a lot."

"They are manually operated battle robots," Thurston told him. "I have one set aside for you if you want in."

Brick slapped his dead legs and said bitterly. "You seem to have forgotten something, General."

"What you can't operate with your hands operates mentally, Brick. You don't need legs."

"You mean something like that author Dale Brown wrote? Battle robots that keep you alive."

"These aren't like that," Thurston explained. "You can die in these quite easily."

"I don't need your pity, General."

"I'm not here to give you pity, Brick. I need an operator to go into battle, and that operator is you. Like I said, you'll work for it, none of this wallowing in fucking self-pity. Shit, you might even do a proper fucking job next time. If you're in, I can also get you out of that bastard contraption. Our people have been working on robotic legs. We strap you in them and away you go." Thurston put the beer down on the coffee table and stood. "If you change your mind, you know where I am."

She started toward the door.

"General?"

Thurston stopped and turned.

"Who is running the team?"

"Cara. It was her idea. Kane and Knocker have come back to help out. We lost a man the other day. You'll be replacing him once you're up to speed."

"You really want me, General?"

"I wouldn't be here if I didn't."

"All right. I'll come."

Thurston smiled and gave a nod. "Get your shit together. I'll wait."

———

RIYADH, SAUDI ARABIA

The day had been busy, but not overly so. A meeting with the Saudi King and a visit to a British technology company based in the city. Now they were back at the hotel and Kane was lying on his large bed, staring at the ceiling.

Strike Team Boa had taken the night shift while Rhino rested. Millicent Stride wasn't happy about the two strike teams from Global, having requested all of Reaper and only getting two operators.

She'd protested but wasn't game enough to push it too far for fear of overplaying her hand. Two would have to do. After all, one of those two was the team leader.

There was a knock at Kane's door. He looked at his watch and saw that it was just after one. Reaching beneath his pillow, he retrieved the Heckler and Koch P756 handgun. He came off the bed and walked cat-footed across the room to the door.

Kane looked through the spy hole and stepped back. He lowered his gaze, contemplating his next move. Then he opened the door.

Millicent Stride walked through the opening without waiting for an invitation. She shouldered past Kane and said, "Close the door before people see."

While Kane closed the door, Millicent stopped in the middle of the room and turned back to face him. She was wearing a bathrobe. God only knew what she had on underneath it. Kane was guessing not much.

He said, "What can I do for you, ma'am?"

"That depends on how receptive you are."

He stared into her eyes. She was high. "Receptive for what?"

She dropped the robe and answered the question about what she had on underneath. Kane stared at her.

"Like what you see?"

Kane nodded. "You've certainly got it all, ma'am."

She walked toward him. Her hands touched his bare chest. Millicent stared into his eyes and said, "Shall we get started?"

Millicent was confident and therefore unused to anyone saying no to her. So she was shocked and humiliated when Kane shook his head. "Can't do that, ma'am. Wouldn't be right."

The shock of the refusal was suddenly replaced with anger. "You—you're not going to sleep with me?"

"No, ma'am."

"Even though I'm like this?"

"Don't get me wrong, ma'am, you're a mighty attractive woman, but mixing business and pleasure in my line of work rarely ends well."

"Good Christ. I only want you to fuck me, not bloody walk down the aisle together."

Kane nodded. "I understand, ma'am. Now maybe you should put your robe back on."

There was another knock at the door. Kane stared at Millicent. "Now would probably be a good time."

She stood there like a defiant child. He shrugged and said, "Okay then."

Kane opened the door and found Knocker in the hallway. The Brit walked in and did a double take when he saw a naked Millicent Stride standing there in all her glory. He grinned. "I guess I'm interrupting something."

Kane shook his head. "Not at all. The lady was just leaving."

With a deep guttural growl, Millicent Stride picked up her robe and headed for the door without bothering to put it on. Then she disappeared.

Knocker looked at his friend. "You knocked that back? Are you feeling all right?"

"The name is Kane, not Jensen. Besides, she was high."

"You know what they say?"

The man called Reaper stared at his friend. "I have a feeling you're going to tell me."

"A silly root is a good root."

Kane pinched his nose and shook his head. "I can't believe you just said that."

"Put it this way. If she had come to my room and dropped her gear like that, I wouldn't be here fucking talking to you."

"Why are you here?"

"I can't remember."

"Then go back to your damn room and get some sleep."

Knocker walked toward the door, shaking his head. "I can't believe you knocked her back."

"Fuck off."

WHO WOULD HAVE THOUGHT the desert could be so cold? But the following morning, Kane and Knocker were convinced it was coated with ice, judging by the reception they got from Millicent Stride.

The prime minister emerged from her room and never even acknowledged their presence. She just walked along the hallway with them trailing behind. Kane said into his comms, "We're on the way down."

The ride down in the elevator was just as cold. They stood at the rear of the compartment and waited to arrive at the parking garage under the hotel.

Boa was waiting for them. Millicent took one look at them and said, "I won't be needing you. Just my two personal escorts."

The strike team leader, Pete Holland, glanced at Kane. The Reaper nodded and Boa stood down.

They climbed into the SUV, Knocker behind the wheel. He glanced over at Kane and said loud enough for Millicent to hear, "Cold in here. Maybe you should have played hide the sausage with her."

"If you are quite finished, we should go."

"Which way?"

"There is an airfield outside the city. Go there."

"You know this is highly unusual, right?" Kane asked.

"We live in unusual times. Drive."

They exited the parking garage and were immediately surrounded by a further six vehicles.

"Who are these clowns?"

"Escorts provided by Prince Majed Abdullah. He is overseeing the construction of The Line," Millicent informed them.

Another alarm bell.

In Kane's ear, Cara said, "Can you hear me, Reaper?"

Kane clucked his tongue. The transmission was on a secondary wavelength, piggybacking into his comms.

"We're airborne and tracking your every move. Good luck."

———

THE LINE, SAUDI ARABIA

It was hard to see at first on approach, but once the helicopter was close enough, the distortion caused by the mirrored wall could be made out. But on closer inspection, the walls were actually buildings. One long structure on either side, a green outdoor space between them that was barely two hundred meters wide. The ingenious part was that there was more underground. More living space and the train line. Each section was called a module and was approximately eight hundred meters.

The helicopter circled and settled onto a landing pad atop one of the modules. Moments later, the helicopter was gone, and the three of them were greeted by a bearded man. He nodded to Millicent and said, "Madam Prime Minister, I am Majed Abdullah."

"Pleased to meet you," Millicent replied.

They shook hands.

"Reaper, I'm getting a strange signal that I can't seem to nail down emanating from somewhere inside The Line," Crystal Garcia said in Kane's ear.

He glanced at Knocker, whose expression told Kane he'd got the same message. Kane turned away from the others and whispered, "What kind of signal?"

"I'm not sure. Could be a closed-loop comms channel."

"Roger that."

Majed was surrounded by bodyguards armed with Heckler and Koch compact SMGs. The Saudi must have felt Kane's gaze and glanced in his direction. Knocker whispered, "The prince of happiness is up to something."

"Yes, he is. Might be that he's upset we interfered with his operation and now he wants his pound of flesh."

Majed and Millicent started moving off the landing platform toward the open doorway, escorted by Majed's men. "Bravo, we're on the move."

Entering the building, the group found an elevator car waiting for them. They crammed into it and traveled to the green level. When the car stopped and the doors opened, they were outside once more and in what resembled a parkland with walking paths interwoven among the palms and other trees.

"This is absolutely marvelous," Millicent gushed. "It is exactly what I want for my country. High-density living but with virtually zero footprint to harm the..."

Her words were lost to Kane as Crystal said, "Reaper, I'm picking up chatter that does me no good."

"What do you mean?"

"It indicates a military channel."

"Why is that unusual?" Kane asked, wanting her to spell it out.

"The signal is local, Reaper. Somewhere within The Line. And they're talking about an attack."

"On who?" Kane asked.

"I'm not sure."

"Is it directed at us?"

"Possibly. But it could be targeting the prime minister. We don't have anything concrete," Crystal said.

"Bravo, copy?"

"I'm here, Reaper."

"Please advise."

Knocker glanced at Kane, who waited for Cara to answer. "We can't take the chance, Reaper. Advise the PM that it might be best if you left."

Kane nodded to Knocker, and they started forward toward where Millicent Stride and Majed were standing. They didn't get far before their paths were blocked by the prince's armed bodyguards.

"What the fuck are you doing?" Knocker asked the closest one to him.

"You stay here while they talk."

"No, mate, we have a problem, and we need to talk to the prime minister."

"I don't think so."

The Brit took a step forward, and the man moved to cut him off, placing a hand on Knocker's chest.

Knocker moved with blinding speed, grabbing the man's hand and twisting it savagely. The man buckled with pain, and Knocker hit him with a savage blow, dropping him to his knees. The others unlimbered their weapons and pointed them at the Brit.

"Whoa, just hold it there," Kane said, raising his left hand in an attempt to defuse the rapidly escalating situation. "Just hold it there."

"What is happening?" Millicent demanded.

"We need to talk to you, ma'am."

"You will have to wait."

"Ma'am, there may not be—"

"Reaper, movement at your two."

Kane turned and saw a line of black-clad men,

armed, emerging from a doorway. He looked at Milli-cent and said, "Ma'am, we need to go now."

The British Prime Minister just stood and stared at him, a gleam of triumph in her eyes. Well, now they knew. Kane pulled his 756 and, along with Knocker, ran.

CHAPTER 9

Bullets chopped through the dense foliage as the two men ran through the trees. Branches and leaves fluttered to the ground while angry hornets searched for soft targets.

Kane stopped next to a tree and turned and fired at a figure coming toward him. The shooter stumbled and fell.

Beside Kane, Knocker fired his own handgun. "Where to, Reaper?"

"Inside."

"What about the residents?"

"Have you seen any residents?" Kane asked.

Knocker realized that he'd not seen a soul. "Man, this is a fucking shit show."

Automatic weapon fire ripped through the Green Zone, forcing the two operators to retreat. They ran between the trees until they were forced to a standstill as another handful of shooters appeared in front of them and opened fire.

"This way," Knocker called out, and Kane turned in his direction. He followed the Brit toward a doorway which led inside.

Just as Knocker reached the darkened opening, yet another shooter appeared. Knocker pressed the 756 into the man's middle and pulled the trigger three times. The shooter grunted as each hammer blow crashed into him before falling back. As he did, Knocker shot him in the head.

Bullets peppered the opening around them as they disappeared inside and found two more shooters following the now-dead one.

The two Team Reaper operators opened fire, and the pair of killers died swiftly. Knocker leaned down and grabbed a compact SMG and tossed it to Kane before grabbing one for himself along with some spare ammunition while the Reaper stood in the doorway and loosed what was in the SMGs magazine at their pursuers.

Once Kane's weapon was empty, Knocker threw him a spare magazine, and he reloaded. The Brit said, "Going down?"

Kane fired. "After you."

They had a choice. Elevator or stairwell. Choosing the latter, the pair bounded down the stairs. The door at the bottom burst open onto what appeared to be an underground city. A central sidewalk ran along the center, flanked by stores and other buildings.

"It's all empty," Knocker said as they started along the sidewalk.

"Maybe it's a new section?" Kane surmised.

"Let's not hang around to find out," Knocker said. "I'll take the other side of the—whatever this is."

He jogged over, and they both moved along the storefronts. A shout from behind them was followed by gunfire. A storefront window shattered, and bullets ricocheted off the concrete at Kane's feet. He turned and opened fire at a handful of shooters.

Not waiting to see the results, he turned and ran toward an iron sculpture, ducking behind it as bullets peppered the hard surface. Across the way, Knocker opened fire, trying to draw some heat away from his friend and whittle down the number of killers.

Kane tried his comms. "Bravo, copy?"

Dead air.

He tried again. "Bravo, copy?"

Nothing.

They were on their own.

———

40,000 FEET OVER THE DESERT

"I can't raise them, ma'am," Crystal said as she pounded keys on her console. "Either someone is jamming or they're way below ground. My guess is jamming."

"Find a way around it, Crystal," Cara demanded. She turned and said, "Pat, get a Star Hawk airborne."

"Yes, ma'am."

Houlihan hit a few keys on her console, and beneath Skyhammer, two doors opened. Moments later, she said, "Star Hawk One away."

From the doors, a UCAV was dropped, and once clear of its host, its motor fired and it commenced flying. "Star Hawk One is operational."

Houlihan's screen came to life. "Five minutes until it's over the target area."

"Let me know when it arrives," Cara said.

"Ma'am, I still can't raise Reaper One or Two," Crystal said. "Shall I place the rest of the team on standby?"

"Not yet. If we launch the Vipers, we'll need one hell of a good reason for the shitstorm that will ensue, coming down on us."

"Copy that."

Cara stared at the screen. She could see the activity of armed men in the open part of The Line. "Zoom in on those two."

The picture was pixelated and then cleared to show Millicent Stride talking animatedly with Majed Abdullah. "Can we get a read on what they're saying?"

"Give me a moment," Crystal said.

Then moments later, the voices became clear.

"...said this was going to be straight fucking forward."

"Calm down, my people will take care of it. I should be angry with you. Only two of them, Millicent? I wanted them all."

"They know something is going on."

"I just hope that my employer will be happy with the head of the snake."

"Don't fucking underestimate these people, Majed, they know what they're doing. Shit, I should never have listened to you."

"It is a little too late to back out now, Millicent."

"Just remember, if I go down, you come with me."

"Wow, she just fucked up," Cara said out loud.

THE LINE

Majed's eyes narrowed. The man was poised like a king cobra, ready to strike. "Are you threatening me, Millicent?"

"Just stating facts, Majed. I have staked everything on this venture. My whole prime ministership. I will not let it be sunk because of this."

The prince stared at her, weighing his options. The one he chose could never have been foreseen. He took out a handgun and shot her.

———

ABOARD SKYHAMMER

"Son of a bitch, he fucking shot her," Crystal gasped.

"Gather yourself, people. It was inevitable the moment she threatened him. The question is, how will he explain it?"

"He'll blame Kane and Knocker."

"That's my guess," Cara agreed.

"If that happens, it'll blow back on us," Houlihan said.

"It sure puts us in the frame. Did we get that on camera?"

Crystal hit some keys. "We should have. Everything records from—ah fuck."

"Tell me we have it."

The computer tech looked helplessly at her commander. "We don't have it. Something glitched, and the recording stopped."

"How does that happen, Crystal?" Cara asked, her voice clipped.

"I don't know."

"Then find out and fix it."

"Ma'am."

"Get Reaper Three and Four geared up. No Vipers, there won't be enough access for them. Tell them I'll meet them in the weapons' bay."

"Ma'am, there are vehicles inbound. My guess is they have more men in them."

Cara looked at Houlihan. "Take over, Pat. Get Skyhammer closer to the target."

"What are our rules of engagement?" Houlihan asked.

"If we call, you give us everything."

"Roger that."

―――――

CARA SLIPPED into her exoskeleton body armor and put her full-face ballistic helmet on. She looked more like an alien than a soldier. Packing extra ammo and grenades, she looked over at Grace and Ryan. "Are you ready?"

They nodded.

"This is going to be a very hot LZ," Cara explained. "There are more X-rays inbound."

"Has there been any word?" Grace asked.

"Nothing. We think they're being jammed." Cara slapped a magazine into her G550 and charged it. "Let's go."

―――――

THE LINE

They'd been on the ground for thirty seconds and were already deep in a firefight. As soon as Cara had landed on the sidewalk in the middle of the Green Zone of The Line, she'd hit the release for her parachute and been engaged by a squad of shooters.

Cara dropped to a knee and opened fire at the shooters. She felt a blow from a bullet in her armor and ground her teeth against the pain. She shifted her aim and shot the culprit.

By now, the other two were down and engaged in the firefight. Grace moved sideways and found cover behind a tall palm. Bullets chewed scars in the soft bole. She opened fire, and another shooter died.

Like trying to hold back a tide, the two dead were replaced by four more shooters.

"Fuck it," Grace growled and reached for a grenade. She pulled the pin and threw it. "Frag out!"

The explosion rocked the Green Zone and took down four shooters. Ryan moved in beside her, and between himself and Cara, they took out the rest.

"We need to get underground," Cara said. "Follow me."

She moved through the Green Zone toward a doorway. As she approached it, she walked past a dead shooter. Cara paused and crouched beside the body. She looked it over. "Bravo Three, can you see what I'm seeing?"

"Yes, ma'am."

"Search the database and see what you can find. This guy isn't Saudi army. He may be dressed that way, but there is no way."

"On it."

Cara stood and headed toward the doorway. She had just entered when Crystal came back to her.

"Your friend came back as Mexican. Special forces. Used to be special forces, I should say. He died five years ago. I guess Majed is using dead people."

"Or his boss is," Cara said. "Keep digging."

The three of them went down the stairwell to the first level. When they arrived, they found chaos.

———

KNOCKER THREW the SMG onto the ground and drew his handgun. He looked across the gap to where Kane had just done the same. Coming toward them through the smoke of a burning store were ten shooters. Knocker said, "They're like fucking ants."

Kane was about to speak, when above them the fire system came on, dumping water like a summer storm.

"Great, now it's bloody raining," the Brit growled.

The modules of The Line each had their own separate fire systems. Water was stored in large tanks pumped all the way from the ocean.

Kane fired at a figure appearing from the gloom. The shooter disappeared into a storefront opening. Kane said, "Fall back."

Walking backward to cover any threats, they retreated until another stairwell was reached. This one, however, was like the ones they'd seen for the London Underground. Without another word, they took the stairs downward into the railway station.

They ran along the platform, under and past the timetable boards hanging perpendicular to the wall, ready for when the rail line opened.

A shout was followed by gunfire. Bullets chipped

concrete from the walls, many screaming past the two Team Reaper operators. They ducked behind two pillars and returned fire.

More bullets chipped away at the concrete and snapped past. Kane looked across at Knocker, who was reloading. He glanced back and said, "Last mag, Reaper."

"Into the tunnel," Kane called back. "I'll cover you."

Knocker nodded.

"Go! Go!"

Kane opened fire while his friend ran for the edge of the platform. He jumped down and turned, crouching below the edge of the platform. "Go, Reaper!"

Kane turned and followed his friend, letting Knocker cover his retreat by opening fire. He leaped down, bullets fizzing all around him. He pressed his back against the platform and said, "Let's go."

Both ran along the line and into the gaping maw of the underground tunnel.

———

"REAPER ONE, COME IN." Nothing. "Reaper Two, come in."

Cara's voice was greeted with silence. It was not hard to see where their teammates had been as they walked forward along the sidewalk between the stores, following a trail of destruction. The fire suppressors had stopped spraying, and everything was soaked.

"Still nothing," Cara said.

The sound of gunfire reached out to them. Ryan said, "It's coming from below."

Cara nodded. "They're in the rail system. Let's go."

They started moving once more and reached an entrance to the transit system on the next level down. They were about to descend the stairs when a mighty explosion rocked the building below.

———

"WHAT DID YOU DO?" Kane asked through racking coughs from the blanketing dust cloud and smoke.

"I fucking shot a guy, that's all."

Part of the tunnel had collapsed from the explosion, and another part looked to be burning. "He must have been carrying explosives."

"Who the fuck carries explosives that go off like that from being shot?" Knocker growled.

The gunfire had stopped, and Kane decided to take advantage of it. "Let's have a look."

The lighting in the tunnel was still operational, which was helpful as he crouched over a body. He studied the dead shooter and said, "Not Saudi."

Knocker nodded. "Looks Central American."

"Reaper One, copy?"

Kane looked at the Brit, who said, "I heard it too."

"Reaper copies."

"Thank God. Where are you?"

"Are you on the ground?"

"Affirmative."

"Follow the smoke."

"On our way."

They emerged from the gloom looking like stormtroopers out of a Star Wars movie. Cara took her helmet off and said, "Are you alright?"

"We're still breathing."

"That's good, because we have a problem."

Kane frowned. "What is it?"

Cara told Kane about the murder of the prime minister. "We think they're going to lay it at our feet."

"So, we need to get him," Knocker said.

"Yes."

"Then we're wasting time here. Let's get to it."

CHAPTER 10

"We've got three bandits inbound, range two hundred miles," Molly Wilson said over their intercom.

"Who are they?" Houlihan asked.

"At first I thought they were Saudi Air Force, but their signature says otherwise."

"What otherwise?"

"Sukhoi Su-35s," Molly replied.

"Russians?" Houlihan asked skeptically.

"Once, I would have said yes. Not now. I'm thinking our prince has his own private air force."

"What's their approach speed?"

"Nine hundred knots. Range now is one hundred and fifty miles."

"All right, let's get our weapons ready and—"

"I've got a missile launch."

"Put Ripper to work. What I'd give for a Black Cat at the moment. Damn—"

"I've got a second missile launch."

"Put them down," Houlihan growled. "Eugene, can you get a fix on those flankers?"

"We're working on it."

"Good luck."

Moments later, Ripper came to life, and the two incoming missiles exploded midair."

"Missiles destroyed," Molly said.

Houlihan felt the Stratomaster shift beneath her feet as the big plane started her turn. Moments later, Houlihan heard over her comms, "Raptor away."

The Raptor was an AA-696 hypersonic air-to-air missile. Beneath both wings, the Stratomaster had two hardpoints where the Raptors were fitted. Not ideal for such a big aircraft, but effective in a pinch.

Molly tracked the missile on her panel. Moments later, she said, "Target destroyed."

She tracked the remaining two flankers on her radar as they turned away, given pause by the destruction of their comrade's aircraft. But that wouldn't hold them for long.

"Pat, the flankers have turned, but they'll be back—missile in the air. Damn."

Her fingers danced across the console keyboard again as she prepared the compact Phalanx anti-missile system. It tracked the incoming missile until the last moment, and it opened fire, smashing the aerial spear.

"Eugene, can you do something about those remaining planes?" Houlihan asked.

"I'm driving a battleship, not a race car, Pat," the pilot reminded her.

"I'm well aware of the fact. But we were given hard points for a reason."

The pilot ignored the testy comment. "Mike, we'll take a long-range shot if you can guide it on?"

Tanner flicked a switch on his console and grabbed his joystick. "Ready when you are, Eugene."

"Raptor away."

"I've got another missile inbound. Time to impact, ninety seconds—"

BOOM!

Everything on Molly's console went out. "No, no, no. Fuck, fuck, fuck."

"Talk to me," Houlihan snapped.

"I've lost power on my console. I'm blind."

"Shit, get it fixed. Mike, are you still up?"

"Yes, ma'am. Raptor acquired and on course."

"Eugene, ready countermeasures. We've got a missile inbound, and defense systems back here are down. Time to impact approximately sixty seconds."

No sooner had the words passed her lips, Skyhammer started a lumbering turn. Up front, Potter and Leslie Groves spoke calmly even as the threat bore down on them.

The missile streaked toward the beast, and at the last moment, Eugene put Skyhammer into a dive, while Leslie hit the chaff button.

The missile flew into it and exploded, neutralizing the threat. Meanwhile, Molly's console was still dark. "Useless piece of shit."

"Raptor tracking to target. Impact in three...two... one. Splash another Flanker."

"How are we looking, Molly?" Houlihan asked.

"I'm still blind."

"Incoming missile, twelve o'clock," came the call from Eugene Potter. "Everyone, brace for impact."

———

THE LINE

Majed was becoming concerned. The whole plan should have played out by now, but his people were being slaughtered, and the aircraft he'd called in were dropping from the sky like vultures on a carcass. Smoke rose skyward from the multiple fires in The Line.

He looked at the man beside him and said, "Report."

"There is nothing else since the three commandos came from the sky." The man's voice was heavily accented Central American.

"The plane should have been picked up before this happened."

"The plane—"

The man's head crashed back as a hole appeared in the center of his forehead. He slumped to the ground, blood pooling on the concrete. Majed's head snapped up, and he saw five figures coming toward him. He froze. Three were clad in a type of body armor. The other two were the bodyguards of the now-dead British Prime Minister.

The prince started to turn, flight foremost in his mind. "Don't," Kane snapped. "You'll be dead before you take three steps."

They couldn't afford to shoot him; the team needed Majed alive. But he didn't know that, and he froze once more. Grace put zip ties on him to make him secure.

Knocker smiled at him. "You've been a bad boy, cock."

"Do you know who I am?" Majed asked defiantly.

Knocker looked at Kane. "Can I answer that?"

"Be my guest."

"You're a dope-peddling asshole."

"I am part of the Saudi Royal Family, and you will not leave this country alive."

"I'm sure once they know what you are, they'll be willing to cut you loose," Cara said.

"You are all doomed."

"He sounds like some idiot bad guy out of a B-grade movie," Grace growled.

Suddenly an alarm sounded, and Cara brought up the satellite link on her HUD inside her helmet. "We've got more incoming X-rays. Looks to be a hundred or more."

Kane cursed. "Great. Knocker, scrounge us up some weapons."

"We can't make a stand against that many without help," Cara pointed out. "And I can't raise Skyhammer."

"Then," replied Kane, "we go down again. Red, the Prince of Doom, is all yours. Remember, we need him alive."

———

MOLLY CURSED VEHEMENTLY and smashed a fist down upon her console. Suddenly, everything lit up as it came to life. "You bastard."

"Ten seconds to impact."

Ripper sprang to life and spewed forth its devastating fire. Rounds impacted the missile, which exploded in a ball of fire.

"That was close," Houlihan growled, relieved that they were all still alive. "How does the radar look?"

"All clear. Flankers are down."

"Crystal, see if you can make contact with the others."

"Yes, ma'am."

"Ma'am, there are X-rays inbound. Looks to be a hundred or so," Molly informed Houlihan.

"Do our people know?"

"Yes, ma'am. The information was transmitted to the boss's HUD."

"Roger that."

"I have something you need to look at," Crystal said into her mic.

Houlihan walked over to her console. "What is it?"

Crystal replayed a recording from a SAT feed. It showed the team taking Majed into custody. It was followed by a discussion, and the team, along with their prisoner, disappeared inside a doorway.

"It looks like they've gone underground," Crystal pointed out.

"They must have decided to do that after finding out about the incoming fighters. At least they have Majed. I need to talk to Mary."

Moments later, Houlihan was hooked through to Thurston. "What is it, Pat?"

"We have what you might class as an issue. The Line was a trap, and Majed executed Millicent Stride."

"Jesus Christ. Where is Cara?"

"On the ground."

"She would be. Keep going."

"The team has Majed in custody, but they've been forced underground. The command platform was also attacked by Su-35s."

"How many?"

"Three. All were shot down. They were not Saudi aircraft."

"What do you make of the murder of the prime minister?"

"We figure she was working with Majed and had become a liability."

"Do you think he aims to lay the blame at our feet?" Thurston asked.

"That would be my guess. The objective is to bring Majed in alive."

"Is there any indication who the supplier of Happy Days is?"

"None as yet."

"Do you want me to dispatch a strike team?"

"No, ma'am. We can handle it at the moment."

"Keep me updated."

"Yes, ma'am."

The link was disconnected, and Houlihan patched herself through to the cockpit. "Leslie, how much fuel do we have?"

"A hundred thousand pounds, give or take, Pat."

Houlihan did a quick mental calculation. Skyhammer, the beast that she was, burned 30,000 pounds of fuel an hour. That gave her just over three hours of flight time, and Aan hour and a half on station. She hoped they didn't need it. "Thank you, Leslie."

Houlihan looked around the TOC. "Listen up, I want a full inventory of what we're looking at and anything unforeseen. Mike, find out where the hell those flankers came from. Get to work."

———

THE LINE

They made their way steadily along the underground rail line, the path illuminated by the flashlights attached under the team's weapons. Red Ryan pushed Majed along in front of him. The prince staggered and then righted himself. He swung around, anger etched in his face. He took a step toward Ryan, and the Australian hit him in the stomach. "Take it easy, mate. Keep it up, and you'll get a headache to go with your bellyache."

Majed gasped for air and managed to say, "You are a dead man."

Knocker appeared and gave him a shove. "Fuck off. Move."

They continued forward, with Kane and Cara bringing up the rear. The Reaper looked at her and said, "Things get boring in the sky?"

"I miss the thrill."

"Yeah, right."

"How are you and Knocker doing?"

"Banged up a little, but it's nothing we aren't used to."

A shout was followed by the eruption of gunfire. Tracer rounds ripped along the tunnel and forced them to scatter.

Ryan pushed Majed down, the sharp edges of the stone bed biting at exposed flesh. They started to return fire, and Kane called back to Ryan, "Keep moving. Get him the hell out of here. Take Grace with you."

With bullets flying all around, Grace and Ryan dragged Majed to his feet and kept moving.

Emptying the magazine of a weapon he'd taken from a dead shooter earlier along the tunnel, Kane dropped the magazine out and reloaded. Then he opened fire.

A rocket-propelled grenade came from the depths, and he threw himself to the ground. The others did the same, and the small projectile hit the side wall and exploded.

The bullets kept coming.

Cara reached for a grenade and pulled the pin. Her HUD changed to infrared, and she could make out targets in the darkness beyond the light. She threw the grenade, and the firing was disrupted long enough for them to fall back.

After fifty meters, she squatted down and placed a tripwire across the tunnel. Then she followed the others.

Moments later, one of their pursuers tripped the boobytrap, and it detonated with a loud roar. "That should slow them down."

More gunfire erupted and Cara grunted, staggered, and fell to a knee. Kane dropped beside her. "Are you okay?"

"Took a round to my body armor. I'll be fine."

He dragged her up and said, "No sense in hanging around here. We need to get up top for extract?"

"Yeah," said Cara. "About that."

Racing through the tunnel to the next platform, they climbed up onto it and then made their way up the stairs, bypassing the living level and emerging in the Green Zone.

Back in the direction from where they had come, dark smoke stained the sky. Cara tried her comms. "Bravo One, copy?"

"Copy, Bravo. Good to hear your voice."

"We need immediate extract."

"That could be an issue."

"I'm well aware of the fact. Will take hot extract."

"Oh, Christ," Knocker growled. "I fucking hate those things."

Cara looked around and pointed at the top of a wall. "There. Everyone up."

The Brit looked at his friend. "This is bad."

"Think of it as an amusement park ride."

"I hate fucking amusement parks. Remember the last one we were in?"

Kane remembered. They were going toe to toe with Albanian drug runners, which turned into a bloodbath. Both Kane and Knocker had been wounded, Interpol officers were killed, and almost all the Albanians had followed each other to hell.

Then there had been Russian mercenaries with their own agenda, that being the kill or capture order on the two men. Every one of the Russians had been killed, and a good portion of the amusement park had been destroyed.

They reached the top and dispersed. Grace and Ryan covered the Green Zone while the others prepared for the hot extract. A long rope was laid out with reinforced clips attached to it. The other end was loaded into what resembled an oversized sawn-off shotgun. Then it was set out, ready for use.

"Contact?" Grace called out as she opened fire.

Down in the Green Zone of The Line, shooters appeared. Ryan joined her, and they started to lay down, suppressing fire.

Cara turned to Knocker and said, "Get him hooked up."

Knocker shoved Majed toward the rope and grabbed up a harness from the ground. He held it out and said, "Put it on."

The prince looked at him defiantly. The Brit's eyes narrowed. "Don't make me fucking put it on you, mate. You fucking don't want that. I might do it wrong, and you'll end up splattered across the desert like raspberry fucking jam."

Majed climbed into the harness disobligingly, taking his time. As he did, Kane, Cara, and Knocker followed his movements and put their own on. Kane looked at Cara and said, "Why do I have a feeling you expected things to go this way?"

"What makes you think that?"

He tightened his harness. "I wonder."

Knocker and Kane switched places with Grace and Ryan while they put on their own harnesses. The gunfire from the Green Zone was still incoming but less intense. Then Knocker saw a handful break from cover and run for a doorway. "We got friendlies on the way up."

Cara tossed him a grenade. "Slow them down."

He ran across to the doorway, which led into the stairwell.

Cara said into her comms, "Bravo, we're ready when you are."

"Five mikes out, ma'am. Hang on to your G-string."

"She doesn't wear one," Kane replied.

Cara stared at him as a chuckle from Houlihan reached their ears. "I won't ask."

"A wise choice, Bravo One. We're standing by."

"See you soon."

"All right, everyone, prepare for extract. Knocker, get ready to run."

"Just reserve me a seat," the Brit growled.

"I'll save you one next to me."

They all gathered around the strung-out rope and hooked themselves to it. This was going to be one hell of a ride.

The sound of thunder from out across the desert reached her ears. Cara turned and saw Skyhammer in the distance, flying directly toward them, no more than fifty feet above the sand.

Majed looked wide-eyed at the oncoming beast. "What—what are you going to do?"

Kane said, "You are going to love this. You thought Happy Days was a buzz. That's nothing compared to what is about to happen."

The Stratomaster grew closer. Knocker kept the shooters at bay in the stairwell. Kane picked up the firing mechanism and waited.

Cara said, "If you're coming, now is a good time, Raymond."

"On my way," he said as he sprayed the last of the rounds held in his weapon's magazine down into the stairwell.

He ran over to the rope and hooked himself up just as the thunder overhead reached a screaming, deafening crescendo. Kane fired, and the rope unfurled as it flew skyward.

Hanging below the open ramp was a retractable hook. The rope picked it up and flowed faster. Meanwhile, Eugene and Leslie had pulled back on their columns, and the big bird was climbing severely toward the blue sky above.

The snatch rope stretched to accommodate the weight placed on it by those attached to it so they wouldn't suffer severe whiplash or injury. But when it had stretched to its capacity, it whipped every one of them skyward, leaving them feeling their guts had been left behind them.

The other downside was the G-forces were severe enough that each of them passed out before they were even one hundred feet in the air.

CHAPTER 11

They stared at their prisoner on the screen. Thurston, Cara, and Kane remained silent as they watched him fidget. It was the former general who broke the silence. "Has he mentioned anything about Millicent Stride?"

"Not a thing," Cara replied.

"We have twelve hours before we have to hand him over to Oliver Preston. Get what you can out of him. I want to know who is responsible for Happy Days and what we have to do to shut the operation down."

Kane said, "Knocker and I will do the interrogation."

"Remember, he's Saudi Royal Family," Thurston pointed out.

The big man stared at the prisoner. "I won't forget."

———

KNOCKER HIT him again and wrung his hand. "Bastard has a hard fucking head."

Kane stared at the bloody face. There was a time when he wouldn't have gone for treatment like this. As the saying went, different times called for different measures. These days, the drug lords dismembered bodies while their victims were still alive. They were adept at cauterizing wounds to prolong the agony so they wouldn't bleed to death. They raped wives in front of husbands and killed children in front of their parents before they did the same to them. Rats were put in bags over the heads of victims who had been smothered in a special paste, which drove the animals into a frenzy. By the time the rodents were finished, noses were missing and eyes were consumed before the frenzied animals had eaten their way into the prisoner's brain.

Politicians were murdered live in front of cameras, and judges were treated worse. Police changed sides quicker than they changed their underwear, and lawlessness was the only order of the day.

"You want me to hit the cunt again?" Knocker asked.

Kane nodded.

WHACK!

Kane said, "This can all stop when you give me a name."

"I know nothing," Majed said and spat blood on the floor.

"All right, Sergeant Schultz," Kane said and drew the P756. The weapon roared, and a bullet tore through the Saudi's leg.

Majed screamed in agony, jerking against the bonds as though it would drive the pain away. Kane stared at him and said, "I'm not going to ask the question again, Majed. I'm just going to shoot you until you tell me."

The gun thundered again, and another round punched into the prince's leg two inches from where the other one had entered. Majed jerked wildly and screeched, "*All right! All right! I'll tell you! I'll tell you!*"

Kane holstered his weapon. Knocker shook his head. "I thought you were going to let me do that."

"Changed my mind."

"Fine." The Brit crossed his arms in acceptance.

Kane leaned in close to Majed. "Who?"

"Fernando. Fernando Torres."

Kane froze. He looked over at Knocker. The Brit raised his eyebrows. "Did he say..."

Kane nodded.

"Oh, shit. Things just got really interesting. What are you going to do?"

"My job."

"The guy operates a fucking army. Not to mention the next time he sees you, he'll bone you out like a fucking butcher."

Kane turned to Majed. "Tell me about his operation."

"I just organize transport. The pipeline into England, Europe, and Asia."

"What about his end?"

Majed shook his head. "I know nothing about it, just what I control."

"What about Millicent Stride?"

Majed snorted and said bitterly, "She was a whore. Getting to her was easy. A night of sex and drugs and she was mine. It took one shot of Happy Days, and it was all over."

"You used her to help get drugs into the country?"

"She was the prime minister; she could do anything I wanted her to."

"But you murdered her."

"She had become a liability."

"So you killed her to set us up and kill us too," Knocker said.

Majed nodded, sweat dripping from his face. "You were trouble."

"I guess we can tell the boss she can hand him over now," Knocker said.

"I will not be kept for long." The bitterness was back in Majed's voice. "And when I am released, I will come back and kill you all and your families as well."

Knocker shook his head. "You just couldn't quit, could you?"

Kane drew his weapon and shot him.

———

HEREFORD, ENGLAND

"You didn't have to kill him," Thurston growled. "I thought I raised you better than that."

"The guy would have got away with it. This way, the world is better off, and Majed just disappears."

"Let's hope so. What now?"

"Fernando Torres."

The former general frowned. "Why do I figure I know that name?"

"Reaper killed his brother while he was screwing his wife," Knocker supplied.

Kane glared at him.

"I can see why that would be a problem."

"The guy is one of the biggest cartel bosses in the Hot Zone."

"Nothing a bomb won't fix," Knocker said.

Thurston shook her head. "I want him alive so there is a face to the monster. I want him to face a public trial for all the people he's killed."

"Easier to kill him," Kane replied with a shrug.

"I agree. But if it can be done, I want it done that way."

"All right, but it could mean playing the long game. Infiltration, everything like that."

Thurston nodded. "I'll talk to Cara about it. In the meantime, take a couple of days. You've all earned it."

"Yes, ma'am."

Kane turned and winced. "Is there a problem, Reaper?"

"Tweaked my back on the extract. Not as young as I used to be."

"Get it checked out."

"Yes, ma'am."

"And one more thing. We're training a new team member on the Vipers."

"Who?"

"Go and see. He's over in the training hangar."

———

The Viper moved like an oversized Bruce Lee under the watchful eyes of the engineers. It rolled and came up stealthily before turning and doing another roll. Once that was completed, the minigun appeared and then the 30mm cannon.

"The guy looks like he's been doing this a while," Knocker observed.

After a few more movements, the Viper stopped and opened. Kane and Knocker glanced at each other. "I'll be fucked," the Brit said.

What surprised them even more was the fact that Richard 'Brick' Peters climbed out with the help of his mechanical leg supports. Once he was clear of the machine, he walked over to them, the legs making a mechanical squeaking sound. He stopped in front of them and said, "Fucking surprise."

"You're the new team man?" Knocker asked.

"That's right." His expression changed. "By the way, thanks for coming to see me after what happened. Great fucking friends you were."

Kane and Knocker looked sheepish. They felt guilty and deservedly so. Sure, they'd intended to go visit him, but something always came up. Besides, they wouldn't have known what to say even if they had. Like now.

There was a long awkward silence before Brick said, "You guys have got it easy as shit with these new beasts."

"The battle platform of the future," Kane said.

"Shouldn't you two be too old to be doing this shit?"

"Shouldn't you be fucking invalided out?" Knocker shot back and immediately regretted saying it.

They stared at each other in a tense silence before Brick laughed. "I got new legs, old son. Man, these techs at Global can do anything."

Kane and Knocker grinned. Kane held out his hand. "It's good to see you, Brick."

They all shook hands, and a voice said, "I heard you were back, stud."

Cara walked up and wrapped her arms around him. "They tell me you're coming to work for me. How's it progressing?"

Brick slapped the robotic braces. "These things are amazing. The Vipers are something else."

"How long before you're cleared for duty?"

"Another week or two. From what I've heard, you've been busy."

Cara nodded. "You could say that. Maybe we'll catch up for a beer later."

"That would be good."

The team leader looked at Kane and Knocker. "You two, with me."

They left Brick and followed Cara to one of the many lounges in the Global complex. "You and the team are taking time off for a couple of days."

Kane nodded. "That's what the boss said."

Cara nodded. "She also told me about the fly in the ointment."

"It just means when we find a way in, I won't be able to go," Kane told her.

"We'll need someone on the ground to work out his movements and where he is. Or someone who knows all of it. I'll get the intelligence people right on it."

"You look tired," Knocker said, surprising them.

Cara studied him and saw the serious expression on his face. She nodded and said, "I'll be fine."

"Tired can get you dead, Cara. Take some time for yourself."

"I will, daddy."

"Good." He looked at Kane. "Come on, oh great one, time for a beer. I'm buying."

———

HER TARGET HAD BEEN KANE. What she got was the tiresome Brit. Not that it mattered, either one would do.

It was a honey trap with a sting in the tail. Manuela Gonzales had once been Mexican intelligence. Now she worked as an assassin for the cartels in the Hot Zone.

She had dark hair which hung down past her narrow shoulders. Her body was athletic, and muscles rippled with her every movement. And she used what she had.

Manuela found them in the pub—no, not found, followed them there.

She had worked on Kane first and got nowhere. So, when she turned her attention to Knocker, he welcomed the attention with open arms. Just as they were about to leave the pub together, Kane warned his friend, "There's something about her."

The Brit grinned. "Reaper, old mate, she's going to take me home and fuck my brains out. Then she's going to try and kill me. I can see it coming from Mayfair."

"Just be careful."

"Maybe someone should tell her."

"I'll try to bring her in alive."

And that is what happened. They went back to Manuela's room, had sex, and then she tried to kill him.

Violently.

One thing Knocker had learned in the military was to sleep with one eye open. Which meant when Manuela made her move with a razor-sharp knife, he was ready.

By the time the blade was plunging down through the moonbeams illuminating the hotel room, the former SAS operator was rolling. He sucked in a sharp breath as the keen edge nicked skin on his back, drawing blood. He came to his feet on the other side of the bed and stared at the woman kneeling on the mattress with a maniacal grin on her face. He said, "I guess I'm slowing down in my old age."

"You won't get any older, so you needn't concern yourself."

"Torres send you?"

"You do not need to know."

"I'll take that as a yes."

Manuela launched herself from the bed like a leaping panther. The knife flashed, and Knocker turned himself away, letting her fly past. He looked down at his chest and saw the thin line where the knife had parted his skin. "Oh, you're good."

"And you are slow."

She came back at him, and he waited, catching Manuela off guard. His right fist shot out and caught her on the jaw. She staggered back and grinned as she gathered herself. The assassin had blood on her teeth.

"You could quit now," Knocker said. "I promised my friend that I would try to take you in alive."

Manuela spat on the floor and attacked.

They did the dance of death for five minutes, each getting in their own blows. The lamp beside the bed was smashed, as was a picture on the wall, which crashed to the floor as Knocker threw her light frame at it. The wall-mounted television came down with a crash, and the mirror shattered when the Brit staggered into it.

Their dance moved from the bedroom to the suite's living room, and the coffee table shattered under their weight. Both were bleeding from various cuts and abrasions, and bruises were already forming. Manuela licked at a stream of blood running from her nose and grinned once more, revealing straight pink teeth.

Knocker said, "As much as I enjoyed the sex and

this little dance, I've had just about enough. Now, do you surrender?"

"Fuck you, motherfucker," she sneered.

"Suit yourself. Let's get it over with then."

Manuela came at him again. This time, however, she was tired, careless. Knocker sidestepped, and as she slid past, he brought his elbow around and clipped her solidly. The assassin fell to the floor, out cold.

"Man, but you're a feisty one."

———

ROSANNA MORALES FINISHED CAUTERIZING the last of the cuts and added a salve to help it heal faster. She said, "That's it, Raymond. Next time you take a young woman home, you might want to check her for sharp objects."

"Thanks for the tip, Doc, but I kind of expected this might happen."

She shook her head. "And yet you still went ahead."

The door to the exam room opened, and Grace walked in. "Hey, stud, someone told me you were pretending to be a leg of ham."

Knocker grunted.

"Are you alright?"

"I'm fine. Where is Reaper?"

"He's watching the interrogation."

Rosanna touched the Brit's shoulder lightly. "Just be careful for a day or so until they start to knit."

Knocker nodded. "Thanks, Rosanna."

He slid off the table and put his shirt on as she left the room. Staring at Grace, he asked, "What can I do for you?"

She shrugged. "Just making sure you're alright."

"I'm fine."

"Why did you have to sleep with her?" Grace asked, anger in her voice.

"Bait."

"It was a stupid thing to do," Grace growled. "You could have got yourself killed. Damn fool."

He stared at her. "If I didn't know better, Grace, dear, I'd think you were jealous."

"Fuck off. Can't you be serious for once?"

"I take my life very seriously," Knocker replied. "It's just when you've seen as much death as I have, there's always a coping mechanism somewhere."

"And what if I did?"

"Did what?"

"Care."

"Don't you go doing shit like that to me, girl. Just slow your damn roll. You've seen how fucked up I am."

"So? You should see me on a good day."

"Shit, Grace."

"Don't tell me you haven't noticed it."

"I was trying to ignore it," he said succinctly. "If we were in some other kind of work, I'd hump you like a fucking rabbit—"

"Charming."

"But we aren't, and there is a good chance I could get killed doing this job."

"Or not."

"It doesn't work, Grace. Ask Reaper and Cara. They tried more than once. It doesn't work."

She sighed, and a broad grin split her face. "Gotcha."

Knocker shook his head. "Fucking bitch."

"You really were thinking about me that way?" Grace asked.

"Go away."

"Come on, I'll buy you a beer."

"You owe me more than that, girl."

"Get me drunk enough, and I just might pay what I owe."

———

KNOCKER ROLLED over in bed and opened bleary eyes, trying to work out who the owner of the Chinese dragon tattoo across their back was lying beside him. Then he realized and closed his eyes again. "Fuck."

As he lay there, he remembered the night before. Beer and sex. The bed rocked, and he opened his eyes. Grace was staring at him, wide awake. "How are you feeling?"

He groaned. "Like I've had the shit kicked out of me."

"Don't blame me; you were the one who wanted to keep going."

"Shit, and I wasn't even drunk."

"I wouldn't have slept with you if you were," Grace stated.

Knocker lay on his back and stared at the ceiling. A long silence lingered between them. Grace rested her head on his chest, and he wrapped his arm around her.

"Don't get thinking this is going to be a regular thing. You were a means to an end."

"Bloody hell, I feel so used," Knocker replied.

She bit his nipple. "Get over it."

He rolled over on top of her and started to position himself when his cell rang. "Bollocks."

Knocker leaned over and grabbed it. "Yeah?"

It was Kane. "Get your ass in here, we've got action-able intel."

"Bloody hell, I've only just woke up," he growled.

"Good. Tell Grace to come in too."

He winced. "I'll see you in twenty."

He disconnected the call and said, "Christ."

"What's up?"

"Actionable intel."

"Great."

"And he knew you were here."

"Fuck."

CHAPTER 12

They were all gathered in the briefing room waiting for Thurston, Cara, and Crystal. Kane was next to Knocker in a soft recliner, and there were large screens on the walls and a long table in the center of the room. Their voices were a low murmur as they all talked among themselves. Knocker said, "I don't see Brick."

"He's still training."

"Oh."

After another drawn-out silence between the two men, Kane said, "It doesn't work, you know?"

"What?"

"Sleeping with—"

"Whoa, slow your roll, Dr. Isabelle. Just because we had a stress relief moment doesn't mean that there is anything going on."

"Are you sure? I don't need to be playing psychologist to the broken hearts club when it all fucks up."

"It was nothing like you and Cara," Knocker

assured him. "Speaking of which, when was the last time you slept with her, mate? Huh?"

"Fuck off."

"I rest my case."

Thurston led the others in, but there were an extra two bodies: Preston from MI6 and Polly Yates from MI5. The former general stopped at the front of the room and said, "Thank you all for coming at short notice. You all know our friends from British intelligence."

She paused.

"All right, this is what we know. The main force behind Happy Days is Fernando Torres." A picture appeared on the big screen, and her eyes fixed on Kane. "Some of us know him better than others. Torres is one of the biggest exporters of products in the Hot Zone. Up until now, we thought it was just cocaine. But apparently, he has climbed the ladder and is now, according to him, dominating the world market. We, ladies and gentlemen, are going to stop him. The plan is to capture and bring him in."

Knocker raised his hand.

"Yes, Raymond?"

Fuck! Whenever she used his Christian name, he knew he was in trouble.

"General, this is a big mistake. To capture him, we need to put boots on the ground. Speaking from experience, as you well know, the only ones capable, with the experience we have, is me and Reaper."

It wasn't arrogance, it was fact, and everyone knew it.

Thurston nodded. "It will be up to you and Mr. Kane to form a plan for his extraction when the time comes."

"Yes, ma'am."

"John?"

"We can do it, General, but you better be prepared for a possible mass casualty event."

The response was blunt and straight to the point.

"Noted. But hopefully we can avoid that by having a person on the inside. Crystal?"

The screen changed, and Kane took in a sharp breath. "This is Maria Torres. She is Fernando's sister-in-law."

Knocker glanced at his friend and saw the concern.

Crystal continued. "She is currently in the Caribbean, holidaying with her child."

The screen changed, and a picture appeared of Maria and Ana playing on the beach. Knocker said, "How did we get these pictures?"

"MI6 has them under surveillance. Once it was known they were there, they put people on them."

"They won't be there alone," Kane said, composing himself.

"They have six bodyguards," Preston said. "I believe you know the woman in question?"

"That was a long time ago," Kane lied.

"Then you are the perfect person to make contact with her."

"No one makes contact with her without making her back scratchers nervous," Knocker said.

"You will have to find a way," Cara said. "You want to stop a slaughter? This might be the way to do it. She will have information no one else has."

"What about the girl?" Kane asked.

"What about her?"

"She doesn't need to be caught up in this."

Cara nodded. "That will be up to you and Raymond."

"Me and him?"

"Yes, you'll be going in alone. Your only backup will be an MI6 operations team. This isn't an extract, Reaper. You flip her and get out."

"We'll be wasting our time," Kane said. "She'll be too scared of him."

"Then you'll have to convince her."

"We'll need to put something on the table."

Thurston stared at Kane. "Explain that we'll get her and her daughter out."

"Where is she?" Kane asked.

"Barbados."

"I need everything you have on the bodyguards. No surprises. And if this goes wrong, we pull her and the kid out anyway."

"Agreed."

Kane looked at Crystal. "You come with us."

"I need Crystal here," Cara stated.

"And I need a tech on the ground I can trust."

"All right."

"Great," Knocker said. "This is going to be fun."

Thurston looked at the Brit. "Was there a heavy hint of sarcasm there, Raymond?"

"No, General. Sun, surf, babes in bikinis, and men with guns. What could possibly go wrong?"

Kane slapped his friend on the back. "Well, you just fucked that up."

———

BARBADOS

White beaches, turquoise water, sun, sand, and tourists. Kane sat on a towel, watching Maria build a sandcastle with Ana, just like many other families on the beach. Except the other families didn't have six men in suits standing in a perimeter around them.

"You're going to have to be the invisible man to get close to her, Reaper," Knocker said over his earbud. "She still looks as good as she did back in the day."

Kane remained silent. His friend was right. She looked just as good, if not better, with age. He said, "We're wasting our time here. Let's go back up to the bar and rethink it."

"I'm with you," Knocker replied.

Crystal said, "If you can't get close enough, I might be able to hack into her cell and you can talk to her that way."

Kane looked sideways at Crystal, who was lying stomach down in a white bikini twenty meters from where he was seated. He said, "To the bar, my dear Crystal. There's no way of doing it out in the open here."

They walked back up the beach and met at the open-air bar where they all bought beers. They sat there and discussed what they should do next, coming up with the whole sum of not much. Kane had just ordered another beer when a voice said beside him, "Boy, it's hot out there."

It was a voice he'd know anywhere. He remained silent, not trusting himself to look. Maria continued, "Don't you think?"

It was Knocker who spoke, trying to distract her. He moved around the other side and said, "You'll have to excuse him, he's ignorant. Me, on the other hand, I'm just a genuine conversationalist."

Maria smiled. "I'm glad someone is. Although, the John I remember could talk just fine."

Kane turned his head slowly and stared at Maria.

"Hello, John."

The bartender stopped in front of her. "Can I help you, miss?"

"Two Cokes, please."

"Hello, Maria."

"Don't talk to me, John, just listen. Tomorrow, Ana and I will be on an island cruise. I assume you are here to see me, and I assume it is about Fernando. If you want to talk to me, be on it."

"Which one, Maria?"

The bartender arrived with the drinks, and she paid for them. She picked up the full glasses and said, "I'm sure you can work it out."

Once she was gone, Knocker said, "That was unnerving."

Kane sighed. "Tell me about it."

———

"THE BOAT they are booked on is called *The Osprey*," Crystal said. "I've fiddled the bookings so that we're on the boat as well and most of the bodyguards are not."

"Most?"

"There will still be one. That way hopefully they will let her go."

"What if they try to stop her from going?" Knocker asked.

"We'll have to deal with it. I've got an earwig ready to go for her to use. All you have to do is slip it to her."

Kane nodded. "Let's hope this works. No weapons."

Knocker and Crystal agreed.

Crystal looked at Kane thoughtfully. "Since I'm involved, would you like to tell me what the history is?"

Knocker said, "Some years back, while Kane and I were running some ops for MI6, we came across Fernando Torres and his brother, Victor. Victor's wife was Maria. Kane used her to get inside the operation. Things happened."

"Things?"

Kane said, "She developed feelings for me. Maybe I did for her too."

"Complicates things," Crystal said.

With a sigh, Kane said, "It did. But it got me where I wanted to go."

"Where was that?"

"Fernando's inner circle. Victor was always suspicious of me, but I had the trust of Fernando so what Victor thought didn't matter. While I was inside, Knocker was running things outside with the help of an MI6 black ops team."

"We had a lot of hairy moments," Knocker explained. "But once we were in, the intel Reaper was getting out was invaluable. All the while, he was getting in deeper with Maria."

"What happened?"

Kane said, "I got caught with Maria by Victor. When it was over, Victor was dead, and I was on the run."

"What happened to Maria?"

"I don't know. This is the first time I've seen her since that happened."

"Did she know who you were?" Crystal asked.

"No. Not until I killed Victor."

"And here we are."

"That's right. I wish I knew how she was going to react."

"I guess we'll find out."

Kane sipped the beer in front of him.

———

THE DAY STARTED out gray and overcast before the steel-colored clouds drifted away and the sun came out. The dock was constructed of old wood reinforced by steel girders. Passengers were lined up, including Kane, Knocker, and Crystal. Not that the line was moving; there was trouble at the front as Maria's bodyguards tried to sort the mess of not enough bookings.

Not helped by Knocker. "Hurry up, you clowns."

Two of the guards turned and stared in his direction. Both had tattoos visible on their necks. They glared at the Brit who glared back at them. A couple of minutes later, Maria, Ana, and one of the bodyguards boarded the boat while the others walked back along the jetty, turning angry gazes on Knocker.

The line moved smoothly after that and once the trio were on board, they separated. As Crystal walked past Maria, she brushed lightly against her, pressing the earwig into her hand.

Ten minutes later, the boat was sailing across the bay toward the open ocean. Watching Maria, Kane saw her press the earwig into her ear. He said, "Can you hear me?"

A fleeting alarmed expression flickered on her face before she regained her composure. "Yes," she whispered.

"Just act naturally and—"

"Act naturally," she hissed. "You used me, killed my husband, and left me to pick up the pieces."

Ana looked up at her mother, curiosity on her face. Kane looked at the bodyguard who was further along the rail and saw that he was watching her, frowning.

"Wait, your friend is looking."

Maria froze before turning at the rail and looking out to sea. Kane said, "Just relax. Give him time to lose interest."

Knocker watched him from where he was. "Looks like he's relaxing again."

Kane gave him a few more moments. "All right, we can talk. Just make sure that your daughter doesn't blow this thing up."

"What do you want, John?" Maria asked. "To use me again, then cast me aside?"

"It was never like that—"

"Bullshit."

"How bad do you want to get yourself and Ana out of Fernando's grip?"

Silence.

Kane turned his head and saw her staring in his direction.

The bodyguard was looking too.

They waited.

Then he turned away again.

"Well?" Kane asked.

"You already know the answer to that, John. I wanted to be gone the last time, but you disappeared."

"I had to. You know that. After killing Victor, things went to shit."

"Then why now, John?" she asked bitterly. "Why now?"

"Because everything has gone too far, Maria.

Fernando has gone too far. His people killed the British Prime Minister. His drugs have killed millions. It's time he was stopped. We want his manufacturing facilities, but most of all, we want him."

"You mean kill him?" There was hope in her voice.

"No, we have to take him alive so we can put him on display."

"What do you need me for?" Maria asked.

"You can give us information from the inside," Kane replied.

"And then once it is done, you forget all about me. Only this time, I will be killed."

Kane shook his head. "No. This time I get you out. I promise."

"You promise, John? I have heard your promises before. But maybe this time I have something that will ensure that your promise remains true."

Kane frowned. "What do you mean?"

"Look at Ana, John. Really look at her."

Kane stared at the little girl.

"Oh, Christ," Knocker said softly, already putting the puzzle together. "Reaper, she's—"

"My daughter," Kane finished for him.

"That's right," Maria said. "Ana is your daughter. Now, how far will you go to protect her?"

The man known as Reaper felt as though he'd been gut shot. He tried to read Maria's face from a distance to see if she was lying, but she wasn't. He already knew. The child's age, the dark hair, even her eyes. "How long have you known?"

"From the night she was conceived."

"Does Fernando know?"

"No, he thinks she is Victor's."

"It doesn't change anything, Maria. We'll get you

both out."

"I hate to interrupt," Knocker said. "But this changes everything, old mate. Your kid is in the mix. We need a new plan."

"He's right," Crystal said in agreement.

"How many more days do you have left?" Kane asked.

"We leave the day after tomorrow," Maria replied.

"Not much time, but I can deal with it. Throw your earwig over the side. I'll be in touch."

———

"WE PULL them both out now and use what she already knows," Kane said irrationally.

"It doesn't work that way, Reaper, you know that," Knocker said sympathetically. "They have to stay in play."

"She's my daughter, Raymond."

"Don't start that fucking shit," Knocker shot back at him. "You know it's the only play."

"We might be able to do it another way," Crystal said.

"After we hit his manufacturing plants, we kidnap the girl. Use her to draw him out. If he still thinks that she's Victor's daughter, it might just work."

Kane hated the idea, but he couldn't think of a better one except dropping bombs on the bastard, and that wasn't allowed. His encrypted cell rang. He looked at the caller ID and stared at his friends. "It's Cara. Who blabbed?"

"There was nothing else I could do," Crystal replied guiltily. "I'm sorry."

Kane shook his head. "It saved me telling her."

He moved off to one side to answer the call. Crystal glanced at Knocker. "There wasn't, was there?"

He shook his head. "You did the right thing."

Meanwhile, Kane was surprised by Cara's reaction. "Are you alright?"

"I guess," he replied doubtfully.

"What's the plan?"

"We leave them both in play." He went on to tell her about the partial plan. "It might just work."

"Break it all down so that we can understand it, and we'll go from there."

"Yes, ma'am."

"What's she like?"

"Ana?"

"Yes."

"I don't really know. I haven't talked to her."

"Does she look like you?"

"Yes."

"Poor kid."

Kane sighed. "You know, for the first time in my life, I'm actually scared."

"A big boy like you? Who gets shot at all the time?"

"This is a lot different to being shot at, Cara."

"I know. Kid, remember?"

"Yes, sorry."

"Don't be sorry. It's a big thing. And they're both in the middle of hell."

"Cara, if anything happens to me—"

"Don't start that bullshit, Reaper, I need you with your head in the game. Just know that if anything does happen, they have family right here."

The call finished, and Kane returned to the others. "All right, now that we know what we're doing, I need to get into that bungalow."

CHAPTER 13

BARBADOS

It was a drunk that got him inside. It was the oldest trick in the book, and it worked. Knocker splashed himself with half a bottle of rum like it was aftershave and proceeded to stagger right up to the first armed guard and berate him for not letting him inside his bungalow.

"Get the fuck out of my way, mate. This is my bungalow, and I'm fucking going to bed."

"No, this is not yours," the guard told him. "Is Mrs. Torres' bungalow."

The Brit stared at him. "What the fuck is she doing in my bungalow? Wait. Is she good-looking?"

"Go away."

"Why? This is where I sleep. The bungalowwww is fucking mine. Number thirty-four."

"This is number forty-three."

"That's what I said."

They were joined by the second guard on duty. "Who is this fool?"

"He thinks that this is his bungalow."

"Tell him to fuck off."

Knocker's eyes narrowed. "That's not very nice, mate. You know what your problem is? Huh? Too many tattoos on your face. All that ink fucked your brain up."

A gun appeared, and Knocker held his hands up at shoulder height. "Whoa, dude, the fuck? If you want this bungalow, take it. Can I just get my stuff?"

"It's not your damn bungalow."

"Okay, got it."

He walked away with the two guards staring after him.

Meanwhile, Kane had come in under the bungalow and up the steps. He slipped inside and found Maria sitting on a sofa. She stared at him in surprise. "What? How?"

Ana appeared and saw the strange man. She opened her mouth to scream, but Maria's fear gave her the speed required to stop the sound from coming out. She wrapped an arm around her daughter and placed her other hand over her open mouth. "No, baby girl. Quiet. He will not hurt us."

"It's okay, Ana, I'm an old friend of your mother's. Do you mind if I talk to her for a moment?"

Ana looked at him with big, round eyes. She nodded. "Okay."

"But this has to be our secret, okay?"

"Okay."

Maria whispered something into her daughter's ear, and she hurried off into the bedroom. Once the door was closed, Maria's expression changed. "What are you doing? If they catch you here..."

"I won't be long." Kane looked at the closed door. "She's a cute kid."

"She takes after her mother."

Kane bowed his head in thought.

"Tell me why you're here, John."

He glanced up, his eyes focused on her. "We need you to relay information to us so we can take action."

"About what?"

"Fernando's operation."

"Are you crazy?" Her voice became high-pitched. "He would kill me."

"We need to know where he manufactures the drugs," Kane explained. "Do you know where that is?"

She shook her head.

"Then you need to find out."

"You ask the impossible, John. Why can't you find them?"

"Because everyone is in his pocket. You are the only one in a position that can find out and get the information to us."

"I can't."

"Listen, Maria, once we get the production centers, there is another part to the plan."

"What?"

"We're going to kidnap Ana."

"What?"

"We'll get her and take her out of harm's way."

"And what about me?" Maria asked.

"We need you in place. It's the only way. We'll make a ransom demand and try to draw Fernando out. Once we do that, we'll sweep him up and get you out as well. I promise Ana will be fine with my people."

Maria stared at him. "Are you sure this is the only way?"

"Yes."

She nodded. "I'm scared, John."

He reached out and took her hand. "It'll all be fine. I promise. Now, tell me about Ana. I have a couple of minutes."

———

HEREFORD, ENGLAND

Kane, Knocker, Grace, Cara, and Thurston were gathered around the electronic map of Central America on the table. Kane touched the map table and zoomed in on Honduras. "Torres has a large compound here in the interior of Honduras. As we know, he has an army of fighters on his payroll. Tanks, fighter jets, ground-to-air missiles, and five thousand troops along with his own special bodyguard. It's a new world. When the time comes, it will be hit and run."

"We still have no idea where he manufactures the stuff," Thurston said.

Kane shook his head. "I'm hoping we might get something soon."

"How is she reaching out to us again?" Cara asked.

"Ana plays an online game with a chat room. It's old school. Terrorists used the method back in the teens."

"And it's secure?"

Crystal nodded. "We've set up a room which is encrypted, and we are the only ones who can access it."

"So, we wait."

"Yes."

"What about the elephant in the room?" Thurston asked Kane. "Is it going to be a problem? Do I need to replace you?"

"I'm fine."

"Work on an emergency extraction plan. Just in case."

"Yes, ma'am."

Thurston sighed. "All right, dismissed. Kane, stay with me for a moment."

When the room was cleared, he looked at Thurston and said, "If this is about—"

"No. It's about Brick."

"Okay."

"He's been cleared as operational. But I need a no-BS assessment on how you feel about it."

"What does he say?" Kane asked.

"He says he's right to go."

"As long as I've known him, he's never put himself in harm's way if he hasn't got his shit together."

"I'll take that as you clearing him."

"You can."

"Fine, then he's all yours."

"Thanks, boss."

Kane left her and went immediately to find Brick. He was in the gym, standing on his new robotic legs and punching a bag. "Hey."

The former SEAL turned, sweat drenching him. "Hey."

"The boss says you're operational. How are you feeling?"

Brick nodded. "I feel good. The best in a while."

Kane stared at him.

Brick shrugged his shoulders. "Out with it, Reaper. We both know why you're here."

"All right. I've got reservations about you in the field. I don't think you can do it. Not in that condition."

"Don't hold back," Brick grunted.

"It's nothing against you, Brick. You were a damn good operator. But now, I don't see how you can be."

"I wouldn't clear myself unless I didn't think I could do it, Reaper. You know that."

"Yes, but part of me wonders if you're trying to prove that you can still do it."

"I guess we'll see in time."

"This is no time for fucking experiments."

"I never said it was."

After a moment of silence, Kane turned and walked away. On the other side of the doorway leading out of the gym, Cara was waiting for him, and she fell into step. "Bit harsh, weren't you?"

"He needed to hear it."

"I've seen him training, Reaper. He can do this. Give him a chance."

"Torres won't give him one."

"You are not Torres."

"There is a good chance he'll get killed."

Cara stared at him. "If he had a choice of dying on the mission or dying in that chair, I know which he would choose, John. He's not asking you to babysit him. All he wants is to be a man again."

Kane grunted and kept walking.

———

TORRES COMPOUND, HONDURAS

It took all of Maria's willpower to stop herself from physically shaking as she went through Fernando's desk, looking for information. He was at a meeting with a man from Europe out near the pool, which didn't give her much time.

She flipped through folders and singular papers before she found what she wanted. A sheet of paper, which was a bill of lading for chemicals that were delivered somewhere in the south of the country. But there was no name on it. That would have been relayed to the driver at the time of delivery. But this was a place for them to start.

She'd just closed the drawer when the door to Fernando's office opened, and he walked in. He glared at Maria. "What are you doing in here?"

She hoped the fear on her face didn't show, but somehow she doubted it. "I—Ana was in here this morning and left one of her dolls behind."

"Ana? In here?" The expression on his face was one of skepticism.

"Yes. Ah—here it is." Maria leaned down and picked up the doll. It had brown hair and droopy eyes.

"Tell her not to come in here anymore," Torres growled. "Nor you. My office is off-limits. Remember?"

She nodded. "Yes, Fernando."

He stared at her as she left his office and closed the door behind her. In the hallway, Maria paused and let her heart slow. Then she went to find Ana, who was playing her online game.

———

WILLIE MULLER WAS a German-born robotics scientist from Berlin. His meeting with Fernando Torres wasn't about drugs or transportation; it was about a new generation of remote-controlled robotic soldiers. When Fernando Torres reappeared, he had a compact laptop which he placed on the table and opened it beside where Muller was seated.

Muller passed him over a thumb drive, and Torres plugged it in. Moments later, he was watching a demonstration of a remote-controlled battle robot.

"That is the HP 433 Armored Battle Droid. It carries a belt-fed minigun as well as anti-tank capabilities. They are like a military platoon all on their own. If you have a handful...well, I think you know what they would be capable of."

Torres watched in silence, his face not displaying the excitement he was feeling, until it was over and asked, "How many do you have?"

"Thirty operational."

"I will take them all."

"It will take a while to train your men and ship them."

"Ship them immediately and send the men with them who will train my people. It is simple."

"Then there is the matter of payment."

"How much?"

"Two hundred million each," Muller said.

"Give me your account number and I will transfer half now and the rest when I have seen a demonstration."

The German was stunned. "Why, of course. But—"

"I have the details."

"Fine. It will be done."

"Good. It has been a pleasure doing business with you."

———

HEREFORD, ENGLAND

"We have contact," Molly Wilson said, poking her head around the corner of the recreation room where Kane and Knocker were playing eight ball. "She made contact through the chat room twenty minutes ago."

They followed Molly to the ops center, where Cara and Crystal were waiting for them. The latter looked up and said, "She made contact under the name Rapunzel. It was only a few lines, but basically she said that one of the manufacturing plants was in southern Honduras."

"Do we know where?" Kane asked.

Cara shook her head. "No. We're using everything we have to try and locate it."

"So, he only has one?" Knocker asked.

"She thinks two. She'll try her best to get to the other location. Meanwhile, we picked up another piece of intel."

"Good or bad?" Kane asked.

"Oh, definitely bad. It seems Fernando's competition is about to make a move into Italy. The Martinez brothers have two shipments of cocaine coming off two ships at midnight tonight."

"Two ships?" Kane asked. "Is that right?"

"That's correct."

"And the Italians are reaching out *now* for help?"

"No. We stumbled across it by chance," Crystal said. "We came across some chatter on the dark web. A couple of us ran it down and came up with a handful of candy."

"Security force?"

"Fifty, maybe sixty."

"But that's not the main problem," Cara said.

Knocker sighed. "It never is these days. Fucking bastards are better equipped than most countries."

"Bring it up, Crystal."

A picture of a ship appeared, and the deck was laden with shipping containers. "This is the *MV Constellation*. Looks just like an ordinary merchant vessel. However..."

The picture changed, and things appeared. "X-ray showed us this."

Knocker shook his head.

Kane said, "What do we have? Surface-to-air missiles, a helicopter, suicide drones, and auto-loading 150mm guns."

"And we can expect the second one to have the same," Cara said.

"Can we sink them?" Knocker asked.

"No, they are already docked close to the cruise terminal in Genoa. Should something go awry, then, well, you get the picture."

"What do we do?" the Brit asked.

"Drop on top of them," Cara replied. "Two Vipers per ship and assault teams to take both bridges."

"I don't like it," Kane said.

"If you're talking about the plan—"

"No. I don't like the mission full-stop. We're changing over ops while we still have one in the pipeline."

"We can't do anything until we find out where the plant is," Cara reminded him.

"What if something else happens?"

"We'll send a strike team."

Kane nodded. "Saddle up."

GENOA PORT, ITALY

Kane led the assault team on the *MV Constellation,* while Knocker led the one on the other vessel, the *MV Baron.* Both teams consisted of four shooters. Meanwhile, the four Vipers were manned by Grace, Ryan, Cara, and Brick.

The Vipers went first, touching down on deck one minute before the strike team. This was to secure the landing zone. Onboard the *Constellation,* Grace swept the bridge superstructure with her minigun as the alarm screamed throughout the ship.

Meanwhile, Ryan moved toward the bow of the ship where the helicopter was concealed among a multitude of fake shipping containers.

From the superstructure, a heavy machine gun started to thump. Grace felt the impact of the large caliber round on her armor and turned her head. The HUD automatically targeted the threat, and the minigun did the rest.

"Heavy weapon on the bridge is neutralized."

"Copy," Kane replied. "Team twenty seconds out."

When Kane and his team landed, they were wearing the same body armor that Cara and the others had been wearing when they jumped into The Line. He gathered them as he unslung his HK 550, and they started toward the bridge.

Light assault weapons opened fire from the top rail outside the wheelhouse. Kane felt the glancing blow of a bullet as he looked for the shooter. He found him and put him down. "Everyone, follow me. We don't stop until the wheelhouse is secured."

Meanwhile, on the second ship, Cara opened fire on an X-ray with a shoulder-launched rocket. The

rounds from her minigun tore him to shreds, chunks of flesh creating a macabre mural on the bulkhead behind him. Beside her, Brick scanned toward the bow, and he caught sight of a target with a second rocket launcher and let his HUD do its thing before he opened fire.

"Damn, this thing is good," he said over an open channel, not realizing it was.

"It gets better, Brick, old son," Knocker said as he touched down on the deck. "Just don't think you're invincible in the thing."

"Like you, Knocker, huh?" Cara said.

The Brit detached his parachute. "Darling, I am invincible."

"Oh, please. Take your team and clear the bridge."

"Yes, boss."

Knocker led his people inside the superstructure. In the stairwell, he came upon three shooters armed with automatic weapons. One of them opened fire, spraying bullets everywhere. The Brit calmly brought up his 550 and put him down before picking a new target and doing the same.

However, the last shooter was smarter than his companions and used the grenade launcher slung under his weapon.

"Fuck, look out!"

Knocker threw himself backward, taking the next operator in line with him. The explosion ripped through the stairwell, the concussion blast rocking the Brit to the core. A female voice said, "Get the fuck off me, old man."

Knocker groaned. "I saved your life and still no respect."

Jessie Nelson shoved him off her. She was former British Army. She climbed to her feet and helped

Knocker up. "I thought you SAS types were tougher than that."

"Like you said, I'm an old man. Get up those fucking stairs."

Jessie led the way, and Knocker followed. She put down the shooter and kept moving. Five minutes later, the bridge was secure, and things got worse.

Much worse.

CHAPTER 14

Houlihan being in command of Skyhammer was becoming a familiar scenario, and as the Stratomaster banked lazily around, Crystal said, "Pat, you need to look at this."

"What have you got, Crystal?"

"I'm not really sure. Bravo Four, maybe bring your toys online."

"Roger that," Molly replied.

Houlihan crossed over to the console where Crystal was working. "What do you have?"

"Ten contacts moving fast toward the port. Designated X-ray One through Ten."

"See if we can get a closer look at them, Crystal."

Crystal tapped the keys on her console, and the picture on the screen changed. For a moment, they stared at the X-rays before working out what they were watching.

"Are they what I think they are?" Crystal asked.

"Robots. Armed like our Vipers."

"Fuck."

"Bravo to all callsigns, you have ten X-rays inbound. Heavily armed and heavily armored."

"Are they tanks?" Knocker asked over the net.

"No, they're robots."

"They're fucking what?"

"You heard me. They are one mike out. Prepare for heavy contact."

"Fuck, I hate this war."

————

GENOA PORT, ITALY

"Fuck, I hate this war," Knocker growled as he reloaded his 550 with a fresh magazine. "Everyone out on the bridge wings. Let's see what we have got."

The four of them went outside and stared into the semi-darkness. "I can't see shit," Jessie said.

Knocker changed over to night vision and saw them approaching. He grabbed Jessie's arm and pulled her to the deck. "Down! Everyone down!"

The night was ripped apart by the sound of minigun fire. Of the Brit's four-person team, Jessie was the only one he saved. The other two operators died under the scything fire. They crawled back into the bridge.

Knocker growled, "This is Reaper Two. I have two, repeat, two people down. We're pinned down on the bridge."

He looked at Jessie. "Are you alright?"

She nodded, a little shaken. "Y-yes, thanks to you."

The Brit came up and fired through a shattered

window at one of the robot warriors. His bullets ricocheted off its armor, and it turned its minigun onto the bridge. Bullets smashed at the metal exterior, some passing through the opening where the window had been.

"That was a bad idea," Knocker growled.

"Do you think?" Jessie snapped. "Not a smart idea to draw their attention to us."

"Cara, I need some help."

"Be right with you, Raymond," came the reply.

"Ah, bollocks," he growled.

"What's the problem?" Jessie asked.

He stared at her through his helmet. "We're fucked."

———

KANE WAS JUST AS MUCH in the same predicament. They were pinned down on the bridge with heavy incoming fire. He had lost one shooter, and the other was wounded. He reloaded his weapon and said, "Grace, Red, you need to kick it up a little, we're pinned down."

"I don't know where the hell these things came from," Grace said. "But I sure as shit know where they're going."

She came out from behind the cover of a shipping container stack, and her HUD picked up a target immediately. She brought up her arm and fired the 30mm housed there.

The impact was sensational as the attacking robot exploded into pieces. The rest of it crumpled to the dock and was done. "Eat that, motherfucker."

WHAM!

Her Viper was punched back, warnings flashing on her display. Through her comms she heard Crystal say, "Reaper Three, sitrep. I've got warnings on my screen. Armor compromised down to sixty-five percent."

"You should see it from where I am," Grace groaned. "I'm still in the fight."

Ryan appeared and gave her cover while Grace brought her Viper erect. A rocket exploded close by, driving them into cover. Ryan leaned out, and his Viper's 30mm exploded to life.

Suddenly the shipping container stack collapsed toward them, falling like a house of cards. "Look out!"

The shipping containers came down on top of the two Vipers, forcing them to the deck. The ship vibrated with explosions. For a moment, the scrambled pile of containers never moved, then one of them lurched aside as Grace's Viper shoved it out of the way. "This is bull-shit. Red, are you okay?"

"I feel like I've been kicked in the nuts."

"Bravo, this is Reaper Three. Copy?"

"Copy, Reaper Three."

Grace heaved another shipping container away. "What the hell is going on?"

"I wish I knew, Three."

Another robot appeared and Grace opened fire with her minigun. The metal beast lurched violently and went down. But not for long, it came erect and opened fire with its own minigun.

Rounds hammered into Grace's Viper, shaking it wildly. "Christ."

Meanwhile, as its slaughter machine rotated, it prepared to launch a rocket. Ryan saw what was about to happen and moved swiftly. "Look out, Grace!"

The Australian's Viper crashed into his counterpart's, knocking her sideways. The rocket, which was meant for her, smashed into Ryan's Viper and exploded.

"Red!"

The Viper was shattered, torn apart by the explosion. Inside the twisted mass of metal and body armor, the Australian had taken the full force of the rocket and lay shattered. Grace said into her comms, "Bravo, Reaper Four is down. I say again, Reaper Four is down. I need vitals ASAP."

"Copy, Reaper Three. No vitals, I repeat, no vitals. Four is KIA."

Anger surged through her, and just as she looked up, another rocket came out of the night, straight at her.

Grace's HUD lit up, and her minigun came to life. A hailstorm of 7.62 rounds smashed into the incoming rocket which exploded violently. She raised the arm of the Viper and fired a flurry of 30 mm rounds and used them to fall back. "Reaper, we need to get out of here."

"Copy. Regroup on the dock. Bravo, we need some cover down here."

"Copy. One, will see what we can do. Standby."

———

MEANWHILE, Cara and Brick were doing their best to hold their position. However, the ship was holed and had already started to list. The call that Reaper Four was KIA weighed heavily on her. Add in the other team members as well and the operation was quickly going to shit. Then came the call for them to withdraw.

"Reaper Two, sitrep?"

"We're still pinned down, boss."

"Give me a moment. Standby to move."

"Roger that."

"Brick, we need to give them some cover."

"On it, ma'am. The sooner we get off this sinking tub, the better."

"Open fire."

They both let loose at the dock with their 30mm weapons. Cara said into her comms, "Move now, Reaper Two."

"Roger that."

Incoming fire from the robots on the dock intensified and hammered into the ship's superstructure.

40,000 FEET OVER GENOA PORT, ITALY

"Pat, the Scorpion is inbound. Five mikes until RV."

Houlihan looked at Crystal. "Thank you. Molly, let's give them support. What do we have?"

"We can launch a Star Hawk."

"Do it. Mike, do what you can."

Tanner nodded. "Roger that. Molly, ready when you are."

What took only thirty seconds seemed like an eternity. "Star Hawk away."

Tanner said, "I have control. Now, let's kick some Terminator ass."

"Reaper One, this is Bravo One. We have a Star Hawk on its way to you. Keep your heads down."

"Copy, Bravo One." Over the open channel, Houlihan then heard Kane say, "Everyone mark your positions. We don't want Joystick John putting a Lucifer down our throats."

"I'm hurt, Reaper One, that you could contemplate such a thing. Standby. Lucifer away."

A handful of heartbeats later, the missile hit.

"Target destroyed. Bravo Two to all callsigns, there is an opening to your south. I'll try to hold them back while the Scorpion comes in for extract. ETA, two mikes. Good luck. Lucifer away."

Tanner brought the UCAV back around and looked for another target. He picked it out and fired another Lucifer. Meanwhile, the team was making their way to the Scorpion. Moments later, he heard Kane say, "Ground team now aboard LCV. Three souls still in the field. All KIA."

"Copy," Houlihan said. "We'll see what we can do about them. Come home, Reaper One. Come home."

They'd had their asses handed to them, but more importantly, someone out there had robot soldiers which packed as much of a punch as their own. The playing field had just been leveled, and that was bad.

HONDURAS

"I'm sorry, Mr. Torres, but it would seem that whoever it was we engaged got away," Muller said apologetically.

"Never mind, Mr. Muller. I consider the experiment a success. We have forced them to flee, as well as killing some of them. I consider that a great success."

"Yes, sir."

"Now, how soon can you have them delivered?"

HEREFORD, ENGLAND

Kane and Knocker watched the feed over and over, coming to the same conclusion. The new robots were a definite threat to the Vipers. Knocker let out a sigh. "We need to find out where these things came from so we can put them out of business."

Kane nodded. "There are but a few places in the world working on things like this that we know of."

"But what about the ones we don't?"

"That would be the big question. You can bet your last dollar that these are from a black-market developer."

"They have to have a weakness," Knocker said. "They're not quite as big as the Viper but heavily armed."

The door to the ops room where they were working opened, and Crystal came in. Kane looked at her. "Any luck in retrieving the fallen?"

"It's been done."

The Reaper nodded. "Good."

"Any luck?" she asked.

"Not yet. We figure there has to be a weakness somewhere."

Knocker said, "If we could find out who made them, we might be in with a show."

"It would have to be someone on the dark side."

"That's what we figured."

"There was one thing I found going back through it all," Crystal said. "A signal."

"What kind of signal?"

"Low frequency, almost undetectable."

Kane stared at the screen. "Could they be remote controlled?"

"That would be my guess."

"Can you trace the source?" Knocker asked.

"With some luck."

Kane nodded. "Good. Now, anything from Honduras?"

"We think we might have a location. We'll station a satellite and gather as much intel as we can before sending in a team."

The door to the room opened again, and Cara stepped in. "We've got contact with Maria."

They hurried to the main ops room where Houlihan was talking via the chatroom. "She says that there was a German scientist there, but he's gone now. They were talking about robots."

"Bingo," Knocker growled.

"Ask her his name."

Houlihan typed quickly and waited.

The screen flashed, and they read her answer.

"Who the hell is Willie Muller?" Knocker asked.

"German robotics engineer," Crystal replied. "He was very good in his field. He got caught selling secrets to the Chinese and disappeared. I guess we know what he's been doing."

"What do we do about him?"

"Find out if he's still there."

Houlihan typed.

Maria answered.

"No."

"How many did Torres buy?"

More typing.

Another answer.

"Thirty."

"When will they be delivered?"

A few moments later, another answer. "She doesn't know. She wants to know what to do."

"Tell her to sit tight and stick to the plan. Expect some news in the next couple of days."

The chatroom closed, and Maria was gone. Cara looked at Kane. "This changes everything."

"No. We stick to the plan. We destroy his factory and kidnap the girl. Then we go after him."

"Yes, but by the time we get there, he's going to have the extra hardware."

"Then we throw what we have at him. If he wants a war, we give it to him. It's cost us too much to get this far. I'm not going back now."

———

KANE AND KNOCKER used their trained eyes to look over the photos of the supposed factory. Knocker placed a finger on a point and said, "Roving patrols. Looks like pairs."

Kane nodded. "Four lots. Looks like they have towers and a couple of machine gun nests. Regular fortress."

"Tell me why we can't bomb it."

"Because we need the intel. We take the Vipers in, secure it, and the strike team will do the follow-up."

"We're back down to four again."

"Yes."

"What about Ivan? He's an extra half."

Kane nodded. "Yes."

"Brick?"

"I think so."

Grace appeared. Knocker looked at her and asked, "How are you doing?"

"All right, I guess. Still can't believe he's gone."

"You get used to it," the Brit said, sounding callous.

"What?"

"I know it sounds harsh, but it's true. Reaper and I have been in this boat so many times that you learn to compartmentalize it. Put it in a box and leave it there. It's brutal but necessary."

"But he died because of me."

Kane shook his head. "He died for you, not because of you. There is a difference. I'm sure that if the shoe had been on the other foot, you would have done the same."

The door opened, and Brick entered, wheeling himself in his chair. "Team meeting?"

Knocker said, "Just explaining a few things to the kid about death."

"Ryan?"

Kane nodded.

"Shit, if it comes down to it, we'd all do the same thing without thinking," Brick said, staring at her. "Compartmentalize and move on, Grace. You can't do that, it'll screw your brain."

"How can you all be so cold?"

"Practice. We grieve, we celebrate, we move on."

"Amen," said Knocker.

"Since when did you become so wise?" Kane asked the former SEAL.

"Only recently," he allowed. "If it wasn't for the general, I'd still be buried in a bottle."

There was a moment of silence, and Kane asked, "Do you think you can handle Ivan next time out?"

"The big prick?"

"Don't let him hear you calling him that, his feelings will be hurt." Knocker grinned.

"I'll drive him into hell if you want," Brick replied.

"Let's hope it doesn't come to that," Kane replied. "How are your planning skills?"

"A little rusty."

"Have a look at this and tell me what you think."

Brick wheeled himself over to the table. He looked at the photo and said, "Normally I'd say put a sniper on this ridge and take out the shooters in the tower before breaching. But since we have the Vipers, I say two points on ingress. Here and here. Have a Black Cat hit the towers before we go in, just in case they have launchers. Wait."

Kane frowned at Knocker. "What is it?"

"Look here," Brick said, pointing at something indiscriminate. "SAMs."

"What?"

"Right here. Looks like they're well camouflaged, but they're there."

"They'll have to be taken out before we can get Skyhammer in position," Kane said.

"Black Cat," Knocker agreed. "We can do the towers and then anything else. Have the strike team hold back until you give the order. Well picked up, Brick."

The former SEAL nodded. "I may not have the use of my legs, but my eyes are still sharp."

"There you are." They all turned to see Rosanna Morales entering. "I've been looking for you everywhere."

"I'm around. Not like I'm running away," Brick replied.

The doctor held up a needle and vial. "I need to get these blood samples done for the researchers."

"Fine, have at it."

Kane said, "Are you all right?"

"They're using me as a guinea pig. Apparently, the Global scientists are working on some kind of spinal cord regeneration. They believe that the pathways can be regrown."

"What does that mean?" Knocker asked.

"Doc?"

"It means that if it is successful, there is a good chance that he will get some movement back in his legs."

"Some?" Kane asked.

"We don't want to be too hopeful."

"Are you talking able to walk again?"

"Nothing is certain."

Kane stared at Brick, who shrugged. "It ain't like I have anything to lose."

"But a lot to gain."

"Let's hope so."

"All right, let's go over this plan again."

CHAPTER 15

The Black Cat came in low over the jungle, its turbines screaming. It followed the contours of the land until, at the last moment, Tanner pulled it up and fired two missiles.

The F-60 turned savagely, flipped, and then righted itself as it came back in for a second run at the targets.

"We have a second SAM site camouflaged within the compound, Mike," Houlihan snapped from where she sat.

"Damn it. Give me a target, ma'am."

"There."

"I have it. Lucifer away."

"SAM fired. Missile in the air."

Tanner pulled back on his joystick, and the Black Cat came into a steep climb. He then hit the chaff button, and the countermeasures exploded from the back of the fighter bomber.

The missile flew into the decoys and exploded

instantly. Meanwhile, the Lucifer smashed into the SAM launcher and destroyed it.

"Launcher down," Tanner said in a calm voice.

Cara nodded. "All Vipers move in. Weapons free."

ON THE GROUND, SOUTHERN HONDURAS

"All callsigns move in," Kane said over the comms channel. "Watch your backs."

The Team Reaper commander started forward out of the jungle, Brick at his shoulder in Ivan. The twin miniguns opened fire as a target came up on the HUD. It was a vehicle with a heavy caliber machine gun on the tray.

With it destroyed, they closed in further. One of the machine gun nests opened up, and bullets cut through the jungle like knives through a stick of butter.

Kane opened fire with his AT, and the nest was silenced.

Meanwhile, on the other side of the compound, Knocker had used the AT on his Viper to take out a communications hut and power substation. He scanned the compound with his HUD, and the display triggered a warning that a shoulder-launched missile was about to be fired.

"Not so fast, mate."

The minigun ripped, and the shooter disintegrated as though he were filled with explosives that detonated within. Beside the Brit, Grace said, "I'm getting a trigger warning for explosives, Two."

"A what?"

BOOM! BOOM! BOOM! BOOM! BOOM!

A line of explosions started heading their way and fanning out as it approached. "Oh bollocks."

"Electronic mines," Grace snapped.

"Move."

They started running, the explosions chasing them. Knocker knew they weren't going to make it and said, "Get down, Three."

They let their Vipers fall flat, hoping that neither of them was on a mine. Suddenly, the explosions were all around them, a heavy shower of debris raining down.

Knocker's HUD lit up with a warning as his Viper felt as though it had been slapped by a giant hand. It moved six feet to the right and stopped. "Christ, that was close."

"Reaper Two, copy?"

"Roger, Bravo Three."

Crystal said, "I'm reading that your armor is compromised down to eighty percent and your heart is showing an irregular beat. Are you all right?"

"Give me a minute."

Knocker brought the Viper erect and was immediately hit by heavy caliber gunfire. He dropped back down and asked, "How is that, Bravo Three?"

"Heartbeat reads sinus rhythm."

"All better. Grace, girl, where are you?"

"At your six, Two."

"All right, let's clear a path for the strike team."

The pair went to work with their machines, taking out strongpoints and other threats. They pressed further into the compound until Knocker said, "Cougar One, copy?"

"Read you Lima Charlie, Reaper Two."

"Bring your people in and clear the factory. Just watch for booby traps."

"Cougar inbound. Switching markers on."

"Reaper One, copy?"

"Read you, Two."

"Cougar inbound to clear the factory, over."

"Copy. We're Charlie Mike. Perimeter this side is almost secure."

"Break! Break! Break!"

"Go ahead, Bravo."

"Four bogeys inbound. Look to be Su-35s. Keep your heads down. Bravo out."

Knocker shook his head instinctively, and the Viper followed his movements. "Reaper, looks like things are about to get interesting."

"Tanner will take care of them with the Black Cat."

"Black Cat down, I say again, Black Cat down."

"Bollocks."

———

OVER SOUTHERN HONDURAS

"Molly, get air defense online," Cara ordered. "Eugene, we're in your capable hands."

"Strap yourselves in, Bravo, this might get bumpy. Bravo Four, call them as they come."

"Copy, Eugene." Then, hot on the heels of the reply, Cara said, "Missile launch. Distance twenty kilometers."

"I have it," Leslie Groves replied. "Preparing to launch countermeasures. Engage Ripper."

"Ripper ready," Molly replied.

"Launching countermeasures...now."

The chaff flared from the Stratomaster, drawing the

missile in toward it. Ripper tracked its path and opened fire. The missile exploded midair.

Then came Eugene's voice. "Raptor away."

Cara looked at Houlihan. "Did Houdini get wired in before we left?"

"Yes, ma'am. But we haven't tested it."

"Then it's time to act like a Klingon bird of prey."

"Are you sure, ma'am?"

"No time like the present."

Houlihan nodded. "Eugene, we're activating Houdini."

"Copy."

"In three...two...one...activating."

And just like that, Skyhammer disappeared.

Cara looked along the line from her chair. "Talk to me, people."

"Looks good," Houlihan said calmly.

"Everything is fine," Crystal agreed.

"Molly?" Cara said.

The weapons tech stared at her screen in silence.

"Molly?"

"Wait one. Raptor is on target. We have impact. Splash one Flanker."

"What are the others doing?" Cara asked.

"They seem to be holding."

"Can they see us?"

"I don't think so."

"All right. Eugene, our friends can't see us. Let's shake them up."

"On it."

Moments later, Skyhammer fired two Raptors. "Missiles away."

Molly tracked them on her screen. "Raptors flying true. Flankers are taking evasive action."

She stared at the screen, willing the explosive lances on toward their targets. "Thirty seconds."

"Do they know where we are?" Cara asked.

"They're sweeping, but they can't pick us up. Ten seconds."

"Impact missile one. Missile two still flying. Searching. Missile two has lost target."

"Are we still invisible?"

"Yes, ma'am."

"Get those last two fighters."

———

ON THE GROUND, SOUTHERN HONDURAS

"Cougar One, sitrep?" Kane said over his comms.

"We've breached the factory, Reaper One. Resistance is minimal."

"Get what you can and then plant the charges and withdraw."

"Roger that."

While Cougar was doing what they were assigned, Team Reaper and their Vipers were holding the perimeter. It wasn't until an urgent call came through that things livened up even more. "Reaper One, copy?"

"Are you still fighting off buzzards, Bravo?"

"We're good for the moment. However, you have a column of vehicles headed your way. Looks like a cartel QRF."

"Numbers?"

"Upward of twenty."

"Copy that. Knocker, on me. Cougar One, finish up. We've got visitors inbound."

Both men acknowledged the transmission. Kane

said to Brick, "Post sentry here. When I say come, we're headed south."

"Roger."

Kane met up with the others. He said, "Secure our exfil south. We're about five mikes from being clear."

"Roger that," Knocker replied.

"Cougar One, are you done yet?"

"Just setting the last charge, Reaper."

"Good. Head south of the compound. We'll meet you there."

"Roger that."

"Bravo, this is Reaper One. We're pulling out."

"Copy, Bravo One. Will have the helos pick you up at the LZ. Out."

"Brick, time to go."

"Roger that. Let's get the fuck out of Dodge."

———

TORRES COMPOUND, HONDURAS

Torres shot the first man because he held him responsible. He shot the second because he wanted someone to shoot. The third was killed because Torres was still feeling irate. The fourth was lucky. Torres had calmed enough from his murderous rage to being just plain mad. He looked at the fourth man and said, "Get the fuck out of my sight."

"S-si."

Someone had destroyed his drug factory. His pill press, his chemicals, everything. Reports came in that his quick reaction force had been tardy in their arrival, and his planes had been shot down. All of them. His workers manufacturing the drugs and guarding the factory—all dead.

Torres walked over to the outdoor bar and poured a glass of tequila. Two tall, broad-shouldered men appeared and stared down at the three bodies. Torres waved his glass in the air. "Get rid of them. Fucking assholes."

The men did as they were asked and left Torres to himself. "They wouldn't have done this if I had my fucking robots."

He reached for his cell and dialed a number. When the call connected, he said, "I want all security measures increased for the foreseeable future. This will not happen again!"

———

HEREFORD, ENGLAND

Kane stared at the screen.

> *Lena:* He lives on Majorca.
> *Mike:* Where?
> *Lena:* A villa overlooking the sea.
> *Mike:* You need to be more specific.
> *Lena:* His name is Ruiz. He has access to all of the codes for the money.
> *Mike:* Where is the villa?
> *Lena:* I'm not sure, I have only seen a picture.

Kane gave a frustrated sigh. He typed again.

> *Mike:* Can you remember anything about it?
> *Lena:* It has a red gate and a blue roof.

Mike: Anything else? Anything at all that could help.

Lena: The bay it overlooks is like an inlet.

Mike: Thank you. How are things?

Lena: He is mad. He scares me when he gets like this.

Mike: I will get Ana out soon. If we can get at his money, it should draw him out.

Lena: I hope so.

Mike: What is she like?

Lena: She is like you.

Mike: Is that a bad thing?

Lena: I have to go.

Mike: OK, be safe.

The chatroom died, and Kane leaned back in his seat. He looked over his shoulder at Crystal. "This could be actionable intel."

"What do you think?"

"It will need to be kicked up the chain."

"I'll take it to Cara," she replied.

Once Crystal was gone, Kane typed once more into the chatroom.

Mike: Are you there, Lena?

He waited for a response, but nothing came.

His finger hit a different key, and a picture appeared. It was of Maria and Ana. Kane zoomed the camera in to look closer at his daughter. Maria was right, she looked like him. Suddenly, he felt the urge to get to know her better. The need to know what his daughter was like. What she liked to do, what she liked to eat, her favorite color.

"Hard to believe, huh?" Knocker said from behind him.

"I still don't believe how it's possible."

"Well, once upon a time—"

"Shut up."

Knocker grinned. "Don't worry, Reaper, we'll get her out, and you'll have all the time in the world to get to know her."

Kane nodded. "Yeah."

"Now, get your head in the game."

"Yes, mother."

———

It was the old firm plus one. They sat around the table discussing plans for the upcoming mission. Grace watched how they worked together, all of them having their say, and felt a newfound respect for what they were and had achieved over countless years.

Kane looked across the table at Brick and said, "Sorry, Brick, you'll have to sit this one out."

The former SEAL nodded. "Understood. Maybe if this thing works, I'll be back up and running."

"If we need you, we'll holler."

"You don't have to explain. I'll sit back and watch."

"Bollocks, you will," Knocker said. "You're on over-watch. You're calling the shots for the mission."

Brick looked at Kane, who nodded. "You know what something like this takes. There's no one I'd trust more to make the hard operational calls."

"Thanks, Reaper."

"Don't thank me yet. Not until we're all back safely. Now, tell me what you think."

Brick pointed at the satellite pictures they were using. "Water infil. UDVs. After dark. Get in, get what you need, and get out the same way. Taking the HVT alive is a must."

Kane nodded. "So far, intel has numbers upward of twenty X-rays on-site. They really want to look after this guy."

"How are we thinking his shit is stored?" Knocker asked. "Electronic or old school?"

On the screen behind them, Grace brought up a picture of their target. "Ruiz Fernandez. In his forties, likes McHale's Navy and Hogan's Heroes. I'm going to take a punt and say he has both."

Cara nodded. "I guess it doesn't matter if we get results."

Brick said, "Go in heavy, Reaper. Kill them as you encounter them. Hide the bodies as you go."

"Tell me why?" Kane asked. He knew the reason but wanted confirmation.

"It makes for less numbers when Knocker fucks up and wakes the natives."

"You have to love the scouser's confidence in a man," the Brit replied, shaking his head that people's opinions of him were that low.

Brick grinned. "I'm confident, all right."

"Me too," Kane said.

"We'll need all communications in the area jammed up," the former SEAL said. "We don't want Torres learning about this until after the fact. Stealing his money should make his day."

"We can do that," Cara said.

"An op just like the old days," Knocker said. "Nothing better."

"Don't get complacent," Kane said. "Remember,

this is a different age. These guys play by different rules now."

"The same ones we play by," Knocker said. "No rules."

Kane said, "Tell me more about Ruiz."

Grace said, "He used to work in Spain as a taxation adviser. You know, the ones who know where to hide all the money, false accounts, overseas havens, stuff like that."

"A legal criminal," Knocker growled.

"The very same." Grace continued, "Then shit changed. His wife left him for a younger man she'd been seeing on the side, and Ruiz got involved with an illegal online gambling scheme. Lost all of his money and was hired out on the dark web to do some free-lancing to make it back. That's where everything gets murky. I'm assuming Torres found him there two years ago because his bank accounts skyrocketed. Now—well, you know where he lives and the security he has."

"Looks like his wife left at the wrong time," Knocker stated with a grin.

"That's the kicker. She and her lover were found murdered in their condo about the same time that Ruiz's life got back on track."

"Ouch."

"There is one more thing."

"There always is."

Grace brought up another picture. "This is his new wife. Yulia Nosenko."

"Looks like money buys a lot of things," Cara said, looking at Ruiz's wife who somewhat resembled a supermodel.

"Nosenko is the daughter of Ilya Nosenko, the Russian Oligarch. You can bet that most, if not all the guards on the grounds are former Russian special forces or mercenaries."

"All the more reason to shoot them," Brick said.

"Heavy weapons?" Knocker asked hopefully.

"None as such," Cara said.

"Okay, what can't we see?"

"That's the big question." A red overlay appeared. "There is something below the villa, we're just not sure what. We think the only way in is through the main house."

"Reach the house, and find out what's under it," Kane said. "Nothing is ever easy."

"No. But judging by the heat signature it's putting out, I'm going to guess servers."

"Servers?" Knocker asked.

"Yes. What better place to store all of his electronic documents without the threat of being hacked"

"You want us to destroy them if they are?"

"Once you get what you need, yes," Cara replied. "Anything else?"

They looked at each other in silence.

"Then I guess we gear up and go say hello."

CHAPTER 16

Darkness enveloped them as the black-clad wraiths came out of the water, wearing their exoskeleton body armor. "Feet dry," Kane said softly into his comms.

They stashed what they didn't need in the rocks and prepared to move. Knocker adjusted the HUD display on his helmet and scanned the immediate area for threats. He brought up his suppressed G550 and started forward. "I've got point."

The HUD switched to white phosphorous mode, which instantly changed his view to day, unlike the old green haze of the past. Knocker moved silently for a few meters before Brick came to him over the comms from Skyhammer. "You've got two X-rays headed your way, Reaper Two. Twenty meters behind the bushes."

Knocker clicked his tongue in acknowledgment. He felt Kane come up beside him, both crouched in the firing position, ready to kill the two guards. When the hapless men appeared, Kane said, "Send it."

Both suppressed weapons fired twice, and the guards dropped where they stood. Kane said, "Brick?"

"You're clear."

Both operators hurried forward and each dragged a body to hide them under the bushes. With that done, they moved again.

Keeping to the shadows, both men pressed toward the main house which was surrounded by smaller bungalows. Knocker crouched beside the corner of a building and peered around. "Tell me what you see, oh great one."

"You've got a sentry on the rooftop of a bungalow. He's walking patrol back and forth. You'll need to take him."

"Roger that," Knocker replied.

He let his HUD find the target, then brought up his weapon. Setting the sights on the X-ray, he squeezed the trigger.

The target dropped and disappeared. "X-ray down."

"You've got another two to the east, coming your way," Brick informed them.

"I've got them," Grace said and disappeared into the undergrowth.

Moments later, they heard her suppressed weapon fire, and she said, "Two X-rays down."

Grace rejoined them and Kane said, "Get up on that rooftop. You should see the villa from there. Cover us."

"Roger that."

"There's a sentry near the pool, Reaper One."

"Copy."

Grace climbed atop the bungalow and settled in to provide an overwatch. She swept the area and found the target near the pool. "I have eyes on the pool boy."

"Drop him."

"Sending."

Thwack!

"Pool secure."

Knocker moved in quickly and hid the body, then he and Kane walked around the pool toward a large area with a pergola covering the scattered outdoor furniture.

"Hold," Brick said. "Danger close."

Knocker and Kane dropped to a knee and held their position.

"You've got an X-ray ten meters to your west. He's facing your way. Just hold, and we'll see what he does."

"I have a shot, Reaper Five," Grace said calmly.

"OK, take it."

Thwack!

"X-ray down."

"Roger that."

Again, Knocker hid the body while Kane took up a covering position. He said, "What else do we have, Five?"

"We're getting heat signatures from inside the villa and others from the far side, away from your position. You're clear to proceed."

Knocker took one step and then the jig was up, floodlights coming on and sirens blaring. "Bollocks, no one mentioned motion sensors."

"Grace, take out the lights," Kane snapped. "Brick, are we jamming?"

"Like a square peg in a round hole."

"Someone kill the power."

"Working on it," Crystal said.

Kane said, "Knocker, press forward to the villa. We need to secure the HVT."

"Moving."

The Brit started swiftly toward the villa, encountering a shadowy figure with a weapon, and he opened fire. Three rounds hit the bad guy center mass, and he crumpled to the ground.

A second man appeared, but their guardian angel was watching, and Grace dropped him beside his comrade.

Shouts could be heard. "They're definitely Russian," Kane said.

"They're mentioning something about an escape route," Knocker said.

"Reaper Five, are there any vehicles or helicopters that you can see? Our friend is going to fly the coop."

"There is a vehicle on the opposite side of the villa. Looks to be an SUV. No movement."

"Moving to that location," Kane replied. "Knocker, on me."

They moved swiftly to the other side of the villa, past palm trees and lush vegetation along sandstone walkways. A shooter appeared on Kane's left, and his G550 spat death.

Knocker's HUD flashed a warning, and he rolled instantly. Gunfire ripped through the air above him. He swung his weapon around and sent a burst at the shooter. The guard fell as bullets ripped through flesh.

Meanwhile, Grace was picking targets at will, covering the others as they went.

Knocker came around the corner of a bungalow and found the SUV. He approached it cautiously and found no threats. He said, "The SUV is clear."

"Shit." They heard Brick breathe over the comms.

"What is it?" asked Kane as he stood beside Knocker.

"I have an in-ground door opening to your north," Brick replied. "Wait one. You've got shooters inbound near your position. Standby."

Kane dropped out his magazine and reloaded a fresh one. "Five, what about the door?"

Nothing.

"Five, the door?"

"Well, we found the helicopter," Brick replied.

Moments later, the deafening sound of a helicopter taking off shattered the night. Then it appeared and flew low over the villa toward the ocean. Annoyed with what he was seeing, Knocker flicked the fire selector on his G550 and let it rip with a long burst at the helicopter. "Fucking bollocks."

"Bravo, HVT has gotten away. Please advise next."

"Copy, Reaper One," Cara replied. "Stay on mission. Clear the villa and see what you can find from the servers."

"Roger that." He looked at Knocker. "Phase Two, Winston."

Knocker snorted. "Do I look like a bald, fat fuck?"

"At your age, it won't be long."

"Screw you, dad."

Knocker led the way toward the villa. They cleared as they went and soon reached a side entrance. Blocking their path was a sliding glass door. Knocker tried it but found it locked, but not for long. A shooter appeared and opened fire, shattering the glass obstruction.

Knocker felt his body armor take rounds, but he remained upright. His weapon fired, and the shooter fell.

The pair entered through the opening. The shooter

lay on the floor, gasping for breath as he lay there, slowly dying. The Brit helped him on his way when he drew his P756 and shot him in the head.

"We need to find a way down into the server room, Five. Any ideas?"

"Start checking doors or look for a hidden elevator."

"And here I was thinking you were an asset to the team," Knocker growled.

"You want me to do all your work?" Brick asked.

"Just some of it."

"Also, you might want to hurry. Once that helicopter is out of jamming range, you'll have visitors."

It took another ten minutes before they found what they were looking for. It was behind a bookcase in the study. Knocker said, "Cliché much?"

"Then why didn't you look here first?"

"Who looks in the obvious fucking places?"

"Grace, sitrep?" Kane asked.

"All clear."

"Roger that."

Descending the stairwell, they found themselves in a long hallway with rooms running down either side. Each room contained a bank of servers. "Bravo, we've hit the jackpot here. Six rooms, all full of servers. Please advise."

"Wait one."

Knocker walked over to a server and stared at it. Kane said, "Don't touch anything."

The Brit sniffed. "What's going to happen? The thing blows up?"

He pressed a button to make his point. At which time, on a small screen to his right, a digital timer began counting down from two minutes. "You have got to be fucking kidding."

"I fucking told you," Kane growled. "But no, you had to prove your fucking point."

"You want to start running now or wait until it gets a bit lower?" Knocker asked.

"Asshole."

Then they ran.

As fast as they could.

Up the stairs and through the villa. Then out onto the pool area where they leaped into the water.

Just as the villa exploded, a ball of fire erupted.

Their heads broke the surface of the pool, and both men stared at the burning structure. Over their comms came Grace urgently asking them if they were okay. "We'll live," Kane acknowledged.

"What happened?"

"Curious George decided to play what does this button do," Kane replied.

"Why is it my fault?"

"Idiot."

They dragged themselves from the pool. Cara said from 40,000 feet, "Which one of you screwed up?"

"Give you one guess," Kane replied.

"Mr. Bean?"

Knocker paused. "I resent that."

"Whatever. We might have been able to get something if you hadn't screwed the op."

"Can we track the helicopter?" Kane asked.

"We can try. Standby for extract. Mind you, I should leave your sorry asses there after that."

Moments later, after Grace had joined them, Crystal came back to them. "It looks like we're in luck, Reaper. The helicopter has made a forced landing two miles north of your location. It turned back. Get yourself some transport."

———

"Be aware. I'm picking up five heat signatures around the helicopter and three moving north at pace," Brick said. "I do believe that would be our target."

"Copy," Kane replied.

They had found a Land Rover SUV at the villa, and Knocker, having superior car theft skills, managed to get it going. They had been guided to the target from above and were now approaching their destination.

Knocker eased the SUV to a halt, and they climbed out of the vehicle. "Reaper, take the HVT. Grace and I'll clean up here before coming after you."

"Keep your fool head down."

Kane disappeared into the darkness, and the Brit turned to Grace and said, "Left or right?"

"Left."

"Good hunting."

"Brick, old cock, talk to me."

"You've got a target behind a tree to your left, around fifty meters."

Knocker's HUD changed for heat signature. He scanned the immediate area and saw his target. Remaining low, he used the trees to cover his advance. He circled around and came in behind the unsuspecting shooter.

The Brit let his G550 hang and took out his combat knife. Moments later, the shooter lay bleeding out on the ground, his wound pumping ferociously.

"X-ray down. Moving to the next target."

"Twelve o'clock, forty meters."

"Roger that."

———

OVER MAJORCA

"What do we have?" Cara asked, looking at the screen.

Brick pointed. "That's Grace about to take down a shooter, and Knocker is circling around this guy here. Kane is up here closing in on what could be our HVT, his other half, and what could be a bodyguard."

As they watched, Grace closed in and shot the target with her handgun. "Target down."

"You've got a hostile to your east, Three, twenty meters. He looks like he's facing—wait, he's moving. I think he heard that last kill."

"Copy." Her voice was lower. "I have him."

While they watched, both Knocker and Grace took down their second targets, leaving one more. Brick said, "Well done, people. The remaining target is fifty meters west of the helicopter and circling right. Keep an eye out."

"Brick, you need to listen to this," Crystal said. "I'll patch it through."

Radio chatter. It was Russian. "Shit. Reaper, I hate to rush, but we've got chatter lighting things up. From what I can gather, the Russians are on the way. Do what you need to and get out."

"Roger that."

"Grace, break off from Knocker and help Reaper. He's moving north of your position."

"Copy, heading now."

"We've got units moving in from the northwest, ma'am," Crystal said.

Cara was about to speak when the Stratomaster vibrated from turbulence. She waited. Sometimes following the smaller ones came bigger ones. When nothing came, she asked, "How many?"

"Five. Looks like they have armed shooters inside. ETA, ten mikes."

"This is going to be tight."

———

MAJORCA, SPAIN

Kane fired his G550 at the bodyguard. Just stroked the trigger twice and heard the bullets impact their target. He switched his aim and saw the other two targets, and one of the men turned to fire. Kane stroked the trigger once more, and the target shouted in pain. Collapsing and grabbing at his leg, the man then gestured at the third figure which Kane assumed was the woman. He was waving her away, and she turned and ran.

The Reaper said into his comms, "The woman is squirting. Let her go. HVT is down. Get us an extract in here, now."

"Doing what I can," Brick replied from Skymaster.

Kane kneeled beside the moaning man and said, "Ruiz, how are you this wonderful evening?"

Ruiz looked up at the suited man in horror. "Who— who are you?"

"Me? I'm the only way you get out of this alive."

"What?"

Grace appeared beside them. "Where's the woman?"

"Gone," Kane replied. "Help me get him up."

They put cable ties on Ruiz and dragged him to his feet. He yelped in pain. "Brick, how far out are our friends?"

"Five mikes, Reaper."

"And extract?"

"Too far."

"All right, we'll wing it. Knocker, we're coming back to you. Have the SUV ready. We're going to need it."

When they reached their ride, they shoved Ruiz into the back seat. Kane looked at Grace and said, "Keep him alive. We need what he knows."

She climbed in after him and turned to the criminal. "Try anything, asshole, and I'll cut your balls off."

"Knocker, you drive," Kane ordered as he climbed into the other side, opposite Grace and Ruiz.

The Brit floored the gas pedal, and the SUV shot forward. Almost immediately, Kane hit Ruiz in the ribs savagely with his elbow. The man howled in pain, and the operator said, "That's a taste of what you'll get if you don't talk. Understood?"

"What the hell are you doing?" Ruiz howled.

"Where are the codes and numbers for Fernando Torres's accounts?"

"What?" Fear replaced any pain he had been feeling.

"Account numbers. You heard me."

The SUV bounced, and Ruiz winced in pain.

"N-no, I can't. I won't."

"You don't have a choice," Kane replied.

"You don't understand. Torres will kill me."

"He's going to kill you anyway, especially now that you're compromised."

"No."

Kane hit his wounded leg, and Ruiz almost shot through the SUV's rooftop. "Tell me!"

"No."

"Tell me!" Kane hit him again.

"Nooo!"

"Stop the car," Kane snapped.

Knocker trod hard on the brakes, and the vehicle came to a shuddering stop. "We don't have time for this, Reaper."

"Get out," Kane snapped.

"What?"

"Get the fuck out. Torres can have you."

"But you said he would kill me."

"I don't give a shit," Kane snarled.

Knocker said, "Reaper, we need to make a call. Those vehicles are getting closer."

"Get out," Kane snapped again.

"I-I can't."

Kane opened his door and started dragging Ruiz out.

"Reaper, we don't have time," Grace said.

He kept going. "I don't need much fucking time."

"5-4-4-6-7-7-3-A-9-9-4-F-F-5-4-3-T," the wounded man cried out.

"What's that?"

"One of Torres's accounts in the Caymans."

"Crystal, check it."

A few moments later, she said, "Reaper One, looks like he's telling the truth. I have an account with two hundred and fifty million in it."

The Reaper didn't hesitate. "He's lying."

"What?"

Kane drew his P756 and pressed it against the side of Ruiz's head. "I told you."

"Okay, okay. I lied."

"What is it?"

"My father-in-law's account."

"Crystal, clean it out."

"No," Ruiz gasped.

"The cost of lying, my friend. Now you're totally fucked. Number."

"6-7-5-4-G-G-9-2-3-H-1-2-0-4-7-T."

"Three?"

"Holy shit. I have an account in the Bahamas that has billions in it."

"Clean it out," Kane said.

Kane closed the door. "Knocker, drive."

Brick came over the comms. "Reaper, I have an extract for you off the coast. You'll be picked up at these coordinates."

"Roger that."

By the time they reached the coast, Crystal had emptied two more accounts. Total monies added up to north of one hundred and fifty billion dollars. "That should get his attention," Cara said.

"Yes," Kane replied. "But we may have only just unleashed the beast. We need to get Maria and Ana out."

———

HEREFORD, ENGLAND

The first reaction came the following day. Yulia Nosenko's body was found hanging from a streetlamp in Majorca. Her father's body was found hanging inverted from a bridge in Moscow without a head. His bodyguards were discovered dead at his apartment.

The manager of the bank in the Bahamas was found with his wife and children in their saltwater pool with two tiger sharks in it.

A British politician was assassinated, along with two DEA agents and their families. Retribution was swift and a bloodbath, and it had been triggered by the actions of Global. It brought back memories of a mission when they had been hired to steal money from another drug cartel boss.

"Well, retribution came swiftly and violently," Preston said as he entered Thurston's office accompanied by Polly Yates.

Thurston nodded. "I guess in a way it was to be expected."

She nodded at the large screen on the wall, playing a cycle of news about Millicent Stride's murder and drug addiction. "Was that you?"

"Joint effort."

"Takes the heat off us. I'm grateful for that."

"What's your next step?" Yates asked.

"My people are going to stage a kidnapping in Honduras to draw Torres out. Once we've done that, we take Torres alive, and you can put him on public display. Behead him, hang him, do whatever you want."

"You're going to send your people into Honduras?"

"Already done it recently. We destroyed one of Torres' factories."

Yates frowned. "That was before you stole billions of his money and really pissed him off."

"That's right. We needed to get him excited so he would make an error. What we didn't anticipate was the extent of his desire for retribution."

"What is the plan?" Preston asked.

"We kidnap his brother's wife and her daughter, posing as just a gang of miscreants. We offer them up for ransom. Draw him out and sweep him up."

"Just like that?" Yates asked.

"Either that or it'll royally fuck up, and we'll be burying all of our people. Take a look at this."

Her large screen changed, and footage from the op in Italy appeared. They could make out the Vipers and then the other robots. "This is footage from a recent op. What you see are HP433 Battle Droids. They're manufactured by German scientist, Willie Muller."

"Battle robots," Preston said. "Are they any good?"

"More than capable. And right now, Torres is in possession of some. To get to him, we're going to have to go through these."

"Can you do it?"

"I guess we'll find out, but ever since we went to war with Torres, we've been losing people. And I don't like it."

"Why not drop a big bomb on him?"

"Because Global still needs to completely clear itself from the stink that has been sprayed on it from the get-go. The only way to do that is to put Torres on display. If we don't, then we die trying."

———

Mike: Two days from now. We will strike on the way to school.

Lena: Fernando is worse. Why did you have to steal all of that money? I'm really scared. Maybe we should forget it.

Mike: It has come too far. We will get you both out, I promise.

Lena: He has doubled the security and keeps changing the route that is taken.

Mike: Let us worry about that. Just make sure you are with her.

Lena: He will get suspicious.

Mike: You need to think of a good story and stick to it. Don't show him you are afraid.
Lena: Easy for you to say. It is not your life at stake. We could both end up dead because of you. Why I let you back in, I will never know.

KANE IMAGINED her hitting the keys forcefully.

Mike: Take it easy.

There was a long pause. Kane frowned and worried.

Mike: Are you still there?
Lena: I am here.
Mike: I'm sorry.
Lena: No, it is I who am sorry.
Mike: It will be over soon, I promise.
Lena: I hope so.

The chat room closed, and Kane looked over at Crystal. "We need to get them out before this goes all to hell."

"We are, remember?"

"Yeah. We need to get this briefing done before we fly out. Get them all together."

———

TORRES COMPOUND, HONDURAS

"I am going to school with Ana the day after tomorrow to talk to one of her teachers, Fernando," Maria said.

Torres stared at her. "Why?"

"I think she is worried about Ana's grades."

"She has only just started school," Torres snapped angrily.

"It is better to get these things early, Fernando."

"Fine. Tell her teacher if they do not do better, then I will come and visit them."

"Thank you, Fernando," Maria said and left him to his mood.

She went and found her daughter in her room. "What are you doing?" she asked Ana.

"Just thinking."

"About what?"

"About that man in Barbados."

"No," Maria said hurriedly. "You must forget about him. Forget he even exists."

"He seemed nice."

She grabbed her daughter and pulled her close. "Oh, Ana. Once maybe, but that was a long time ago. He has changed. But maybe it is there somewhere."

She shrugged.

Maria said, "The day after tomorrow, I am coming to school with you to talk to your teacher."

"Miss Domingo?"

"Yes."

"She is wonderful. She is also very smart."

Maria smiled at her daughter. "I'm sure she is."

———

HEREFORD, ENGLAND

"Gather around," Kane said, calling everyone together. "Take a seat, and we'll get started."

He was running the briefing with Crystal, who had

helped him nut out some details with the assistance of Knocker and Cara.

A hologram map appeared before everyone was seated. It was voice-activated, designed to recognize different commands. Most of the time, he and Reaper liked the old-school briefings, but today they needed Abbey, as they called her. Kane said, "This is where Torres's compound is. It is on the outskirts of San Salvador. The school is here."

The hologram changed. "These are the possible routes that the convoy can use. We have to guess the right one."

"What happens if we get it wrong?" a bearded, tattooed man asked.

His name was Denver, a former Ranger who led Strike Team Walrus. Each of the five men were highly qualified operators who specialized in covert work, such as the mission they were about to complete.

Kane said, "Then we work around it until we get the mission complete. My people will go after the targets. Denver, I need your people to keep the area secure."

"Copy that. Extract?"

"We'll have a Falcon Five on station to pick us up. If everything really goes to shit, Brick will drop in with Ivan to save our asses."

"What about the battle droid things that Torres has got his hands on?"

It was Cara's turn to speak. "If they pop, then Skyhammer will have its say. Other than that, we're only there as a command platform."

"Roger that. I guess we're going into Death Valley."

CHAPTER 17

TORRES COMPOUND, HONDURAS

Maria opened the door and allowed Ana to climb into the rear seat of the SUV. She waited until her daughter slid into the center and then followed her in. Inside her chest, her heart beat fast as her anxiety started to rise. She grabbed Ana's hand and smiled nervously at her.

"Are you all right, Mama?"

"I'm fine."

The other three doors opened, and the driver and two bodyguards climbed in. All were serious-faced former military specialists from the Mexican military. Doors slammed, and the motor started.

The SUV fell into line behind two others. Without looking, Maria already knew there would be two more lined up behind them.

The vehicle bounced over the driveway until it reached the road, and then it turned left. On its way to a meeting with destiny.

40,000 FEET OVER HONDURAS

"Be advised, Reaper One, the convoy has left," Cara said into her comms. "Five vehicles, target is in the third SUV. Three X-rays in with them. Eleven all told. Tracking."

"Roger that, standing by. Reaper One out."

Cara turned to Houlihan. "Pat, launch a Star Hawk. I want to be ready just in case."

"Yes, ma'am."

"Brick, is Ivan ready?"

"Yes, ma'am."

"Molly, weapons primed?"

"Ready to rock, ma'am."

"Stark Hawk launched. Callsign Cobra One."

"Thank you, Pat. All ground callsigns, over."

"Read you Lima Charlie, Bravo," Kane replied.

"We have a Star Hawk in the air. Callsign, Cobra One."

"Copy. Cobra One."

Cara stared at the screen, and the Stratomaster rocked as it hit some turbulence. "Crystal, how are we looking with Houdini?"

"All good, ma'am."

"Update on the convoy?"

"Approaching first waypoint," Crystal replied.

As she watched, the convoy approached the first of the intersections where three possible routes could be taken. All told, there were three of them, and they wouldn't know until the convoy hit the third where the strike team could position. However, after watching ISR feed, they'd narrowed down the possibilities to two.

Which had left them with an educated guess regarding the last one, and they'd chosen one. They named it Broadway.

"Target has taken East End," Crystal said over the net. "Making toward the next waypoint."

There were only two possible routes to take from waypoint two. One was named Chicago, and the other was London Bridge. As the convoy made its way toward the next intersection, the countryside started to give way to urbanization. Or rather, suburban slums.

"Convoy headed into the suburbs."

It continued its approach until it slowed.

"Target has reached waypoint two...London Bridge. I say again, target has taken London Bridge."

Crystal looked at Cara. She said, "I guess we'll find out if we were right."

"I guess so."

EN ROUTE, HONDURAS

Maria watched as the landscape gave way to houses and streets and slums. Everyone she saw on the street, every vehicle, she wondered if they were part of the plan.

"Mama?"

She looked at Ana. "What is it?"

"You're hurting my hand."

She released it. "I'm sorry. I was doing it again."

The small convoy sped up as the road smoothed out. Up ahead, there was a large roundabout. It had three offshoots in addition to the thoroughfare they were on now. The vehicles slowed as they approached. The lead vehicle entered the roundabout and exploded.

———

40,000 FEET OVER HONDURAS

"Oh my god," Crystal said as she watched the first SUV disappear in a ball of flame.

"What the hell just happened?" Cara growled.

"Someone is hitting the convoy," Crystal replied. "I'm picking up heat signatures and gunfire all around the convoy."

The rear SUV suffered the same fate as the lead one. Other vehicles scattered as drivers tried to get away from the twin infernos. "Who the hell is this?" Cara snarled.

"There are at least twenty hostiles closing in, maybe more. The bodyguards have stopped and are making a stand outside the SUVs."

"Damn it. Reaper One, copy?"

"Copy, Bravo."

"Abort current mission and proceed to waypoint three. The convoy is under attack by unknown hostiles. Estimate upward of twenty X-rays. Move your ass."

"Damn it, we're ten minutes out," Kane said.

"I'm aware of that fact."

"Shit, Reaper One out."

Another explosion could be seen on the ISR feed. Crystal said, "They have rocket launchers. Ma'am, they aren't going to last long if this keeps up. Who knows what will happen to the HVTs."

"Send me," Brick said over the intercom. "I'm ready to go."

Decision made. Cara nodded. "Launch Ivan."

"On my way."

"Pat, until he gets there, can you give some cover with Cobra One?"

"How close, ma'am?"

"Nothing happens to the HVTs. Do whatever it takes."

"Yes, ma'am."

———

HONDURAS

"Mama, what's happening?" Ana cried as the gunfire grew louder.

Maria covered her daughter with her body and prayed that it would be over soon. She heard bullets rattle like hail as they punched dents in the armored exterior.

Then there were the cries of the wounded and dying. Suddenly the door opened, and a big man, one of the bodyguards, shouted, "Out. You cannot stay here."

"We cannot go out—"

BOOM! Another rocket exploded close by.

"We cannot go out there."

"If you stay here, you will die. I am the only one left." He opened fire with his assault weapon at an unseen enemy.

"But—"

WHAP! WHAP!

The bodyguard jerked as bullets hammered into him, and he died, his weapon clattering onto the asphalt.

Suddenly, things fell quiet. The shooting had stopped. Maria slowly looked up and saw a line of armed, tattooed men coming toward the SUV. They were speaking Spanish, so they weren't John's people. Which meant they were Fernando's enemies.

Which meant they were here for Ana because Maria being here was, more or less, last minute.

"Mama?"

"Stay down, Ana."

Maria reached under the seat and felt around. Her hand locked onto the butt of a Glock she knew was there. She looked up and saw the shooters closing in. She raised the handgun and fired.

Five shooters disappeared into a boiling fireball. Then moments later, a giant robot landed.

———

"Ivan is down," Brick said as soon as he landed. "Time to go to work."

The twin miniguns opened up at targets as they lit up his HUD display. Figures disappeared in bloody sprays of red as the rounds tore them to shreds. While the metal monster fired, he walked toward the SUV where Maria and Ana were hiding.

A rocket reached out and slid past Ivan. Brick found his target and raised the Viper's arm to fire the anti-tank weapon. The rocket man had time for a breath before his world turned to darkness, the anti-tank round sending him into the abyss.

More bullets peppered Ivan, and his armor integrity started to wane. Another rocket landed close and knocked the big Viper back and down.

"Damn son of a bitch," Brick growled. He managed to get it back up and heard Crystal say, "Reaper Five, are you alright?"

"Still in the fight, Three."

"I'm showing elevated heart rate and significant armor integrity reduction."

Ivan was still fighting like a behemoth. His miniguns found targets and ripped them apart. His flame thrower hissed, and attackers screamed as they did the dance of flaming death. The Viper stood like a sentinel as it and Brick did all they could to protect the woman and girl. The Viper's left arm came up to fire when a rocket cut through the air and took it off.

Ivan staggered, and warnings went off on Brick's HUD. "Motherfucker."

"Brick, are you alright?" Crystal asked, emotion in her voice.

"I've got a little problem, Bravo. I'll be fine."

"Get out, Brick. Kane and the others aren't far away."

"I can hang on."

"Brick, damn it," Cara said as she came on the net. "Get your fucking ass out of there."

The HUD on the Viper showed that armor integrity was down to five percent. Another good hit and it was done. He looked at the SUV and knew what he had to do. "Sorry, Cara, can't do it. I'm grateful for everything you've done for me. I guess it's not my time. Just get this kid out."

"Brick, damn it!"

He turned to face a new threat, and as he did, the miniguns opened fire and tore through flesh and bone. Not long after that, another rocket fired and Ivan took it full on.

———

40,000 FEET OVER HONDURAS

"Brick!" Cara cried out. She looked at the shape of the destroyed Viper and turned to Crystal. "Please tell me you have something."

Crystal shook her head. "No vitals at all, ma'am. He's gone."

Cara stared at the screen, her eyes welling with emotion. "Damn you. How far out is Reaper?"

"Three mikes."

"Still too fucking long. Pat, get Cobra One back in there. Plaster those bastards."

"Roger that."

HONDURAS

Maria saw the big robot get hit and explode, pieces blowing in every direction. The sound was deafening, and against her, Ana trembled with every noise that shattered their world. Then there was a lull, and she looked again and saw the attackers closing in once more.

Two of them ran forward and reached in to drag Maria from the SUV. The Glock in her hand came up and she fired five times. Both attackers reeled back with bullet holes in their chests.

Behind them, a loud explosion rocked the vehicle as a missile from Cobra One smashed into the ground.

As the roiling orange and black cloud cleared, Maria made her first mistake. Instead of staying inside the SUV, she climbed out. Her idea was to take Ana and run. A plan that was foiled by the bullet that hammered into her back.

She dropped to her knees, reaching for her daughter.

"Mama!"

"It's okay, baby. It's okay."

———

THE TWO VANS containing the Global teams hit the roundabout and separated. Walrus would do what they could to cover the extraction, while Reaper would get Maria and Ana.

Knocker brought the van to a shuddering halt near the SUV, and Kane leaped from the rear, followed by Grace who immediately dropped to a knee and opened fire. Kane rushed to the SUV and found Maria wounded and holding onto her daughter's hand.

"John, I—"

"Don't talk."

He checked her wound quickly and knew there was nothing they could do for her. He stared into her eyes. "Maria—"

"I know. I can feel it. Take Ana."

"No, Mama, no."

"Go with him. He will make sure you're safe. Remember him from Barbados."

Bullets punched hard against the SUV.

Ana screamed. "I can't."

"You can trust him, Ana, he's your father."

She stared at Kane in disbelief. "No."

"Yes, baby. He is."

"We'll have to discuss this later," Kane said. "I'll take her, then come back for you."

"John, I—"

Kane grabbed Ana and dragged her from the rear seat. She started to cry and scream, but he wasn't letting her go. With one last look at Maria, he said, "Just hang on."

Through the chaos, Kane started to carry Ana to their van. He made it halfway before an explosion knocked him sprawling on the asphalt, and he was forced to let his daughter go. Immediately, she ran back to her mother in the SUV.

Kane came to his feet to follow her when machine gun fire ripped through the space between them, forcing him to take cover. He dove behind the van and saw a battle droid appear.

"Where the fuck did they come from?" Knocker shouted.

Kane cursed and looked at Ana and Maria. The little girl was locked onto her mother, but Maria wasn't responding; she was already gone.

"Bravo, I need to know what the hell is going on."

"Wait one, Reaper One."

"Christ. Denver, what's your situation?"

"We can't hold against all this, Reaper. We need to get out of here."

Kane looked over at Ana, who was crouched down, scared. "Roger that. Knocker, Grace, cover me."

"Say when," Knocker replied.

"Now."

Kane lurched forward and made it three steps before he was forced back. "Damn it. Give me a fucking break."

"Reaper One from Bravo. You need to get out. The place is a damn war zone, and Torres has at least six battle droids in position."

Again, his gaze went to Ana. "I'm not leaving her, Cara."

"You've got no choice. And you are no good to her dead."

In the middle of the carnage, Knocker appeared beside him. "Come on, Shag, time to go. We've lost the initiative and Brick as well."

Kane's head snapped around with a questioning stare. "Brick?"

"Yeah. No one else today. Maria and Brick are enough. We'll get Ana. I promise. Even if I have to do it myself."

Kane looked once again at Ana, who was now looking at him. He mouthed, "I will come for you," and turned away. "Everyone mount up. We're getting out of here while we still can. Bravo, we need extract."

"On the way."

They climbed into the van which was starting to look like swiss cheese. The windows were gone, though luckily, the motor still ran. Moments later, they sped away, the remaining combatants still fighting each other.

"Bravo, who were those people?" Kane asked.

"I'm not sure who ambushed the convoy, but we know who the battle droids belonged to."

"Keep an eye on Ana. See what happens to her."

"What about Maria?"

"She's dead."

Then there was silence.

———

TORRES STARED at Maria's body with indifference. He neither cared nor was concerned about her death. She'd been his brother's wife and had been caught sleeping with the one called Kane, the man who'd eventually killed his brother. However, she'd been pregnant at the time with his brother's child, so instead of killing her, he'd kept her around for the simple fact that he had no compunction to care for the kid.

Now she was dead, and he felt nothing.

He looked at the child who sat alone on the curb. He walked over to her, and she looked up at him. There was no relief in her eyes. "Mama is dead."

Torres nodded. "I can't do much about that."

"But who will look after me?"

"I will find someone."

"What about my father?"

The cartel boss stared at her. "Your father is dead. He died before you were born."

Ana shook her head. "No. He came to Barbados; he was here when those men attacked us. He tried to rescue us."

"Who said the man was your papa?"

"Mama."

Ice started to fill his veins. "Did you hear his name?"

"She called him John."

The cartel boss's head snapped up, and he looked around. It was a futile gesture because the person he sought was long gone. Torres called a man over.

"Sir?"

"Who attacked them?"

"We think it was Domingo Navarro."

"Send some people. Find him, kill him."

"Yes, sir."

"Take the girl back to the compound."

CHAPTER 18

"What happened?" Thurston asked Cara over the video call.

"We were victims of coincidence," she explained. "A rival cartel had the same idea as we did. Brick was KIA and Maria—looks like she died trying to protect her daughter."

"What happened to the girl?"

"We think she is with her uncle. Once his droids showed up, we were screwed. If they hadn't pulled back, we would have lost them all. Not just Brick."

"What are we doing about his remains?"

"Working on it."

"Okay. Replacements?"

Cara sighed.

"Cara?"

"I'm fucking losing everyone," she hissed. "Every time I send them out, someone fucking dies. I've had enough."

"It comes with command, you know that."

"Maybe it's time you found someone else."

"You're tired. Once this mission is complete, take some time. Think about it. If you still want to step down after that, I'll find someone else."

"Yes, General."

Thurston said, "I'll send you a couple more Viper pilots and some additional hardware."

"Yes, General. Anyone I know?"

"Maybe."

The video call was terminated, and Cara leaned back in the chair of the quarters she was assigned. She stared at the ceiling and counted the dull paint spots where patches had been missed. The team had been on the ground for over twenty-four hours. With reinforcements coming in, that would push it out to an extra couple of days. Not that the rest wouldn't be appreciated.

Suddenly, faces from the past came to her. Luis Ferrero, Hank Jones, Axe, Brick, Teller, Traynor—all gone. Brooke had moved on to greener pastures, and Rani, who'd taken over from Brooke, was also gone.

Others had died in the line of duty as well. Many were from the strike teams, others from support.

There was a knock on the door, and Kane walked into the office. He looked around and said, "They set you up."

Cara nodded. "Yes. Are you alright?"

"I'm fine. Want to come for a drink to say goodbye to Brick?"

"I think I need one," Cara replied. "I was just talking to Mary. She's going to send some Viper pilots and such to boost the team back to operational status."

"Not like we can't use them," Kane allowed.

There was a drawn-out silence, and Cara said, "What is it?"

He said, "Once this mission is done, I'm out. I can't give any more. Not that I have more to give."

She nodded. "I think I'll be joining you. I'm done with sending people out to die."

"Where will you go?"

"Somewhere far from anything military. Maybe Derby or Cheshire. What about you?"

"I might go back to the Med. Lay on a beach, drink beer, and sleep."

"That sounds good."

They went silent. An awkward and long silence.

"This is a young person's game," Kane said, eventually breaking it.

"You got that right."

Another knock and the Brit entered. He looked at them both and said, "I can come back."

Cara shook her head. "No need, darling."

Knocker's eyes narrowed. "Are you all right? What did I do?"

Cara smiled. "Nothing, Raymond. We've just been discussing the future and lamenting the past."

"That sounds deep. Anyway, just so you know, once we're done here, I'm out. There comes a time when a man can push the boundaries only so far. I think I've reached it."

They both smiled at him.

"What?"

"Join the queue."

"You too?" He had a quizzical look on his face.

They both nodded.

"Bollocks. Once we get Reaper's kid back, then we're done."

"It would seem so," Cara agreed. "We've lost some good people along the way."

Kane nodded. Knocker said, "I still miss that big bastard."

"Axe?"

"Yeah, he was always good for a laugh."

Kane said, "One last time?"

Cara nodded. "One last time."

Knocker smiled. "Into the valley of death rode—"

"Shut up, Raymond."

"Yes, ma'am."

————

CARA, Kane, and Knocker stood at the base of the Global Loadmaster's ramp and watched as it was unloaded. Ammunition, spares, three Viper replacements, and Ares, Ivan's replacement.

"I want him," Knocker said.

"You sure?" Cara asked.

"As I've ever been."

"Then you shall have it."

The Brit frowned. "Where the hell are our pilots?"

"Hey, Mom," a voice called.

Knocker groaned. "Ah, bollocks. I had to fucking ask."

Cara stared at her son, Jimmy. He was dressed in combat fatigues and aviator sunglasses. Gone was the kid of thirteen when the journey began all the way back in the border town of Retribution, and standing at the top of the ramp was a twenty-one-year-old young man. "Jimmy? What are you doing here?"

"I'm a replacement Viper pilot."

Her jaw dropped. "The fuck you are."

Knocker leaned close to Kane. "This is going to be intense."

Kane nodded and grabbed Knocker's arm. "Time to go."

They turned and started walking away.

"Stand firm, you two," she snapped at them.

The pair stopped. Knocker whispered, "Do you think she knows?"

"The fuck you think?"

"We should run."

They turned.

"Did you two know about this?"

Knocker shrugged. Kane said, "I thought you had told your mother."

"I thought I'd surprise her once my training was done."

Kane winced. "Knocker, you were right. We should have run when we had the chance."

"Is there a problem?"

Mary Thurston appeared beside Jimmy.

Cara stared at her boss. "You might say that. What the fuck is my son doing here?"

"He volunteered to come."

"Then he can volunteer to go right back. This is no place for a trainee operator."

"Mom, I'm fully qualified."

Cara shook her head. "I don't care, Jimmy. This is my command, and I say what goes."

Jimmy looked at Thurston. "General?"

"Go and get your kit. I'll sort things out here."

Jimmy disappeared back inside the loadmaster. Thurston looked at Kane. "Well, Reaper, Cara has made her feelings known, how about you? He'll be on your team."

"It has nothing to do with him," Cara snapped, her color heightening.

"Reaper?"

"Cara is right. This isn't any place for a trainee Viper pilot."

Cara nodded. "I told you."

"But," Kane continued, "I've been keeping an eye on things. He's top at everything he does. The kid is damn good."

"Don't you dare say it, Reaper."

"The facts are there to see, Cara. Out of a bunch of green recruits, he's the best we've got. And we need replacements."

"He's my son," Cara pleaded.

"He's a man. He's all grown up."

"He could die. Haven't we lost enough?"

Kane nodded. "So could we all."

"This is all about your daughter."

The Reaper's face remained passive. "You know that's not true. I tell you what, use him as a QRF. If we need him, he jumps."

The suggestion seemed to work. Cara nodded. "All right."

"What about the other replacements?" Knocker asked.

"You're looking at her," Thurston said.

"What? There's no one else?"

"I brought the best of the rest with me."

"So, we've got Reaper, me, Grace, you, and the kid?"

"And me," said Cara. "I'll be on the ground too."

Knocker grinned, his face a mask of sarcasm. "This is going to be fucking great."

———

THEY SET out part of the base as a training range for the Vipers. Although Cara wouldn't admit it, Jimmy knew his stuff and was well trained. They ran through drills and worked with Walrus. Denver's men were good, possibly the best strike team on the Global payroll.

While this was happening, Global's intel people were trying to get a fix on Torres and Ana. The day after the battle, Torres had left his compound and gone into hiding. Now no one knew where he was.

Kane worked his way through the training course alongside Jimmy. Once they were done, he pulled the kid aside. "You did well."

Jimmy glanced at his mother who was talking to Thurston. "Try telling her that."

"It's been a brutal time for her. For us all. She just wants to see you safe, and this isn't how to do it."

"But I finally found something I'm good at. That I love doing."

"She'll see that eventually; she's just having a hard time seeing that you're all grown up."

"Wait until she finds out you slept with Josie the load master."

Jimmy went red and looked at Knocker who had joined them. "You know about that?"

"We're all family here, kid. We look out for one another."

"Shit."

Kane stared at Jimmy. "You slept with Josie?"

"So? She's nice."

"It's a wonder she didn't eat you alive."

"Hasn't for the past couple of months."

Knocker shook his head. "I've heard enough."

"What's happening?" Cara asked as she walked over to the trio.

Jimmy smiled and said, "We were just discussing—"

"Ants," said Knocker. "Big fuckers around here."

"That's right," Kane agreed. "Don't want them to be getting hold of you."

Her expression was skeptical. She looked at her son and said, "You did well today. It looks like I have some catching up to do with you. Got time for a chat?"

Jimmy nodded. "Sure."

Kane and Knocker watched them walk away. When they were gone, Kane turned to his friend and said, "Josie?"

"Could have been worse," the Brit replied.

"How?"

Knocker smiled. "Could have been someone on his mother's team."

"Don't even joke about it."

Knocker slapped him on the back.

"I'm thinking you two are up to no good," Thurston said as she approached them.

"Just talking about the kid," Kane replied.

"About how he's sleeping with Josie the load master?"

The Reaper shook his head. "Does everyone know?"

Knocker grinned. "Almost."

"What do you think of Jimmy?" the former general asked.

"He's a good operator. Being in combat will tell us more. And we won't know that until it happens."

"Good enough to fit into your team?"

"Time will tell." He didn't mention that it wouldn't be his team for much longer.

———

"How long have you and Josie been seeing each other?" Cara asked her son.

"How…"

"I know everything. Just don't tell Tweedle Dum and Tweedle Dee. They don't think I know."

"Sorry I didn't tell you about everything."

"It is what it is, but we'll deal with it. I've seen your records from training, and you're quite good. But combat is different."

Jimmy nodded.

"I'm going to change things around on the upcoming mission," Cara told her son.

"How so?"

"You will go in with the team. I'll act as QRF."

"Are you sure, Mom?"

"I'm sure."

Jimmy smiled. "Thanks."

"I'll tell Reaper. Just make sure you follow orders and don't do anything stupid."

"I won't."

"Get out of here."

She found Kane and Knocker drinking beers in one of the hangars. "Got a spare?"

The Brit tossed her one, and she twisted the cap off. Cara took a sip and said, "I'm sending Jimmy in with you guys."

"You sure you want to do that?"

"It's time to let go."

"We'll take care of him, boss."

"I know, but not to the detriment of the team," Cara said.

"Deal."

Minutes later, Crystal appeared. "We've got a lead."

————

"WHAT DO YOU HAVE?" Kane asked, an edge to his voice. "Where are they?"

Crystal shook her head. "We're not sure, but this woman might be the key to unlocking the puzzle."

A picture flashed up of a woman in her forties with long, dark hair and meticulous makeup. Her skin was flawless, and her body matched.

"Who is she?" Cara asked.

"Lucia Garcia. She's a television reporter for Honduras News and also a close friend of Torres."

"How close?" Knocker asked.

"Share your bed horizontal tango close."

"You mean they play hide the sausage together?"

"Yes."

"And you think she might know where Torres is?"

"Only one way to find out. Pick her up and ask questions."

"Going into Honduras again isn't my favorite travel plan at the moment," Knocker said.

"That's good because she isn't in Honduras."

"Where is she?"

"Miami. Traveling under the name Ursula Collins."

"Okay," Kane said. "I'll bite. Why is she in Miami?"

"Visiting Eduard Gomez."

A picture came up on the screen of a Central American man wearing long gold chains, tattoos, and designer clothes. Kane's eyes went straight to the small tattoo on his neck. "Los Muertos. The Dead."

"Yes. Get this. Her cover is as a freelance journalist doing a story on Miami gangs."

"I guess we're going to Miami," Cara said.

Kane nodded. "A job for a small team. Two in the field and two in the crib. We take Crystal."

Crystal looked up from the screen. "Oh, I am so in."

Cara nodded. "Let's do it before she flies the coop."

———

MIAMI, FLORIDA

It was late at night, and each of the streetlamps had been smashed, which suited the two men in the SUV. They were virtually in the dark, and no one could see them. They'd been staked out for just over an hour, both armed with suppressed 756s.

"Are we sure this is happening tonight?" Knocker asked for the tenth time. He was starting to have doubts and concluded that whoever had supplied them with the intel had screwed up.

"As far as we know, Raymond," Cara replied.

Knocker looked at his friend. "You think she's getting pissed at me?"

"What do you think?" Kane asked without looking at him.

"Maybe."

"Yeah."

"Heads up, we have a vehicle approaching."

The headlights swept the street as the vehicle rounded the corner. It was a 2027 Chevy Yellowstone four-door pickup.

Knocker said, "That isn't her."

The Chevy stopped outside the well-tagged building and was approached by a man. His hands moved, and the Chevy pulled away. Kane said, "It's another deal."

For the next ten minutes, nothing further happened, and the pair was getting impatient. Kane was about to pull the pin when a 2028 BMW appeared. "This is her."

He reached for his handgun.

"How do you know it's her?" Knocker asked.

"It's her."

The BMW stopped, and the lights were turned off. The motor went silent, and the door opened. Moments later, Lucia Garcia climbed out and was escorted inside.

"Bravo, the target has arrived. She just went inside."

"Copy, Reaper."

"We're moving in."

"Copy, good luck."

Kane and Knocker climbed from the vehicle and started across the street from the building Los Muertos were using. They climbed up onto the sidewalk and jumped the fence into the vacant lot beside it. The drug dealers and gangsters were making a lot of money these days, but it wasn't evident to look at them.

Kane and Knocker crept through the long, dry grass until they reached the rear of the building. Out the back were three gangsters sitting around a fire, the orange flames licking hungrily at the night sky.

The brightness of the fire worked in their favor because it ruined the gangsters' night vision. The two operators came up to the edge of the long grass and stood erect. The gangster closest to Knocker started to turn but was too slow. The Brit hit him behind the ear with the butt of the 756, and the man dropped like a stone.

The other two gangsters, however, were too far

away and therefore unlucky. The only way to silence them was through death. Kane shot them both in the head, and they fell to the dry earth beside the fire.

Using hand signals, Kane directed Knocker toward the back of the building. The Brit walked toward the rear door, keeping to the left of the opening. When he reached it, he peered inside. The lighting was weak, like someone had installed a twenty-watt globe to light a warehouse.

The space was sectioned off by black wooden room dividers, separating them into separate rooms as there were very few walls. It was like an open-plan office, but instead of half walls, they were two-thirds height. And it was large. Not warehouse large, but it had possibly been a nightclub in a previous life.

Knocker stepped inside and started forward. He could hear voices somewhere in front of him, distant, quieter. Then the sound changed to moaning, and it was closer. The Brit shook his head. Someone was having sex in one of the cubicles.

A couple of moments later, they arrived at the one that was being utilized as a boudoir. Now their choices were to push forward or restrain the two within before moving on. Leaving at least one shooter behind them was dangerous. The possibility of taking down two spoke for itself.

Using hand signals once more, Kane indicated what he wanted to do. Knocker nodded and moved to the open doorway and peered around.

As luck would have it, the woman was on top, her back to the opening, oblivious to the threatening presence behind her.

Knocker moved like a cat as he entered the room. He clamped his hand over her mouth and pulled her backward. The gangster she was riding had his eyes closed and was blissfully absorbed in his ongoing pleasure and failed to notice what was happening until it was too late.

Kane, holding a knife, drove it down into the man's throat, cutting off any chance of him crying out in alarm. The knife then savagely moved to the right, severing everything the keen edge touched.

"Do not make a sound," Knocker hissed into the woman's ear. "You do, and you'll be lying next to your boy there."

The woman stopped struggling immediately. They gagged her first and then bound her tight so she couldn't move. Then they moved on.

The voices grew louder. Not raised, just closer. Kane peered around the corner of a partition and saw them seated in a circle. Chairs, beanbags, an old sofa.

Knocker stopped behind his friend and listened.

"Fernando wants to boost sales in Miami. He says that the last six months have dropped away."

"That's because customers keep dying," a second voice said. "Customers are down. Not to mention that the police are stepping up their raids."

"Can't you fight them?"

"It isn't that simple. If we start killing them, they send more, then comes the army, and before you know it, they aren't raiding us, they're killing us."

"There must be a way. Increase prices."

"Tell Fernando I will find a way. But tell him also that he needs to find a way to make Happy Days safer. If it keeps killing customers at this rate, there will be no one left."

"He does not care."

Kane looked back at Knocker. He held up five

fingers, and then another two. Seven people. Knocker nodded.

Bringing their weapons up, they moved.

As soon as Kane was clear of the partition, he shot one of the closest gangsters to him in the head from behind. Blood sprayed, and the dead body crashed forward.

By the time he hit the floor, Kane had moved a further four feet and changed his aim to shoot a second man.

Knocker was hot on his friend's heels and killed a third gangster who was starting to react. He was coming off his seat when the bullet from the Brit's suppressed 756 smashed into his face.

Shouts filled the room as the remaining survivors scrambled frantically to meet the threat. Kane shot an additional would-be shooter, and Knocker shot another. That left two still alive. One was Lucia, and the other was Eduard Gomez.

The gang leader stared at the two men who had their weapons pointed at him. "Who the fuck are you?"

Kane said, "If you just sit back down, buddy, you might just see the sun come up tomorrow. Besides, we're not here for you."

Gomez looked at Lucia, who was stunned to silence by the violence she'd witnessed.

"I'd sit down if I were you, mate," Knocker said. "It's been a bad week, so we're not really happy."

Gomez sat down in the stained recliner he'd sprung from when his people had been dying around him. "Just so you know, you two will never get out of Miami fucking alive."

Knocker shook his head. "You just couldn't help yourself, could you?"

Then the former SAS operator shot him twice in the chest.

Kane stared at Lucia. "Time to go."

"Do you know who I am?" she blustered. "What are you doing?"

Knocker dragged her to her feet and secured her hands before putting a hood over her head. "That's the thing, love, we sometimes leap before we look. In your case, we just jumped off a cliff."

Kane said into his comms, "Bravo, we've got the package, and we're on our way out."

"Copy, Reaper One, we'll meet you at the helicopter."

CHAPTER 19

After landing at Johnson Air Force Base, Lucia was placed in a small interrogation room and left for several hours while they discussed the best way to interrogate her. It was decided to go with the all-female approach, which came down to Cara and Houlihan.

As he looked at Lucia on the screen, Kane said, "She's going to play the scare card, then the tough card."

"Without a doubt," Cara said. "But she hasn't met us before."

A glint came to Houlihan's eye. "She's a pretty little thing."

"Be nice, Pat. We catch more flies with honey."

"Yes, ma'am."

Kane said, "She's got a nervous tap."

"Then we're one up already," Cara replied.

"I'm not so sure. Being nervous will put her on edge. It might make her more guarded about what she's saying."

"Then we get her to relax. Okay, Pat, let's have a run at her."

Leaving the observation room, the two operators entered the interrogation room. On the way in, they passed Knocker, who went to join Kane. "The all-girl team having a crack?"

Kane nodded. "Should be interesting to watch their moves."

The two women entered, and Cara walked around behind Lucia, grabbing a handful of hair, and slammed the beautiful face down into the stainless-steel table.

Kane stared at the screen. "Interesting angle."

Lucia's head bounced back up, blood already flowing. Houlihan stepped forward and grabbed Cara. "That's it, you're out of here."

"The hell you say, this is my interrogation room."

"Not anymore it isn't. Out." Houlihan indicated the door with an extended finger.

Cara stormed from the room, and Houlihan reached into her pocket and took out a cloth. Kane frowned. "Uh-huh."

The observation room door opened, and Cara walked in. Knocker grinned at her. "That kind of fucked everything, boss."

"You're here. Saves me going to find you. You're up. And grab a bottle of booze."

"What?"

"Reaper said we needed to make her relax."

"Slamming her head into the table really did that," Kane pointed out.

"Hence the booze. Go."

———

"WHAT THE FUCK IS HER PROBLEM?" Lucia asked as she wiped the blood from her face.

"She's had a bad week."

"Haven't we all?"

"I doubt you've had one like hers. She's lost people, and one was a close friend."

"I don't care how bad it was. There's no need to do that," Lucia said. "I'm going to report her to the proper authorities when we're done here."

Houlihan stared at her. "Who do you think we are?"

Lucia waved a hand, the handcuffs clinking. "How the hell should I know? I know this, however. You people have made a grave mistake."

"Are you talking about your boyfriend, Fernando?" Houlihan asked.

Lucia was brought up short and went silent.

"I don't understand what you see in him. He's a mass murderer on a grand scale."

"He is a businessman."

"He's rich. You like the money? Is that it? Or is it a power thing? If it's the latter, honey, I'll tell you this: you have no power at all. When Fernando gets sick of you, he'll hang you from something, upside down without a head."

Lucia glared at her indignantly. "He would do no such thing."

"Well, then, if he loves you so much, why has he disappeared and not taken you with him?"

Lucia smiled. "This is what it is all about? You want me to tell you where Fernando is?"

Houlihan just stared at her.

"I do not know where he is."

"I think you are lying."

The door opened. and Knocker entered with a bottle of scotch and three glasses. He smiled. "You lot started the party without me."

Placing the glasses on the table, he filled them from the bottle, passing one to Houlihan who frowned but relieved him of it. The Brit slid one over in front of Lucia and picked up his own, drinking half before speaking again. "Go on, love. Have a go at it. Make the pain in your face go away."

Lucia shook her head. "No. I know what you are doing. Trying to get me drunk."

"What would be the point in that? If you were drunk, you'd ramble, and we'd get fuck all out of you. No, it's just a peace offering before we let you go."

"Let me go?"

Knocker nodded.

"Yeah, right."

He walked over to her and undid the handcuffs. "Sorry about that."

Lucia stood up. "I can just leave?"

The Brit shook his head. "Sure."

Lucia started toward the door.

"There is just one thing," Knocker said.

She turned.

He pointed at the chair. "Take a seat. We'll have to organize some transport for you."

Lucia looked at him suspiciously.

"You know, I had an ex-wife who worked for the BBC years ago," he said.

His comment seemed to put Lucia at ease. She sat back down. "The BBC?"

"Yes. In my opinion, it was the best job she ever had."

"Really?"

Knocker nodded. "Yeah, she was never home."

Houlihan stifled a grin.

Lucia took a drink of whiskey. "She was that bad?"

"Bitch of a thing."

He topped off her glass and then his. "What about you? Have you covered some big stories?"

She nodded and took another drink. "Venezuela a couple of years ago, when the vice president was assassinated by the Americans."

Knocker nodded. "It wasn't the Americans."

Another drink. "Sure, it was. Everyone knows it was them."

The Brit shook his head. "No, it was MI6."

Lucia stared at him. "Really?"

"Yes, really."

"How do you know this?"

"It was me who did it."

"No?"

"Yes."

In the observation room behind the two-way mirror, Cara turned to Kane. "Really?"

Kane nodded. "Six had us both in-country."

"Christ."

Lucia took another drink, rattled by what she'd just been told. "What about Aristov, the Russian minister in Cuba? He was assassinated at the same time. I suppose you will tell me that was you as well? Not the Americans again."

Knocker grinned and took a drink. "It was an American."

"I knew it."

"Working for MI6."

She took another drink, and Knocker filled her glass again. He glanced at Houlihan who nodded.

"I do not believe you."

"It's true. Just like I put Hernandez in the ground."

Lucia's eyes widened as though she had caught him out in a lie. "No. This time I know you lie. It was Fernando who killed this man."

And there was the chink in her armor.

"Sorry, you're right. I have him mixed up with someone else."

Lucia looked at him after a couple more drinks and said, "Where is my car?"

Knocker looked at his watch. "Should be here soon. Then you can chug off to Cuba and be with Fernando."

The remark slipped through the weakened guard, and she said, "He's not in Cuba."

"My mistake," Knocker replied. "I thought he was going there."

"No. Par—" She waved a finger at Knocker. Her glassy eyes showed suspicion. "You almost got me."

Knocker nodded. "Sorry. You're too smart for me. Wait here, and we'll send someone for you when your ride arrives."

Lucia gave a grunt and nodded. "Thank you."

Knocker and Houlihan left the interrogation room, and once they were in the hallway, she said to the Brit, "He's in Paraguay."

"Yes, he is."

Cara and Kane exited the observation room. "Good work."

"Sometimes the old ways work best," Knocker replied.

"All we have to do now is find him."

———

CRUISING over Central Paraguay at ten thousand feet, the General Electric Hanson Rapier UAV scanned everything its sensors touched. Over the past three days, there had been three of them alternating as they monitored the camp being utilized by Torres.

Crystal had located it using satellite imagery and real-time recordings. It was deep in the interior of the country.

Now they were trying to get all they could before committing to an operation.

So far, they had located an airstrip capable of accommodating the handful of flankers that they'd discovered, along with three SAM batteries and a barracks large enough to accommodate a good-sized battalion of Torres' fighters.

On a sweep the day before, Houlihan had picked out a handful of tanks hidden beneath camouflage netting. Then there were the six machine gun posts and anti-tank batteries. But the concerning thing was that they had no idea where the HP433 Battle Droids were. Apart from Torres and Ana, that was the last piece of the puzzle they were trying to slot in.

Then, more by luck than good management, they found them.

Tanner guided the Rapier around for another sweep of the jungle to the east and dropped five thousand feet. Houlihan sat beside him, using the adage that four eyes were better than two. She yawned and said, "Last sweep, Mike, then we call it quits."

"Sounds like a plan, Pat."

The Rapier commenced its sweep of the jungle and was two-thirds through it when Pat said, "What was that?"

"Didn't see a thing."

"I thought I caught a glimpse of something."

Houlihan hit a key and hurried over to a printer, all thoughts of sleep gone. Picking up the picture, she examined it closely. Then she saw it, hurrying back across to where Tanner sat and showed him the picture. "What am I looking at?"

Houlihan took the picture back and circled the area in question. "There."

Tanner looked again. Frowned, then said, "It looks like a person."

"Yes, but it isn't. It's too tall."

"Robot?"

"I'm going to say yes. Turn the Rapier around and let's scan the whole area again."

While he did as ordered, Houlihan reached for the phone on the desk. When the call was connected, she said, "Sorry to bother you, ma'am, but you need to see this."

She hung up, and five minutes later, Cara appeared. "What do you have?"

Houlihan had been printing off pictures. She grabbed a couple sheets of paper and started to point out what they had found. "We've counted fifteen so far."

"Good work."

"We'll keep going just in case we missed any and there are more."

"That just leaves the cream on the top."

"Yes."

Cara looked thoughtfully at the screen. "I think there is only one way to do that. Send out a memo. I want a briefing for everyone in the morning."

"Yes, ma'am."

———

EVERYONE GATHERED in the briefing room the following day and waited for the meeting to start. Cara and Thurston stood in front with a bank of six large screens. Thurston stepped forward and said, "Right, thank you for all being here. As you know, this operation is not going to be easy, and there is a good chance that some of you will not be coming home. That is the reality of it. I will not bullshit you on any of this."

As she scanned the room, she saw only grim, determined expressions. "Okay, Cara will take over from here. If you have any questions or suggestions, do not be afraid to speak up. The hive mind is sometimes the best."

Cara waited for a moment before addressing those gathered. She let out a sigh and started. "Okay. This is the compound in Central Paraguay where we think—almost certain—where Fernando Torres is. We have yet to confirm it."

"How do we plan on doing that?" Grace asked.

"I have a plan." Her eyes went to Denver. "I need your team, Denver."

"Yes, ma'am."

"I want to drop you in, you set up an OP, and we go from there."

"QRF, ma'am?"

"We'll have assets in the air to support you, out of range of the SAMs. It was just a fortunate thing that the stealth capabilities on our UAVs are good. But, yes, we'll have Black Cats in the area and a gun platform as well."

"Yes, ma'am. We'll get it done."

"Thank you. Once we confirm that both targets are

on-site, you'll note that I said both targets. We are expecting that there will be a small girl as well, then we go in. Once the shit hits the fan, Denver's team will get the job of securing her."

Denver nodded.

"Now, let's get down to defenses. We've counted five flankers, the same in tanks, three SAM batteries, six machine gun posts, some anti-tank batteries, and a large enough barracks to suit a battalion of men."

She looked at Kane and her son. There was no emotion on either face, but she knew Kane would be formulating things inside his head. Each time she mentioned the weapons Torres had at his fingertips, their positions came up on the screens.

Then came the last one.

"These are the battle droids that Torres has purchased. They are hidden in the jungle to the east. We have counted twenty of them but there could be more. Each is operated by remote, like the Black Cats we have."

"Do we know where they are being operated from?" Knocker asked.

"No. If we did, then we could shut them down before they have a chance to be a threat. At this time, we assume that the operators are hidden underground in a bunker."

"Then why not bomb the shit out of them?"

"That's what we plan to do, but they are well spread out, so success won't be complete. Then there are the SAMs. Our targets need to be strategic. Taking them by surprise will help. We'll have two fully armed Black Cats in the air. Taking out the SAMs and the battle droids is the priority. The Vipers will need to be dropped in position before the Black Cats open the ball for us. We even the playing field, and we're more likely to succeed."

Her gaze once more drifted over the people in the room. "We're going to war, ladies and gentlemen. Bring your A-game. Your B will get you killed."

Silence.

"Any questions?"

"When do we go?" Denver asked.

"You drop in tonight."

He nodded.

"Anything else?"

Nothing.

"Okay. You all have jobs to do. Go do them."

———

KANE PAUSED what he was doing and looked over at Knocker, who was loading rounds into the compartment for the twin miniguns of Ares. "Jam them in, the ammo packs will take it. And make sure you have enough AT."

Knocker nodded. "Speaking of AT, it might pay to give the kid the one-twenty."

Kane looked over at Jimmy. "Kid, you used the one-twenty before?"

"Yes, sir."

"Good, load it up to your Viper instead of the minigun."

"Yes, sir," Jimmy replied.

"Don't call me sir. Call me Kane or Reaper."

"Yes, sir."

"Grace, double check your packs."

"Already done it, Reaper."

"Got enough juice for the flamethrower, Knocker?"

"Just need to top it up," the Brit replied.

"Don't forget to check your HUD displays. The last thing you want is for them to go down in the middle of combat."

Knocker grinned. "Gracie, he's like an old mother hen."

"Just missing the feathers."

"Uh-huh."

"I have a question." Jimmy said.

They all looked at him. Kane said, "All right, kid, let's hear it."

"What are we going to do? What's the mission?"

It was a fair question. "We're going to take out everything that Torres has. Whatever it takes to capture the compound."

"What are the battle droids like?"

"Tough. Some are armed with rockets. If they hit you, game over."

"What is with the girl?" Jimmy asked. "I get why we're after Torres, but the girl?"

Kane dropped his gaze. Knocker said, "She's Reaper's daughter."

"Oh. I didn't know."

"Now you do," Kane said. "You and Grace make sure the two Vipers are ready to go for Cara and the general. Fully loaded."

Then he turned and walked out.

Jimmy looked at Knocker. "Did I do something wrong?"

The Brit shook his head. "No, kid, he's been like it ever since he found out Ana was his daughter. Then her mother got killed, and now he's all she's got."

Jimmy shook his head. "Fuck it."

"Yeah, fuck it."

———

MOLLY WAS WATCHING as the ground crew loaded Skyhammer with ammunition for her weapons. She considered them hers because they were under her command. Once the loading was complete, she made sure that the Raptors were loaded onto the hardpoints.

Then she climbed aboard and examined the weapons closely. If they failed in battle, people would more than likely die. Next came the flares.

Once everything was loaded, she went aboard Skyhammer and started to check her console, making sure all the wiring and fuses were good.

"Hard at it?" Crystal asked.

Molly looked up from where she was lying on the floor, checking some wires below her console. "Making sure."

"Yes, I'm going to check my wiring as well. Especially after what happened."

Houlihan appeared. "Great, a mother's meeting."

"What are you up to, Pat?" Crystal asked.

"Console. Make sure the joysticks are working right."

"I guess we're all feeling jittery," Crystal said.

"You might say that." She sat down in her seat behind the console. "You know, all this time we've been together, you have never once talked about yourselves."

Crystal said, "You start."

"All right. I'm from London, was married, and am now divorced."

"No shit," Crystal said. "I'm from Sussex, not married, just seeing a guy at the moment. One of the ground crew back at home."

They both looked at Molly. "The fuck are you lot

looking at?" she asked them as though she had no intention of sharing anything personal.

"Come on," Crystal said.

"Fine. I'm from Leeds. Not married, and I'm mostly gay."

"Shit, we knew that."

Molly stared at Crystal. "How?"

"The way you stare at Josie the load master."

Pat frowned. "I thought she was sleeping with Jimmy."

Molly smiled. "She is. But some nights—well, you know."

"So, she's bi."

"Fine."

"I never knew that."

"Can we change the subject before I find one of the load masters for myself?" Houlihan said.

The three of them looked at each other and laughed. It would be the last time for a while.

CHAPTER 20

Strike Team Walrus had been on the ground for twenty-four hours and still had little to show for their efforts. Billy Holliday guided the UAV, known as the Fly, over the target. They had two more hours left on their clock to confirm the girl was there or the op would commence. They had confirmation of the presence of Torres within the first few hours. The man looked nervous, most likely because he'd not been able to reach Lucia. The Head Shed were now worried that he would rabbit.

It was dark, and the moon was out. A shape appeared outside that was small and erect.

"Hello, what do we have here?"

He took the Fly down lower. The small motor in the microdrone made it sound like a winged bug. He took it closer to the target and changed the view. He smiled and said, "Hello, Ana."

She swiped the air with her hand to make the bug

go away. Holliday lifted the drone and said into his comms, "Denver, wake up."

"What is it?"

"We've got the girl."

"Be right there."

Denver appeared out of the darkness. "What have you got?"

Holliday pointed at the screen. "There."

"You're sure?"

"Yeah."

"All right, wake the others up. I'll let the boss know."

"Roger that."

"Bravo, this is Walrus One, over."

"Copy, One. Read you Lima Charlie. Send traffic."

"Bravo, we have eyes on the prize, over."

"Copy. Does she look all right?"

"Copy."

"Okay. I guess it's time to go to work. Standby for further transmissions."

"Roger that."

JOHNSON AIR FORCE BASE, LLANO, TEXAS

"She's there with Torres, Reaper," Cara told him. "Denver has seen her."

Kane felt his heart speed up. "Then we're going?"

"Just as soon as we can. It's going to be a daylight operation."

"I'm cool with that."

Cara nodded. "Fine, wake them up."

Kane went back to their barracks and turned on the lights. "Everybody up, we're going to work."

"Fuck off," Knocker growled. "I'm busy."

"They've found her, cock."

He sat up immediately. "I'm up."

"You've got five minutes to be ready," Kane said.

"Nothing takes five minutes," Knocker said in a deep voice.

The others climbed off their cots and started dressing. Then, within the five allotted minutes, the operators were hurrying out the door.

Except for Knocker who paused to look around with an expression like it would be the last time he'd see it.

Kane came back. "What's up?"

"Just looking."

"Don't look too long, you'll miss the plane."

After another minute, Knocker reached out and turned off the light, then followed the others.

———

OVER PARAGUAY

"All Reaper elements in position."

Cara looked at the screen and could see the five Vipers in the jungle. The sun had been up for six hours and everything was set. The strike team was prepped, Vipers were in place, Black Cats were just below the horizon along with Skyhammer. Cara said, "Walrus One, copy?"

"Copy, Bravo."

"I need the location of the packages."

"Big package in the main house. The smaller package is in the pool house."

"Are we cleared to launch?"

"Roger that."

"All callsigns standby." She paused, took a deep breath, and turned to Houlihan. "Hit them hard, Pat."

"Yes, ma'am. Mike, let's do this. Cat One and Two inbound. Cleared hot."

Two F-60 Black Cats turned and started toward their targets. Both flew low and fast. Without taking her eyes off the screen, Houlihan said, "I'll take the SAMs, you drop everything you can on the battle droids."

"Yes, ma'am."

The Black Cats crossed the horizon and separated. Each took their own route to their respective targets. But even though they were independent, they would strike simultaneously.

Houlihan said, "Two minutes to target."

"Copy. Eugene, copy?"

"Yes, ma'am."

"Take us in."

"Roger that."

Cara felt the Stratomaster start its turn. "Molly, concentrate on the SAMs first."

"Yes, ma'am."

Meanwhile, the Black Cats were almost in position. "Cat One ready to fire."

"Cat Two ready to fire."

Cara nodded. "Engage."

"One firing."

"Two firing."

Within moments, there were four Lucifers in the air, speeding toward their individual targets. Their explosions rocked the compound as the air-to-ground missiles drove home.

Crystal said, "I have impacts on the ground. One SAM site is down, and it looks like we got a couple of battle droids as well."

"Good work, bring them back around."

"I've got a radar signal from one of the SAMs."

"That was damn quick."

"It's painting the second Black Cat."

"What?" Tanner blurted out. "The damn things have stealth capabilities. It's impossible."

"SAM away."

"Shit. Firing countermeasures," Tanner said as he pulled back on the joystick.

The Black Cat climbed and went into a roll as it tried to escape the incoming threat. The missile flew into the chaff and exploded in an orange ball of flame.

"I have another missile launch from the west. Range three miles."

"What the fuck? How did we miss that?" Cara demanded.

"Not in the area we were looking."

"Shit. Eugene—"

"I have it, ma'am."

"Molly, Ripper?"

"On it, ma'am."

Cara felt the vibrations flow through the Stratomaster as it expelled countermeasures for the incoming missile. Eugene flew it like it was a fighter. Ripper exploded to life, and the incoming SAM disappeared.

Cara looked at Houlihan. "Pat, concentrate on the SAM sites at the compound. We'll worry about the other one."

"Ma'am."

"Second missile launch," Crystal said in a calm voice.

"Countermeasures deployed." This time it was Leslie Groves, the copilot.

"Ripper ready."

"Find me that damn launcher."

"Third missile in the air." Crystal's voice was still calm.

"Christ!"

"Lucifer away," Tanner said.

"Lucifer away," Houlihan repeated.

"Target destroyed." Tanner.

"Targets destroyed." Houlihan.

"First missile time to impact: thirty seconds."

"Molly?"

"Anytime now...missile destroyed. Acquiring second target."

Cara looked at the second large screen. "Situation on the ground?"

"Two SAM sites destroyed and—"

"Missile in the air."

"Damn it. Eugene, put us over that damn site."

"Almost there."

"Second missile destroyed," Molly said stoically. Then, "I have acquired the target on the ground. Firing Thor...now."

The whole plane shuddered as the howitzer cleared its throat. Meanwhile, the third missile that had been fired was within reach of Ripper and was chewed up and spat out by the ferocious beast.

Molly watched her screen and saw the outgoing rounds strike the SAM launcher. She grunted with satisfaction and said, "Target destroyed."

Cara looked around. "Can anyone tell me, with all of our stealth capabilities, why they are still fucking finding us?"

All eyes remained focused on their screens and consoles.

For a moment, Cara lost her composure. "For fuck's sake, find out why before we get blown out of the damn sky."

———

PARAGUAY

"I've got movement to my left, Reaper," Grace said in a quiet voice.

"Check it out. Jimmy, go with her."

"Copy."

The two Vipers started through the jungle while the others remained on station. Knocker's voice came over the comms from Ares. "Let's get in there, Reaper."

"No, we wait for the word from Skyhammer."

"They're too busy with everything going on up there," the Brit pointed out.

"I agree with Raymond," Thurston said. "We're losing the initiative."

"We wait."

Meanwhile, Grace and Jimmy drew further away. She scanned the jungle with her sensors, and her HUD suddenly lit up like a Christmas tree. "Hold it, Jimmy. I've got a bogey one hundred meters ahead. No, make that two."

The Viper crouched down and beside her, Jimmy's did the same. They remained there and watched. The bogeys turned out to be two battle droids. "Now, where are you going?"

"Should we take them?" Jimmy asked.

"No. We don't want them to know we're here yet."

"Okay."

"Reaper One, I have two bogeys close to our position. I'm observing."

"Copy, Reaper Three."

Kane waited, the sounds of the explosions closer than before. "Walrus One, copy?"

"Copy, Reaper One."

"I need a sitrep."

"No sign of both packages, over."

"Copy."

Suddenly, all hell broke loose as explosions erupted through the jungle. "Damn it, they know we're here. All Vipers engage. Let's get some."

OVER PARAGUAY

"Ma'am, the Vipers are engaging," Crystal informed Cara.

"Already?"

"Yes, they came under fire. Torres's people knew they were there."

"Damn it. Keep me updated." A pause. "Pat, sitrep."

"All SAM launchers are down, and some battle droids have been destroyed."

"Some?"

"About half."

"Eugene, I want to get over the target so we can take out the strongpoints."

"Yes, ma'am."

"Molly, we need to take out targets as they come around."

"On it."

"Crystal, what are we looking at?"

"It looks like they're scrambling their tanks, and the men are taking up defensive positions. And their flankers."

"Pat, we need a gun run over the airfield; they're trying to scramble their flankers."

"On it."

Moments later, Tanner expended his last missile into the jungle where the droids were. "Black Cat Two, missiles expended."

"Mike, do a gun run along the defenses where Torres's fighters are digging in."

"Yes, ma'am."

"Walrus One, copy?"

"Read you Lima Charlie."

"If you see an opening, take it. Don't wait for us."

"Roger that. Walrus on the move."

———

"Now, KID," Grace said as she brought her Viper erect. Her minigun came to life and poured rounds at the closest battle droid while what she thought were mortar rounds rained down, smashing and exploding trees, issuing a furious fusillade of slivers scything through the air.

The machine staggered under the onslaught of the

fire. Then she brought up her arm and fired a couple of 30 mm rounds into the monster.

The droid collapsed as though it were a marionette with its strings cut. It started to smoke, then burst into flame.

Beside her, Jimmy followed her lead and smashed the second droid with the AT weapon. It was his first battle kill.

Grace said, "Follow me, kid. Watch my back."

They pushed forward through the jungle while it exploded around them. She heard Kane say over the comms, "We need to get out into the open. We can't fight in here."

Another droid appeared ahead of Grace. She fired the 30 mm at it. The first missed, the second found its target, but not before the droid fired a rocket.

"Look out!" she exclaimed.

Jimmy threw the Viper to the side, and it rolled before coming back up. The rocket slipped by above the Viper and caught the trunk of a large tree, exploding on impact. It blew splinters through the undergrowth while the tree above the impact area leaned and then fell to the ground.

The droid, on the other hand, exploded when the 30 mm hit the ammunition store it carried.

"You okay, kid?" Grace asked as her HUD scanned for more threats.

"I'm good."

"Good, I'd hate for something to happen to you, especially on my watch. Your mother and Josie would kill me."

Once more, they pressed forward through the carnage of war until they broke free of the jungle and out into the battle zone proper. Grace took one look around and said, "Oh, fuck me."

———

KANE FIRED a 30 mm round at a droid while his minigun fired deadly bursts at a machine gun post closer to the compound. Beside him, Ares was hammering a heavy tank which had burst from its camouflage, firing its main gun. One shell exploded near Ares, rattling it and Knocker to the core. Knocker fired more AT, and finally one pierced the armor of the beast and killed everyone inside before the tank started to burn.

Thurston was concentrating on a machine gun post when she was blindsided by a battle droid. But as luck would have it, the rocket it fired missed, but only just.

"Son of a bitch," she said out loud and raised the Viper's arm to fire the 30 mm.

The weapon roared, and the battle droid was punched hard in its armor, destroying it. Another tank appeared. This one was a Soviet-made T-72 which came from Venezuela.

Its main gun spoke with a massive roar, and Thurston could feel herself being thrown backward from the explosion.

Inside the Viper, she had been knocked senseless. Her HUD was flashing warnings, and her armor integrity was down fifty percent effectiveness. Over her comms, she could hear Crystal calling her but didn't have the breath to answer. Then there was the tank. It was still operational, and its gun was about to fire one more time.

————

IT WAS Jimmy who reacted first. He opened fire with the AT and hammered the tank with three shots. All rounds hit the tank and pierced its armor, making a ghastly mess of the crew within.

Grace hurried forward in her own Viper, its minigun spraying a defensive position, killing those hunkered there. "Good work, Jimmy. Now take out the anti-tank battery."

Jimmy changed his aim toward the defensive site to his right. The AT-120 opened fire once more, and the battery disappeared.

Meanwhile in the air, things were about to take a dramatic turn. One which could prove disastrous.

————

ONBOARD SKYHAMMER

"Pat, give me a report on those flankers," Cara said over her intercom.

"Last one has been destroyed on the ground. None were able to get up."

"Great work. Ammunition status?"

"Almost expended."

"Fine. Do one more pass and hand it off to Hereford."

"Yes, ma'am."

"Tanner."

"I'm in the same boat, ma'am."

"Do the same as Pat."

"Roger that."

"Reaper One, sitrep? Over."

"We're pushing toward the main compound. Resistance is heavy, but we're making progress."

"Crystal, give me the status on each Viper."

"One is eighty percent, Two is one hundred, Three is at ninety-five, Four at ninety-five, and Five is down to forty with vitals kicking back an elevated heart rate. That rocket really knocked her around."

"Reaper Five, copy?"

"I hear you, Cara," Thurston replied.

"I need a no-BS assessment on how you are feeling."

"I'm fine."

"You are showing an elevated heart rate."

"I'll manage."

"Leslie, fuel status?"

"One-twenty."

120,000 pounds. They had enough to remain on station for a couple more hours if required. "Copy. Thank you."

"Oh shit," Molly growled. "I have another SAM launch five miles out and closing."

"Damn it. Eugene, do you have the incoming SAM?"

"Copy. But we're out of chaff."

"That's OK. Ripper will take care of it. Molly?"

"Ripper is tracking the incoming."

A cold hand suddenly gripped Cara's heart. A feeling she couldn't shake. She thought for a moment that it might have been some kind of subliminal link to Jimmy, but she was about to find out that it was something entirely different.

"Missile in range—opening fire...fuck!"

"What?"

"Prepare for impact. Ripper—"

BOOM!

The SAM exploded beneath the inner port engine of the Stratomaster, ripping it to shreds. Pieces of debris somehow managed to get sucked into the turbofan of the one next to it, shattering the blades. Within moments, Skyhammer was compromised beyond all flight capabilities. The war bird was going down, and there was nothing to be done about it.

Groves' voice came over the intercom. "All hands, we're going down. We'll try to make the airfield. Get ready to brace. I say again, we're going down."

Cara had been thrown from her feet by the explosion and now crawled along the operations deck to her crash seat. While she was doing so, she heard Houlihan say, "Molly, take everything off-line and get rid of all the excess ammunition."

"Doing it."

"Crystal, let our people on the ground know what's happening. Good luck, everyone. God bless."

ON THE GROUND

"Bravo Three to Reaper One, we are hit and going down. I say again, we are going down. Will try to make it to the airfield. Good luck."

Kane looked up and waited for his HUD to find the Stratomaster as it started to fall from the sky. When he found it, he saw that the port wing was on fire, and it was trailing debris. *Damn it.* "Reaper Five and Three, go to the airfield and secure the crash site."

"Copy."

"Walrus One, where are you?"

"We're approaching the compound, Reaper."

"I need you to get in there, get the package, and get the hell out. Skyhammer is down, and we need to secure the crash site."

"Copy that. We'll do what we can."

Kane thought for a moment. He wished he didn't have to make the next call, but he did it anyway. "Four, I've got tanks to the north. Two of them. They're yours."

"Roger that."

"Knocker, make a hole. Get us into the compound. Now."

———

THE STRATOMASTER WAS COMING DOWN FAST and felt as though it were about to shake itself apart. In the cockpit, Eugene and Leslie Groves wrestled with the dying bird. Ahead of them was the long strip of asphalt they had Skyhammer headed for.

"Gene, we're not going to make it."

"It'll be close enough. Any luck with the landing gear?"

"Negative."

"Can you see the wing?"

"It's still on fire."

"Dump fuel."

Groves flicked a switch, and the Stratomaster began dumping all their excess fuel. "The extra ammo has already been dumped, Molly did that."

Skyhammer lurched and started to yaw to the right. Once more, they fought to bring the plane back.

Leslie looked at the panel. "We're at five hundred feet."

"You're right, we're going to be short. Get them braced."

"Copilot to all hands. Brace for impact. I say again, brace, brace, brace."

The Stratomaster lurched again.

"Two hundred feet."

Eugene's face became a stoic mask of concentration. "Mayday, mayday, mayday. This is Skyhammer One. We are going down. Coordinates..."

"One hundred feet."

"It's been an honor, Leslie."

"You too, Gene."

Then Skyhammer hit.

Hard.

CHAPTER 21

PARAGUAY

When Thurston and Jimmy came clear of the sparse jungle, the sight ahead gave them pause. The Stratomaster had hit short of the runway and dug a deep furrow across the ground. By the time it reached the tarmac, sliding on its belly, it had lost its tail; it had completely snapped off. The port wing, weakened by the fire, had parted ways with it around the same time.

Further along, the starboard wing, which had begun to drag, eventually became structurally challenged and was ripped away as well, leaving the rest of the plane to careen along on its own. As it did, it rolled and began to disintegrate.

By the time the Stratomaster had stopped, the cockpit had separated from what was left of the rest.

"Mom!" Jimmy gasped.

Thurston heard him over the open comms. "Jimmy, listen to me. We can't do anything for them until we secure the crash site. Now, go."

"Yes, ma'am."

"Reaper One, copy?"

"Copy, Five."

"Skyhammer is down hard. I say again, Skyhammer is down hard. Securing the crash site."

"Roger that. Keep me informed."

Jimmy started forward and came under immediate fire. A droid appeared to his right, firing a rocket which flew wide. He brought the AT-120 around and fired twice. The droid exploded violently, adding to the smoke and debris around the crash area. Some of it was from the flankers which had been destroyed on the ground earlier, but most of it was from Skyhammer.

Thurston opened fire with her minigun at a handful of shooters coming out of the brush. Her HUD picked out the targets, and the hand of death touched each of them.

A heavy machine gun opened up from a position close to a large hangar. "Jimmy, shut that gun down."

The Viper turned, and the 120 spoke again. The resulting explosion was devastating. "That ought to shut him up."

A technical appeared, weaving in and out of the debris field. A large caliber machine gun was fixed in the back and started firing. A round hit the armor of Jimmy's Viper and made the machine jerk. A warning appeared on the HUD, telling him his armor's integrity had suddenly dropped by fifteen percent.

The 120 opened up again, and the technical disappeared in a ball of orange flame.

Everything went silent.

Thurston looked at the carnage in front of her and said, "Bravo, copy?"

Nothing.

"Bravo, copy?"

Nothing.

"Any Bravo callsigns, copy?"

Still nothing.

"Jimmy, I need you to stand watch. Anything pops its head up, take it off. Copy?"

"Roger that."

With the sounds of battle raging in the background, Thurston approached the wreckage of the cockpit first. She stopped her Viper and climbed out, taking her sidearm with her.

The cockpit seemed to be in one piece even though it was banged up. She climbed inside and found both pilots still strapped in their seats. She checked for signs of life and found none. Thurston bowed her head, said a quick prayer, and exited.

She went looking for the others, finding Molly first. Thrown clear of the wreckage, Molly was still strapped in her seat. Like the pilots, she was also gone.

The next person Thurston found was Crystal. She was lying under some wreckage inside the section where the op-center was. There was blood on her face, a piece of metal in her right shoulder, and her right leg looked to be broken.

Thurston crouched down beside her. "Crystal?"

She moaned.

"Don't move. You're still alive. I need to check on the others."

Another moan.

Tanner was dead.

She found Houlihan still strapped into her seat, as was Cara. Cara was out cold. There were a few cuts and abrasions, but it appeared as though she had escaped the crash with only minor injuries. Houlihan, however, had a piece of metal embedded in her right side, and both legs were broken. It was lucky she was out of it because the pain would have been intense.

"General?"

It was Jimmy calling her over her comms. "She's okay, Jimmy."

"Yes, ma'am."

Thurston looked around until she found the medical compartment. She took out what she needed and started to triage the survivors. While she worked, she reached out to Kane.

"Reaper One, copy?"

"Copy, Five."

"I have an update for you."

"Send it."

"Both pilots are KIA along with Bravos Four and Two. Bravos One and Three are banged up pretty bad. Cara is out but looks okay. We need to get a medevac in here ASAP."

"Do what you can, General, I'll take care of it."

"Copy. Five out."

"General?"

Thurston turned and saw Cara looking in her direction. "Cara."

"What happened?"

She told her and said, "Just relax, I'll give you something for the pain. Jimmy is on watch, and the airfield is secure."

"What about the others?"

Thurston reached for a morphine syrette. "I'll tell you while I work."

———

DENVER FIRED HIS G550, and the cartel soldier to his front died violently. His men pushed hard for the compound using everything they had to do it. So far, they had been lucky.

On their flank, a machine gun opened fire, spraying the open ground with a deadly fire. The men of Strike Team Walrus dived for cover as the rounds cut through the air above them.

"Lionheart, do something about that gun," Denver growled.

Slung beneath the operator's weapon was a grenade launcher. He pulled the trigger on it, and it gave a low BOOP.

Moments later, the explosive round hit home and blew the two operators in the machine gun pit to pieces.

"Walrus One, this is Reaper One, over."

"Read you Lima Charlie, Reaper."

"I need you to radio for a medevac. We've got three at the crash site who need evac now."

"Copy." The team leader turned to Hammer Lewis. "Hammer, get a medevac to the airfield now."

"Where from?"

"Fucking improvise."

Suddenly, they came under fire from another heavy tank. "This is just fucking ridiculous," Denver growled. "Everyone, move, now!"

They broke from their position and ran across open ground just as the tank fired. A large explosion threw dirt and grass into the air where they had just been. The bow machine gunner from the beast opened fire, and smaller gouts of earth leaped behind them.

"Argh!"

Denver looked back and saw Walrus Four, also known as Lionheart, falling. "No, no, no."

Denver doubled back and crouched by his man. The machine gun bullets were a heavier caliber and had punched through the operator's body armor. The man was dead. "Damn it."

He turned and was about to run again when the machine gunner opened fire, and he was suddenly pinned down and at the mercy of the metal monster.

"Christ," he cursed bitterly.

Then, just as all seemed lost, the tank exploded, and a huge Viper came out of the smoke.

"You going to fuck around there all day or fight this damn war?" Knocker asked.

"Thanks, buddy."

"That's all right. Go find that girl."

"Reaper's down! Reaper's down!"

"Ah bollocks," Knocker growled. "There is always something with that guy. Denver, like I said, find that girl."

———

KANE HADN'T SEEN the battle droid until it was too late. By then, the robot had fired. The rocket impact had rung his bell good and proper; in fact, he was lucky not to be killed.

The Viper went down, its armor compromised beyond all safety aspects, leaving it vulnerable.

However, Grace was right there, and she fired three 30 mm rounds into the droid. The machine blew apart and ceased to function. "Reaper, are you alright?"

"I'm fine. The Viper is screwed. Cover me while I get out."

Grace waited for him to climb free of the Viper. He

had his P756. Looking around, he actually *saw* the battlefield for the first time.

There was debris and wreckage everywhere. Fires burned and smoke rose into the sky, leaving a dirty stain against the blue. He said, "I'm going in."

"Damn it, Reaper, be careful."

He ran toward the compound. The mission wasn't complete yet. The objective was still to take Torres alive, but Kane wasn't even sure he was going to do that anymore.

———

"WHAT IS HAPPENING?" Torres demanded as he looked at the screens which showed different areas of the battlefield through well-placed cameras. He'd been watching the battle ever since it had kicked off and seen his forces slowly decimated by the attackers. "Where are the battle droids?"

A man turned toward him. He acted as a general overseeing Torres's armed forces, and at that moment he had a painful expression on his face. "They are gone."

"All of them?"

"Yes."

Torres paled. "My tanks? My aircraft?"

"Gone."

"But we shot down one of their aircraft."

"Yes."

"My men?"

The man stared at Torres. "Sir, I recommend you leave. They are about to breach the perimeter."

"Send someone to get the girl. We will leave now."

"I will have men meet you at the cars."

"What about you?" Torres asked.

"I have failed. I will stay behind and do what I can."

The cartel boss nodded. "Good luck."

———

Kane caught up with Denver as the three remaining men from Walrus entered the compound. They crouched behind a truck, taking fire from a couple of guards near the main building. Denver rose with Holliday beside him, and they opened fire with their 550s. The two guards dropped and never moved.

Kane said, "I need one of your guys to look for my daughter."

Denver nodded. "Billy, go with Reaper. We'll go and look for Torres."

They separated there, and Kane and Holliday moved through the compound until they reached a smaller building off the main one. According to their surveillance, this was where Ana had been sleeping.

The pair busted in and found it empty. Kane indicated toward the bedroom. "Check in there. I'll check the bathroom."

Kane found the bathroom empty.

"Reaper, get in here."

Kane hurried to the bedroom. No one was there apart from Holliday. "There is a stairwell down through the back of the closet."

"Let's go."

The stairwell led to a well-lit concrete tunnel, so there was no problem seeing. There were very few turns, and by the time they reached the end, they found another stairwell. Kane led the way up, and when they emerged, they found themselves in what looked to be a command bunker.

However, Denver had beaten them there. Almost everyone within was dead except for one man.

"Who is he?" Kane asked.

"The man in charge of the defenses, we think."

Kane looked at him. "Where are they?"

"He's not talking, Reaper."

Kane shot him in the leg. The man cried out and fell. Kane shot him in the other one. "I don't have time to fuck around."

All bravado gone, the man blurted out words that seemed to run together, caused by the burning pain in his legs. Kane looked at Denver. "Three vehicles are in an underground garage at the rear of the compound."

"What are we hanging around here for?"

"Knocker, copy?"

"Roger."

"The rear of the compound. Torres is headed there, and he's got Ana with him."

"On it."

Kane started moving. "Let's go."

They broke out into the day and started toward the rear of the compound. When they reached it, they found nothing. "Where are they?" Kane growled.

Knocker changed his HUD display in Ares and scanned the area. "Here they come," he said.

Kane snapped his head around. "Where?"

The twin miniguns sitting on Ares turned to focus on a large bush. "There."

Suddenly, it exploded as a dark SUV appeared, crashing through it. Ares exploded to life, his miniguns hammering the first of the SUVs. The vehicle shuddered violently to a halt. Then Knocker divided Ares's attention. One minigun for the second SUV, another for the third. Both weapons came into life, causing Kane to hold his breath.

He knew what the Vipers were capable of, but it didn't make it any easier watching what was happening.

The third SUV blew up. One moment it was moving fast, the next it died a catastrophic death. The second one, however, ground to a halt when its wheels were shot away.

Denver led his men forward and secured the vehicle. He wrenched the door open and reached inside, dragging a stunned Fernando Torres out and shoving him face down onto the ground to secure him. Holliday and Hammer secured the driver and passenger.

Kane slowly approached the SUV and looked in the back. Ana was crouched down on the floor, her arms over her head as she cowered, afraid.

"Ana?"

She never moved.

"Ana, it's me. John. You remember me."

Slowly, her head came up, and she stared at Kane. "Are—are you here to take me away?"

"That's right."

"Mama said you were my papa. Are you?"

Kane nodded slowly. "Yes."

Ana reached for him.

———

KANE SURVEYED the carnage around the airfield and shook his head at the probability of anyone surviving, knowing that it was a miracle that several had when Skyhammer came down. There were now two helicopters on the ground to evacuate the injured. Crystal and Houlihan would be out of action but eventually would be back after a lengthy stretch on the sidelines.

Cara lay on a stretcher waiting for her turn to be loaded up, and Jimmy stood beside her. Thurston came over to Kane, who had turned his attention to the medic examining Ana.

"How is she doing?"

"She seems okay."

"Who would have thought? The Reaper as a dad."

He grunted. "Not me."

Thurston looked at the wreckage. "We were lucky today."

"Yeah."

Knocker appeared and handed a piece of paper to Thurston. She frowned. "What's this?"

She opened it up and read the two scrawled words on it. *I quit.*

She cocked an eyebrow. "Really?"

"We figure we've used up all our lives, General," Knocker said. "It's a young man's game."

"We?"

He nodded. "Me and Reaper."

Thurston looked at her team leader. "You too?"

He nodded. "I'm done."

"You two. That means I'll only have Cara left."

"You want to tell her, or shall I?" Knocker asked Kane.

"Don't let me stop you," Kane replied.

Thurston shook her head. "Damn it."

She left them to it, muttering as she walked away. Kane looked over at Ana again and saw that the medic was finishing up. He slapped his friend on the shoulder and said, "Something new to look forward to."

EPILOGUE

IRAKLIA, GREECE—TWO MONTHS LATER

Kane and Cara laughed as they watched Knocker running up the beach with Ana on his shoulders, roaring like some weird kind of monster. Cara smiled at Kane and said, "Who would have thought that somewhere under all that crazy was a soft crazy?"

She had arrived the day before after tying up loose ends in Hereford. Her original plan had been to sequester herself away in northern England and grow old, but Kane had convinced her to come to Greece for a while to see if she liked it. So far, so good.

Kane nodded. "She's been good for him. Ever since we stopped going down range, she's kept him hopping."

"Maybe they've been good for each other."

He nodded. "Maybe."

"What about you?"

"I'm adjusting," he replied. "Melanie has been helping, although she leaves for Malta tomorrow."

"What's she doing there?"

"Something to do with a religious artifact that was found."

"Ana will still have you and Knocker." They ran past again, the Brit screaming like a banshee, and Cara shook her head. "I'll rephrase that. You'll have two children to take care of."

They laughed and stared at the water. Kane asked, "How are the others?"

"Crystal is back on deck. Another month and Pat will be ready to return."

"Lucky."

"We all were."

"Let's hope Torres gets what is coming to him."

Cara stared at him. "You didn't hear?"

"What?"

"I thought you knew, that's why I didn't say anything."

"Knew what?"

"Torres was shanked and killed in prison five days ago."

"By whom?" Kane asked, surprised.

"No one knows."

"Hey."

They both looked up and saw Melanie approaching them. Cara smiled at her and said, "Hey yourself."

A shout of joy, and Ana leaped down from Knocker's shoulders and ran along the beach and into Melanie's arms. "Hey, Pumpkin."

"Hi."

"How are you doing?"

"Uncle Ray is driving me nuts."

Melanie smiled and winked at the Brit. "He does that to everyone."

He gave her an indignant look. "Thanks."

"Do you want to come and get an ice cream?" Melanie asked Ana.

Ana glanced at Kane. "Papa?"

That was still going to take some getting used to. Kane nodded. "Sure."

The excitement inside her grew, and she raced over and gave her father a hug. "Thank you."

"What about me?" Knocker asked.

"Do you want a hug too?"

"No, I want an ice cream."

"Come on then, Raymond," Melanie said with a sly grin. "You can come too."

They started walking up the beach together, Ana between them holding their hands. Cara said, "What have you done to him?"

"Wasn't me," Kane replied. "It was all her."

"Ana?"

"Yes."

"You might want to keep an eye on your sister too," Cara told him.

"Don't go there," Kane said. "I don't need that headache."

Cara reached out and took his hand. "I can fix that headache."

"Really?"

She smiled. "Uh-huh."

"I think I'd like that."

Cara leaned over and put her head on his shoulder. "Me too."

TEAM REAPER IS BACK, AND THIS TIME THEY'RE IN THE MIDDLE OF A FEROCIOUS STORM.

In the heart of Africa, Team Reaper embarks on a mission like no other. Their objective: to train an all-female anti-poaching squad, standing as the last line of defense against the ruthless poachers threatening the region's wildlife.

But as Team Reaper chips away at the edges of this nefarious underworld, they unwittingly awaken a sleeping beast—a force more vicious than the savannah storms that frequent the African landscape. Caught in a relentless tempest of violence and betrayal, every move they make only serves to irritate the very entity they are determined to halt.

With no room for error and no second chances, Team Reaper plunges headfirst into a showdown that will determine everyone's fates.

Brace for impact as Team Reaper plunges into a jaw-dropping storm, where the echoes of their courage will resonate long after the final showdown.

AVAILABLE APRIL 2024

ABOUT THE AUTHOR

A relative newcomer to the world of writing, Brent Towns self-published his first book in 2015. *Last Stand in Sanctuary* took him two years to write. His first hardcover book was published the following year.

Since then, he has written twenty-six Westerns, including some in collaboration with Ben Bridges; several action adventure novels; the novelization to the 2019 movie, *Bill Tilghman and the Outlaws*; as well as scripted a handful of Commando Comics. Not bad for an Australian author, he thinks.

Often up until the small hours of the night, bashing away at his tortured keyboard in Queensland, Australia, Brent loves to lose himself in the world of fiction. If you're interested in sharing your thoughts in more detail, scan the QR code below! Your feedback is invaluable to him—and often helps shape his future writing endeavors.

www.ingramcontent.com/pod-product-compliance
Lightning Source LLC
Chambersburg PA
CBHW010824250626
47169CB00010B/2945